"Look at you. You're young. You're scared. Why are you so scared? Stop swallowing your words. Stop caring about what other people think. Speak your mind. Wear what you want. Listen to the music that you want to listen to." Play it as loud as you can and dance to it. Go out for a drive at midnight and forget you have school the next day. Stop waiting for Friday. Live now. Do it now." Start Living."

IT'S KIND OF A FUNNY STORY

NED VIZZINI

HYPERION
New York

To my mom

You knew you'd get one sooner or later,
and seeing as they're so hard to do, I figured we'd
better make it sooner. I love you.

Text copyright © 2006 by Ned Vizzini

All rights reserved. No part of this book may be reproduced or transmitted in any form or by any means, electronic or mechanical, including photocopying, recording, or by any information storage and retrieval system, without written permission from the publisher. For information address Hyperion Books for Children, 125 West End Avenue, New York, New York 10023-6387.

Printed in the United States of America
First Hyperion Paperbacks edition, 2007
20
Library of Congress Cataloging-in-Publication data on file.
ISBN 13: 978-0-7868-5197-3
ISBN 10: 0-7868-5197-X
ILS No. V475-2873-0-14175
This book is set in Goudy and Rotis Sans Serif.

Visit www.un-requiredreading.com and www.nedvizzini.com

SUSTAINABLE
FORESTRY
INITIATIVE
Certified Chain of Custody
Promoting Sustainable Forestry
www.sfiprogram.org
SFI-01054
The SFI label applies to the text stock

PART 1: WHERE I'M AT

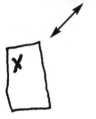

one

It's so hard to *talk* when you want to kill yourself. That's above and beyond everything else, and it's not a mental complaint—it's a physical thing, like it's physically hard to open your mouth and make the words come out. They don't come out smooth and in conjunction with your brain the way normal people's words do; they come out in chunks as if from a crushed-ice dispenser; you stumble on them as they gather behind your lower lip. So you just keep quiet.

"Have you ever noticed how on all the ads on TV, people are *watching* TV?" my friend is like.

"Pass it, son," my other friend is like.

"No, yo, that's true," my other other friend is like. "There's always somebody on a couch, unless it's an allergy ad and they're in a field—"

"Or on a horse on the beach."

"Those ads are always for herpes."

Laughter.

"How do you even tell someone you have that?" That's Aaron. It's his house. "That must be such a weird conversation: 'Hey, before we do this, you should know . . .'"

"Your moms didn't mind last night."

"Ohhhh!"

"Son!"

Aaron lobs a punch at Ronny, the antagonist. Ronny is small and wears jewelry; he once told me, *Craig, when a man puts on his first piece of jewelry, there's no turning back.* He punches back with his hand with the big limp gold bracelet on it; it hits Aaron's watch, clanging.

"Son, what you tryin' to do with my gold, yo?" Ronny shakes his wrist and turns his attention to the pot.

There's always pot at Aaron's house; he has a room with an entirely separate ventilation system and lockable door that his parents could rent out as another apartment. Resin streaks outline his light switch, and his bedsheet is pockmarked with black circles. There are stains on there, too, shimmery stains which indicate certain activities that take place between Aaron and his girlfriend. I look at them (the stains, then the couple). I'm jealous. But then again, I'm beyond jealous.

"Craig? You want?"

It's passed to me, wrapped up in a concise delivery system, but I pass it on. I'm doing an experiment with my brain. I'm seeing if maybe pot is the problem; maybe that's what has come in and robbed me. I do this every so often, for a few weeks, and then I smoke a *lot* of pot, just to test if maybe the *lack* of it is what has robbed me.

"You all right, man?"

This should be my name. I could be like a superhero: You All Right Man.

"Ah . . ." I stumble.

"Don't bug Craig," Ronny is like. "He's in the Craig zone. He's Craig-ing out."

"Yeah." I move the muscles that make me smile. "I'm just . . . kinda . . . you know . . ."

You see how the words work? They betray your mouth and walk away.

"*Are* you okay?" Nia asks. Nia is Aaron's girlfriend. She's in physical contact with Aaron at all times. Right now she's on the floor next to his leg. She has big eyes.

"I'm fine," I tell her. The blue glow of the flatscreen TV in front of us ricochets off her eyes as she turns back to it. We're watching a nature special on the deep ocean.

"Holy shit, look at that, son!" Ronny is like, blowing smoke—I don't know how it got back to him already. There's an octopus on the screen with giant ears, translucent, flapping through the water in the cold light of a submersible.

"Scientists have playfully named this specimen Dumbo," the TV narrator says.

I smile to myself. I have a secret: I wish I was Dumbo the Octopus. Adapted to freezing deep-ocean temperatures, I'd flop around down there at peace. The big concerns of my life would be what sort of bottom-coating slime to feed off of—that's not so different from now—plus I wouldn't have any natural predators; then again, I don't have any now, and that hasn't done me a whole lot of good. But it suddenly makes sense: I'd like to be under the sea, as an octopus.

"I'll be back," I say, getting up from my spot on the couch, which Scruggs, a friend who was relegated to the floor, immediately claims, slinking up in one fluid motion.

"You didn't call one-five," he's like.

"One-five?" I try.

"Too late."

I shrug and climb over clothes and people's legs to the beige, apartment-front-door–style door; I move through that, to the right: Aaron's warm bathroom.

I have a system with bathrooms. I spend a lot of

time in them. They are sanctuaries, public places of peace spaced throughout the world for people like me. When I pop into Aaron's, I continue my normal routine of wasting time. I turn the light off first. Then I sigh. Then I turn around, face the door I just closed, pull down my pants, and fall on the toilet— I don't sit; I fall like a carcass, feeling my butt accommodate the rim. Then I put my head in my hands and breathe out as I, well, y'know, piss. I always try to enjoy it, to feel it come out and realize that it's my body doing something it has to do, like eating, although I'm not too good at that. I bury my face in my hands and wish that it could go on forever because it feels good. You do it and it's done. It doesn't take any effort or any planning. You don't put it off. That would be really screwed up, I think. If you had such problems that you didn't pee. Like being anorexic, except with urine. If you held it in as self-punishment. I wonder if anyone does that?

I finish up and flush, reaching behind me, my head still down. Then I get up and turn on the light. (Did anyone notice I was in here in the dark? Did they see the lack of light under the crack and notice it like a roach? Did Nia see?) Then I look in the mirror.

I look so normal. I look like I've always looked, like I did before the fall of last year. Dark hair and dark eyes and one snaggled tooth. Big eyebrows that meet in the middle. A long nose, sort of twisted. Pupils that are naturally large—it's not the pot—which blend into the dark brown to make two big saucer eyes, holes in me. Wisps of hair above my upper lip. This is Craig.

And I always look like I'm about to cry.

I put on the hot water and splash it at my face to feel something. In a few seconds I'm going to have to go back and face the crowd. But I can sit in the dark on the toilet a little more, can't I? I always manage to make a trip to the bathroom take five minutes.

two

"How're you doing?" Dr. Minerva asks.

Her office has a bookshelf, like all shrinks' offices. I used to not want to call them *shrinks*, but now that I've been through so many, I feel entitled to it. It's an adult term, and it's disrespectful, and I'm more than two thirds adult and I'm pretty disrespectful, so what the hell.

Like all shrinks' offices, anyway, it has The Bookshelf full of required reading. First of all there's the DSM, the *Diagnostic and Statistical Manual*, which lists every kind of psychological disorder known to man—*that's* fun reading. Very thick book. I don't have a whole lot of what's in there—I just have one big thing—but I know all about it from skimming. There's great stuff in there. There's a disease called Ondine's Curse, in which your body loses the ability to *breathe* involuntarily. Can you imagine? You have to think "breathe, breathe" all the time, or you stop breathing. Most people who get it die.

If the shrink is classy, she'll (mostly *she'll*, occasionally a *he'll*) have a *bunch* of DSMs, because they come in different editions—III, IV, and V are the most common. I don't think you can find a DSM II. It came out in 1963 or something. It takes like ten years to put one out, and they're working on VI.

Jeez, I could be a shrink.

Now, in addition to the DSMs, there are an assortment of specific books on psychiatric disorders, things like *The Freedom from Depression Workbook*; *Anxiety & Panic Attacks: Their Cause and Cure*; and *The 7 Habits of Highly Effective People*. Always hardcover. No paperbacks in a shrink's office. Usually there's at least one book on childhood sexual abuse, like *The Wounded Heart*, and one shrink I went to caught me looking at that and said, "That book is about childhood sexual abuse."

And I was like, "Uh-huh?"

And she said, "It's for people who were abused."

And I nodded.

"Were you?"

She had a little-old-lady face, this one, with a shock of white hair, and I never saw her again. What kind of question was that? Of *course* I wasn't abused. If I were, things would be so simple. I'd have a reason for being in shrinks' offices. I'd have a justification and something that I could work on.

The world wasn't going to give me something that tidy.

"I'm fine. Well, I'm not fine—I'm here."

"Is there something wrong with that?"

"Absolutely."

"You've been coming here for a while."

Dr. Minerva always has such amazing outfits. It's not that she's particularly sexy or beautiful; she just carves herself out well. Today she has a red sweater and red lipstick that is exactly the same red. It's as if she went to the paint store to match them up.

"I want to not have to come here."

"Well, you're in a process. How're you doing?"

This is her prompt question. The shrinks always have one prompt question. I've had ones that said "What's up?" "How are we?" and even "What's happening in the world of Craig?" They never change. It's like their jingle.

"I didn't wake up well today."

"Did you sleep well?"

"I slept okay."

She looks completely stone, staring ahead. I don't know how they do this: the psych-poker face. Psychologists should play poker. Maybe they do. Maybe they're the ones who win all the money on TV. Then they have the gall to charge my mom $120/hour. They're very greedy.

"What happened when you woke up?"

"I was having a dream. I don't know what it was, but when I woke up, I had this awful realization that I was awake. It hit me like a brick in the groin."

"Like a brick in the groin, I see."

"I didn't want to wake up. I was having a much better time asleep. And that's really sad. It was almost like a reverse nightmare, like when you wake up from a nightmare you're so relieved. I woke up *into* a nightmare."

"And what is that nightmare, Craig?"

"Life."

"Life is a nightmare."

"Yes."

We stop. Cosmic moment, I guess. *Ooooh, is life really a nightmare? We need to spend like ten seconds contemplating that.*

"What did you do when you realized you were awake?"

"I lay in bed." There were more things to tell her, things I held back: like the fact that I was *hungry* in bed this morning. I hadn't eaten the night before. I went to bed exhausted from homework and knew as I hit the pillow that I would pay for it in the morning, that I would wake up *really* hungry, that I would cross the line where my stomach gets so needy that I can't eat anything. I woke up and my stomach was screaming, hollowing itself out under my little chest. I didn't want to do anything about it. I didn't want to eat. The idea of eating made me hurt more. I couldn't think of anything—not one single solitary food item—that I would be able to handle, except coffee yogurt, and I was *sick* of coffee yogurt.

I rolled over on my stomach and balled my fists and held them against my gut like I was praying. The fists pushed my stomach against itself and fooled it into thinking it was full. I held this position, warm, my brain rotating, the seconds whirring by. Only the pure urge, the one thing that never let me down, got me out of bed fifty minutes later.

"I got up when I had to piss."

"I see."

"That was great."

"You like peeing. You've mentioned this before."

"Yeah. It's simple."

"You like simple."

"Doesn't everybody?"

"Some people thrive on complexity, Craig."

"Well, not me. As I was walking over here, I was thinking . . . I have this fantasy of being a bike messenger."

"Ah."

"It would be so simple, and direct, and I would get paid for it. It would be an Anchor."

"What about school, Craig? You have school for an Anchor."

"School is too all over the place. It spirals out into a million different things."

"Your Tentacles."

I have to hand it to her; Dr. Minerva picked up on my lingo pretty quickly. *Tentacles* is my term— the Tentacles are the evil tasks that invade my life. Like, for example, my American History class last week, which necessitated me writing a paper on the weapons of the Revolutionary War, which necessitated me traveling to the Metropolitan Museum to check out some of the old guns, which necessitated me getting in the subway, which necessitated me being away from my cell phone and e-mail for 45 minutes, which meant that I didn't get to respond to a mass mail sent out by my teacher asking who needed extra credit, which meant other kids snapped up the extra credit, which meant I wasn't going to get a 98 in the class, which meant I wasn't anywhere close to a 98.6 average (body temperature, that's what you needed to get), which meant I wasn't going to get into a Good College, which meant I wasn't going to have a Good Job, which meant I wasn't going to have health insurance, which meant I'd have to pay tremendous amounts of money for the shrinks and drugs my brain needed, which meant I wasn't going to have enough money to pay for a Good Lifestyle, which meant I'd feel ashamed, which meant I'd get depressed, and that was the big one because I knew what that did to me: it made it so I wouldn't get out of bed, which led to the ultimate thing—homelessness. If you can't get out of bed for long enough, people come and take your bed away.

The opposite of the Tentacles are the Anchors. The Anchors are things that occupy my mind and make me feel good temporarily. Riding my bike is an Anchor. Doing flash cards is an Anchor. Watching people play video games at Aaron's is an Anchor. The answers are simple and sequential. There aren't any decisions. There aren't any Tentacles. There's just a stack of tasks that you tackle. You don't have to deal with other people.

"There are a lot of Tentacles," I admit. "But I should be able to handle them. The problem is that I'm so lazy."

"How are you lazy, Craig?"

"I waste at least an hour every day lying in bed. Then I waste time pacing. I waste time thinking. I waste time being quiet and not saying anything because I'm afraid I'll stutter."

"Do you have a problem with stuttering?"

"When I'm depressed, it won't come out right. I'll trail off in midsentence."

"I see." She writes something down on her legal pad. *Craig, this will go on your permanent record.*

"I don't—" I shake my head. "The bike thing."

"What? What were you going to say?" This is another trick of shrinks. They never let you stop in midthought. If you open your mouth, they want to know exactly what you had the intention of saying. The party line is that some of the most profound truths about us are things that we stop saying in the middle, but I think they do it to make us feel important. One thing's for sure: no one else in life says to me, "Wait, Craig, what were you going to say?"

"I was going to say that I don't think the stuttering is like, a real problem. I just think it's one of my symptoms."

"Like sweating."

"Right." The sweating is awful. It's not as bad as the not eating, but it's *weird*—cold sweat, all over my forehead, having to be wiped off every two minutes, smelling like skin concentrate. People notice. It's one of the few things people notice.

"You're not stuttering now."

"This is being paid for. I don't want to waste time."

Pause. Now we have one of our silent battles; I look at Dr. Minerva and she looks at me. It's a contest as to who will crack first. She puts on her poker face; I don't have any extra faces to put on, just the normal Craig face.

We lock eyes. I'm waiting for her to say something profound—I always am, even though it'll never happen. I'm waiting for her to say "Craig, what you need to do is X" and for the Shift to occur. I want there to be a Shift so bad. I want to feel my brain slide back into the slot it was meant to be in, rest there the way it did before the fall of last year, back when I was young, and witty, and my teachers said I had incredible promise, and I *had* incredible promise, and I spoke up in class because I was excited and smart about the world. I want the Shift so bad. I'm waiting for the phrase that will invoke it. It'll be like a miracle within my life. But is Dr. Minerva a miracle worker? No. She's a thin, tan lady from Greece with red lipstick.

She breaks first.

"About your bike riding, you said you wanted to be a messenger."

"Yes."

"You already have a bike, correct?"

"Yes." ··

"And you ride it a lot?"

"Not that much. Mom won't let me ride it to school. But I ride around Brooklyn on weekends."

"What does it feel like when you ride your bike, Craig?"

I pause. ". . . Geometric."

"Geometric."

"Yeah. Like, *You have to avoid this truck. Don't get hit in the head by these metal pipes. Make a right.* The rules are defined and you follow them."

"Like a video game."

"Sure. I love video games. Even just to watch. Since I was a kid."

"Which you often refer to as 'back when you were happy.'"

"Right." I smooth my shirt out. I get dressed up for these little meetings too. Good khakis and a white dress shirt. We're dressing up for each other. We should really go get some coffee and make a scandal—the Greek therapist and her high school boyfriend. We could be famous. That would get me money. That might make me happy.

"Do you remember some of the things that made you happy?"

"The video games." I laugh.

"What's funny?"

"I was walking down my block the other day, and behind me was a mother with her kid, and the mother was saying, 'Now, Timmy, I don't want you to complain about it. You can't play video games twenty-four hours a day.' And Timmy goes, 'But I *want* to!' And I turned around and told him, 'Me too.'"

"You want to play video games twenty-four hours a day?"

"Or watch. I just want to not be me. Whether it's sleeping or playing video games or riding my bike or studying. Giving my brain up. That's what's important."

"You're very clear about what you want."

"Yeah."

"What did you want when you were a kid? Back when you were happy? What did you want to be when you grew up?"

Dr. Minerva is a good shrink, I think. That isn't the answer. But it is a damn good question. What did I want to be when I grew up?

three

When I was four, this is how things were:

Our family lived in a crappy apartment in Manhattan. I didn't know it was crappy at the time, because I didn't have our better apartment to compare it to yet. But there was exposed piping. That's no good. You don't want to raise your child in a house with exposed piping. I remember there was a green pipe and a red pipe and a white pipe, gathered near the corner of the hallway just before the bathroom, and as soon as I could walk I investigated them all, walked up to them and put my palm about two millimeters away from each one to test if it was hot or cold. One was cold, one was hot, and the red one was *really* hot. Two millimeters wasn't enough. I burned myself on it and Dad, who hadn't realized ("It must only get hot in the afternoon"), encased it in dark gray foam with duct tape, but duct tape never stopped me and I thought the foam was fun to pick at and chew so I picked it off and chewed it and then when other kids came over to my house I dared them to touch the re-exposed pipe; I told them anyone who came in *had* to touch it, otherwise they were a *pussy*, which was a word I learned from Dad watching TV, which I thought was great because it was a word with two meanings: the cat that girls liked and the thing you called people to make them do stuff. Just like *chicken* had two meanings: the bird that walked around and the white stuff you ate. Some people touched the hot pipe if you called them *chicken* as well.

I had my own room but I didn't like to be alone in it; the only room I liked to be in was the living room, under the table that held all the encyclopedias. I made it my little fort; I put a blanket over me and worked in there, with a light that Dad rigged up. I worked on maps. I loved maps. I knew that we lived in Manhattan and I had a map of it, a Hagstrom Five Borough Atlas with all the streets laid out. I knew exactly where we lived, on the corner of 53rd Street and 3rd Avenue. Third Avenue was a yellow street because it was an avenue, big and long and important. Fifty-third Street was a little white street that went across Manhattan. The streets went sideways and the avenues went up-and-down; that was all you had to remember. (Dad helped me remember, too, when we went out for pancakes. He would ask, "Do you want them cut in streets and avenues, Craig?" And I'd go "Yes!" and he'd cut the stack of pancakes in a grid, and we'd name each street and avenue as we went along, making sure to get 3rd Ave. and 53rd Street.) It was so simple. If you were really advanced (like I was, *duh*), you knew that traffic on the even streets went east (East for Even) and the odd streets went west (West is Odd). Then, every bunch of streets, there were fat yellow streets, like the avenues, that went both ways. These were the famous streets: 42nd St., 34th St. The complete list from the bottom up was Chambers St., Canal St., Houston St., 14th St., 23rd St., 34th St., 42nd St., 57th St., 72nd St. (there wasn't any big street in the 60s; they got shafted), 79th St., 86th St., 96th St., and then you were in Harlem, where Manhattan effectively ended for little white boys who made forts under encyclopedias and studied maps.

As soon as I saw the Manhattan map, I wanted to draw it. I should be able to draw the place where I lived. So I asked Mom for tracing paper and she got it for me and I brought it into my fort and I pointed the light right down on the first map in the Hagstrom Atlas—downtown, where Wall Street was and the stock market worked. The streets were crazy down there; they didn't have any kind of streets and avenues; they just had names and they looked like a game of Pick-Up Sticks. But before I could even worry about the streets, I had to get the land right. Manhattan was actually built on land. Sometimes when they were digging up the streets you saw it down there—real dirt! And the land had a certain curve to it at the bottom of the island, like a dinosaur head, bumpy on the right and straight on the left, a swooping majestic bottom.

I held my tracing paper down and tried to trace the line of lower Manhattan.

I couldn't do it.

I mean, it was ridiculous. My line didn't have anything to do with the real one. I didn't understand—I was holding the tracing paper steady. I looked at my small hand. "Stay still," I told it. I crumpled up the paper and tried again.

The line wasn't right again. It didn't have the swoop.

I crumpled up the paper and tried again.

This line was even worse than before. Manhattan looked square.

I tried again.

Oh boy, now it looked like a duck.

Crumple.

Now it looked like a *turd*, another word I picked up from Dad.

Crumple.

Now it looked like a piece of fruit.

It looked like everything but what it was supposed to look like: Manhattan. I couldn't do it. I didn't realize then that when you trace stuff you're supposed to have a tracing *table*, lighted from below, and clamps to hold the paper straight, not a trembling four-year-old hand, so I just thought I was a failure. They always said on TV you could do anything you wanted, but here I was trying to do something and it wasn't working. I would never be able to do it. I crumpled up the last piece of tracing paper and started sobbing, my head in my hands in my fort.

Mom heard me.

"Craig?"

"What? Go away."

"What's wrong, honey?"

"Don't open the curtain! *Don't open it!* I have things in here."

"Why are you crying? What's the matter?"

"I can't do it."

"What's the matter?"

"Nothing!"

"Tell Mommy, c'mon. I'm going to open the blanket—"

"No!"

I jumped at her face as she pulled the blanket aside, bringing it taut under the encyclopedias. Mom threw her hands up and held the books in place, saving both of us from getting clobbered. (A week later, she'd have Dad move the encyclopedias.) With her occupied, I ran across the room, streaking tears, wanting to get to the bathroom, to sit down on the toilet with the light off and splash hot water on my face. But Mom was too quick. She shoved the encyclopedias back and loped across the room, swooping me up in her thin arms with the elbow skin that you could pull down. I beat my palms against her.

"Craig! We do *not* hit Mommy!"

"I can't do it I can't do it *I can't do it!*" I hit her.

"*What?*" She hugged me tight so I had no room to hit. "*What* can't you do?"

"*I can't draw Manhattan!*"

"Huh?" Mom drew her face up and away from me, looked me in the eyes. "Is *that* what you were trying to do down there?"

I nodded, sniffled.

"You were trying to trace Manhattan with the tracing paper I bought you?"

"I can't do it."

"Craig, *no one* can." She laughed. "You can't just trace freehand. It's impossible!"

"Then how do they make the maps?"

Mom paused.

"See? See? Someone can do it!"

"They have *equipment*, Craig. They're grown-ups and they have special tools that they use."

"Well I need those tools."

"Craig."

"Let's buy them."

"Honey."

"Do they cost a lot of money?"

"Honey."

Mom put me down on the sofa, which turned into a bed for her and Dad at night, and sat next to me. I wasn't crying anymore. I wasn't hitting anymore. My brain was all right back then; it didn't get stuck in ruts.

"Craig," she sighed, looked at me. "I have an idea. Instead of spending your time trying to trace maps of Manhattan, why don't you make your own maps of *imaginary places?*"

And that was the closest I've ever come to an epiphany.

I could make up my own city. I could use my own streets. I could put a river where I wanted. I could put the ocean where I wanted. I could put the bridges where I wanted and I could put a big highway right across the middle of town, like Manhattan should have but didn't. I could make my own subway system. I could make my own street names. I could have my own grid stretching off to the edges of the map. I smiled and hugged Mom.

She got me some thick paper—white construction paper. Later on I grew to prefer straight computer paper. I went back under my fort and turned the light on and started on my first map. And I did that for the next five years—whenever I was in class, I didn't doodle, I drew maps. Hundreds of them. When I finished, I crumpled them; it was making them that was important. I did cities on the ocean, cities with two rivers meeting in the middle, cities with one big river that bent, cities with bridges, crazy interchanges, circles and boulevards. I made cities. That made me happy. That was my Anchor. And until I turned nine and turned to video games, that was what I wanted to be when I grew up: a mapmaker.

four

"I wanted to make maps," I tell Dr. Minerva.

"Maps of what?"

"Cities."

"On the computer?"

"No, by hand."

"I see."

"I don't think there's much of a market for that."
I smile.

"Maybe not, maybe so."

What a shrink answer.

"I can't take maybes. I have to make money."

"We're going to talk more about money next
time. We have to stop now."

I look at the clock. 7:03. She always gives an
extra three minutes.

"What are you going to do when you leave,
Craig?"

She always asks that. What am I always going to
do? I'm going to go home and freak out. I'm going

to sit with my family and try not to talk about myself and what's wrong. I'm going to try and eat. Then I'm going to try and sleep. I dread it. I can't eat and I can't sleep. I'm not doing well in terms of being a functional human, you know?

Hey, soldier, what's the matter?

I can't sleep and I can't eat, sir!

How about I pump you full of lead, soldier, would that get you motivated?

Can't say, sir! I'd probably still be unable to sleep or eat, just a little bit heavier from the lead.

Get up there and fight, soldier! The enemy is there!

The enemy is too strong. I can't fight them. They're too smart.

You're smart too, soldier.

Not smart enough.

So you're just going to give up?

That's the plan.

"I'm going to just keep at it," I tell Dr. Minerva. "That's all I can do. I'll keep at it and hope it gets better."

"Are you taking your medicine?"

"Yes."

"Are you seeing Dr. Barney?"

Dr. Barney is the psychopharmacologist. He's the one who prescribes me meds and sends me to people like Dr. Minerva. He's a trip in his own way, a little fat Santa with rings embedded in his fingers.

"Yes, later in the week."

"You know to do what he says."

Yes, Doctor. I'll do what you say. I'll do what you all say.

"Here," I hand Dr. Minerva the check from my mom.

five

My family shouldn't have to put up with me. They're good people, solid, happy. Sometimes when I'm with them I think I'm on television.

We live in an apartment—a much better one than the Manhattan one, but still not good enough, not something to be *proud* of—in Brooklyn. Brooklyn is a big fat blob with its own ugly shape across from Manhattan; it looks like Jabba the Hutt counting his money. Its bridges connect to Manhattan and it's split up by canals and creeks—filthy green streaks of water that remind you that it used to be a swamp. There are brownstones—limestone and maroon houses that stand like fence posts and always have Indian men refurbishing them—and everybody goes crazy for those, pays millions of dollars to live in them. But other than that, it's a pretty statusless place. It's a shame we moved out of Manhattan, where all the real people with power live.

The walk from Dr. Minerva's office to our

apartment is a short one, but loaded with mocking stores. Food stores. The absolute worst part of being depressed is the food. A person's relationship with food is one of their most important relationships. I don't think your relationship with your parents is that important. Some people never know their parents. I don't think your relationships with your friends are important. But your relationship with air—that's key. You can't break up with air. You're kind of stuck together. Only slightly less crucial is water. And then food. You can't be dropping food to hang with someone else. You need to strike up an agreement with it.

I never liked eating the traditional American things: pork chops, steak, rack of lamb . . . I still don't. Never mind vegetables. I used to like the foods that come in abstract shapes: chicken nuggets, Fruit Roll-Ups, hot dogs. I liked junk food. I could demolish a bag of Cheez Doodles; I'd have Doodle Cheez so far infused into my fingertips, I'd be tasting it on myself for a day. And so I had a good thing going with food. I thought about it the way everyone else did; when you're hungry, you have some.

Then last fall happened, and I stopped eating.

Now I get mocked by these groceries, pizza places, ice-cream stores, delis, Chinese places, bakeries, sushi joints, McDonald'ses. They sit out in the street, pushing what I can't enjoy. My stomach shrank or something; it doesn't take in much, and if I force in a certain amount it rejects everything, sends me to the bathroom to vomit in the dark. It's like a gnawing, the tug of a rope wrapped around the end of my esophagus. There's a man down there and he wants food, but the only way he knows to ask for it is to tug on the rope, and when he does, it closes up the entrance so I can't put anything in. If he would just relax, let the rope go, I'd be able to give him all the food he wanted. But he's down there making me dizzy and tired, giving extra tugs as I pass restaurants that smell like fat and grease.

When I do eat, it's one of two experiences: a Battle or a Slaughter. When I'm bad—when the Cycling is going on in my brain—it's a Battle. Every bite hurts. My stomach wants no part of it. Everything is forced. The food wants to stay on the plate, and once it's inside me, it wants to get *back* on the plate. People give me strange looks: *What's wrong, Craig, why aren't you eating?*

But then there are moments when it comes together. The Shift hasn't happened yet, maybe it never will, but sometimes—just enough times to give me hope—my brain jars back into where it's supposed to be. When I feel one of these (I call them the Fake Shifts) I should always eat, although I don't; I sometimes stubbornly, foolishly try to hold the feeling and get things done while my mind can operate, and neglect to eat, and then I'm back where I started. But oh, when I slip back into being okay when I'm around food, watch out. It's all going in. Eggs and hamburgers and fries and ice cream and marmalade and Fruity Pebbles and cookies and broccoli, even—and noodles and sauce. Screw you; I'm going to eat *all* of you. I'm Craig Gilner, and I will make myself strong from you. I don't know when my body chemistry is going to line up to let me eat again, so you are all getting in me right now.

And that feels so good. I eat it all, and the man is away from his rope. He's busy down there eating everything that falls inside, running around like a chicken with its head cut off, the head on the floor, munching food of its own. All my cells take the food in and they love it and they love my brain for it and I smile and I am full; I am full and functional and I can do anything, and once I eat—this is the amazing part—once I eat I *sleep*, I sleep like I should, like a hunter who just brought home a kill . . . but then I wake up and the man is back, my stomach is tight, and I don't know what it was that got me to have a Slaughter eating experience. It's not pot. It's not girls. It's not my family. I've started to think it must just be chemistry, in which case we're looking for the Shift and we haven't found it yet.

six

Night is here except for a thin gray at the edge of the sky and the trees are thick with rain and the drizzle is pissing on me as I come up to my house. No sunsets in spring. I lean in and ring the buzzer, streaked bronze from years of use—the most used buzzer in the building.

"Craig?"

"Hi, Mom."

Bzzzzzzzt. It growls deeply, amplified by the lobby. (Lobby. Mailroom, more like, just a compartment for mailboxes.) I throw open one door and then the other. It's warm in the house, and it smells like cooked starch. The dogs greet me.

"Hi, Rudy. Hi, Jordan." They're little dogs. My sister named them; she's nine. Rudy is a mutt; my father says he's a cross between a chihuahua and a German shepherd, which must've been some wild dog sex. I hope the German shepherd was the guy. Otherwise the German shepherd girl probably wasn't too satisfied. Rudy has a pronounced under-bite; he looks like two dogs where one is eating the other's head from below, but when I take him for a walk, girls love him and talk to me. Then they realize that I'm young and/or messed up, and they move on.

Jordan, a Tibetan spaniel, looks like a small, brown lion. He's small and cute but completely crazy. His breed was devised in Tibet for the purpose of guarding monasteries. When he came into our home, he immediately fixated on the house as a monastery, the bathroom as the most sacred monastic cell, and my mom as the Abbess. You can't go near my mother without Jordan protecting her. When she's in the bathroom in the morning, Jordan has to be in there with her, placed up on the counter by the sink as she brushes her teeth.

Jordan barks at me. Since I started losing it, he started barking at me. It's not something any of us mention.

"Craig, how was Dr. Minerva?" Mom comes out of the kitchen. She's still tall and skinny, looking better each year. I know that's weird to think, but what the hell—she's just a woman who happens to be my mom. It's amazing how she looks more stately and confident as she gets older. I've seen pictures of her in college and she didn't look like much. Dad is looking like he made a better decision every year.

"It . . . was okay." I hug her. She's taken such good care of me since I got bad; I owe her everything and I love her and I tell her these days, although every time I say it, it gets a little diluted. I think you run out of I *love yous*.

"Are you still happy with her?"

"Yeah."

"Because if you're not we'll get you someone else."

You can't afford to get anyone else, I think, looking at the crack in the wall next to my mom. This crack in our front hallway has been there for three or four years. Dad paints over it and it just recracks. We've tried putting a mirror over it but it's a strange place to put a mirror—on one side of a hallway—and my sister started calling it the Vampire Mirror to tell if people who came into the house were vampires, and it came down after a few weeks, when I came home stoned and stumbled into it. Now there's an exposed crack again. It's never going to get fixed.

"You don't need to get anyone else."

"How's your eating? Are you hungry?"

Yes, I think. I am going to eat the food my mom made me. I'm still in control of my mind and I have medication and I am going to make this happen.

"Yes."

"Good! To the kitchen!"

I go in, and the place is all set for me. Dad and my sister, Sarah, are sitting at the circular table, knives and forks in hand, posing for me.

"How do we look?" Dad asks, banging his silverware on the table. "Do we look hungry?"

My parents are always looking into new ways to fix me. They've tried acupuncture, yoga, cognitive therapy, relaxation tapes, various kinds of forced exercise (until I found my bike), self-help books, Tae Bo, and feng shui in my room. They've spent a lot of money on me. I'm ashamed.

"Eat! Eat! Eat!" Sarah says. "We were waiting for you."

"Is this necessary?" I ask.

"We're just making things more homey for you." Mom brings a baking pan over to the table. It smells hot and juicy. Inside the pan are big orange things cut in half.

"We have squash"—she turns back to the stove—"rice, and chicken." She brings over a pot of white rice with vegetable bits sprinkled over it and a plate of chicken patties. I go for them—a star-shaped one, a dinosaur-shaped one. Sarah grabs at the dinosaur-shaped one at the same time.

"The dinosaurs are mine!"

"Okay." I let her. She kicks me under the table. "How're you feeling?" she whispers.

"Not good."

She nods. Sarah knows what this means. It means she'll see me on the couch tonight, tossing and turning and sweating as Mom brings me warm milk. It means she'll see me watching TV, but not really watching, just staring and not laughing, as I don't do my homework. It means she'll see me sinking and failing. She reacts well to this. She does more schoolwork and has more fun. She doesn't want to end up like me. At least I'm giving someone an example not to follow.

"I'm sorry. They're trying to do a big thing for you."

"I can tell."

"So, Craig, how was school today?" Dad asks. He forks into the squash and looks at me through his glasses. He's short and wears glasses, but like he says, at least he has hair—thick, dark stuff that he passed on to me. He tells me I'm blessed; the genes are good on both sides, and if I think I'm depressed now, imagine if I knew I was going to lose my hair like everyone else! Ha.

"All right," I say.

"What'd you do?"

"Sat in class and followed instructions."

We clink at our food. I take my first bite—a carefully constructed forkful of chicken, rice, and squash—and mash it into my mouth. *I will eat this.* I chew it and feel that it tastes good and rear my tongue back and send it down. I hold it. All right. It's in there.

"What did you do in . . . let's see . . . American History?"

"That one wasn't so good. The teacher called on me and I couldn't talk."

"Oh, Craig . . ." Mom is like.

I start constructing another bite.

"What do you mean you couldn't talk?" Dad asks.

"I knew the answer, but . . . I just . . ."

"You trailed off," Mom says.

I nod as I take in the next bite.

"Craig, you can't keep doing that."

"Honey—" Mom tells him.

"When you know the answer to something, you have to speak up for yourself; how can that not be clear?"

Dad takes in a heaping forkful of squash and chews it like a furnace.

"Don't jump on him," Mom says.

"I'm not, I'm being friendly." Dad smiles. "Craig,

you are blessed with a good mind. You just have to have confidence in it and talk when people call on you. Like you used to do. Back when they had to tell you to *stop* talking."

"It's different now . . ." Third bite.

"We know. Your mother and I know and we're doing everything we can to help you. Right?" He looks across the table at Mom.

"Yes."

"Me too," Sarah says. "I'm doing everything I can, too."

"That's right." Mom reaches across to ruffle her hair. "You're doing great."

"Yesterday, I could've smoked pot, but didn't," I say, looking up, curled over my plate.

"Craig!" Dad snaps.

"Let's not talk about this," Mom says.

"But you should know; it's important. I'm doing experiments with my mind, to see how it got the way it is."

"What are you *talking* about?"

"Not around your sister," Mom says. "I want to tell you some news about Jordan." Hearing his name, the dog walks into the kitchen, takes up his position by Mom. "I took him to the vet today."

"So you didn't go to work?"

"Right."

"And that's why you cooked."

"Exactly."

I'm jealous of her. Can you be jealous of your mom for being able to handle things? I couldn't take a day off, take a dog to the vet, and cook dinner. That's like three times too much stuff for me to get done in one day. How am I ever going to have my own house?

"So you want to know what happened at the vet?"

"It's crazy," Sarah says.

"We took him in for the seizures he's been having," Mom says. "And you'll never believe what the vet said."

"What?"

"They took some blood tests last time, and the results came back—I was sitting in the little room with Jordan; he was being very good. The vet comes in and looks at the papers and says, 'These numbers are not compatible with life.'"

I laugh. There's a bite on my fork in front of me. It shakes. "What do you mean?"

"That's what I asked him. And it turns out that a dog's blood-sugar level is supposed to be between forty and one hundred. You know what Jordan's is?"

"What?"

"Nine."

"*Ruff!*" Jordan barks.

"Then"—Mom is laughing now—"there's some sort of other number, some enzyme ratio level, that's supposed to be between ten and thirty, and Jordan's is *one eighty!*"

"Good dog," Dad says.

"The vet didn't know what to make of it. He told me to keep giving him the supplements and the vitamins, but that basically he's a medical miracle."

I look over at Jordan, the Tibetan spaniel. Pushed-in shaggy face, black nose, big dark eyes like mine. Panting and drooling. Resting on his furry front legs.

"He shouldn't be alive, but he is," Mom says.

I look at Jordan more. Why are you bothering? You've got an excuse. You've got bad blood. You must like living; I guess I would if I were you. Going from meal to meal and guarding Mom. It's a life. It doesn't involve tests or homework. You don't have to buy things.

"Craig?"

You shouldn't be able to be alive and you are. You want to trade?

"I . . . I guess it's cool."

"It's very cool," Mom says. "It's by God's grace that this dog lives."

Oh, right, God. Forgot about him. He's definitely, according to Mom, going to have a role in me getting better. But I find God to be an ineffectual shrink. He adopts the "do nothing" method of therapy. You tell him your problems and he, ah, does nothing.

"I'm done," Sarah says. She picks up her plate and trots out of the room, calling to Jordan. He follows.

"I can't eat any more either," I say. I've managed five bites. My stomach is churning and closing fast. It's all such inoffensive food; I shouldn't have any problems with it. I should be able to eat three plates of it. I'm a growing boy; I shouldn't have trouble sleeping; I should be playing sports! I should be making out with girls. I should be finding what I love about this world. I should be frickin' eating and sleeping and drinking and studying and watching TV and being *normal*.

"Try a little more, Craig," Mom says. "No pressure, but you should eat."

That's right. I'm going to eat. I slice off the top of the squash, in streets and avenues, a big chunk, and put it on my fork and get it in my mouth. *I'm going to eat you.* I chew it, soft and yielding, easily molded into a shape that fits down my throat. It tastes sweet. *Now hold it.* It's in my stomach. I'm sweating. The sweating gets worse around my parents. My stomach has it. My stomach is full of six bites of this meal. I can take six bites. I won't lose it. I won't lose this meal that my mom has made. If the dog can live, I can eat. I hold it. I make a fist. I tense my muscles.

"Are you okay?"

"One second," I say.

I lose.

My stomach hitches as I leave the table.

What were you trying to do, soldier?

I was trying to eat, sir!

And what happened?

I got caught thinking about some crap, sir!

What kind of crap?

How I want to live less than my parents' dog.

Are you still concentrated on the enemy, soldier?

I don't think so.

Do you even know who the enemy is?

I think… it's me.

That's right.

I have to concentrate on myself.

Yes. But not right now, because now you're going to the bathroom to throw up! It's tough to fight when you're throwing up!

I stumble into the bathroom, turn off the light, close the door. The horrible thing is that I like this part, because when it's over I know I'll be warm; I'll have the warmth in me of a body having just been through a trauma. I bear down on the toilet in the dark—I know just where to go—and my stomach hitches again and slams up at me, and I open up and groan. It comes out, and I hear my mother outside, sniffling, and my dad muttering, probably holding her. I grip the handle and flush a few times, alternating filling the toilet and flushing it. When I'm done I'll go to sleep, and I won't do any homework; I'm not up to it tonight.

And I think as I'm down there:

The Shift is coming. The Shift has to be coming. Because if you keep on living like this you'll die.

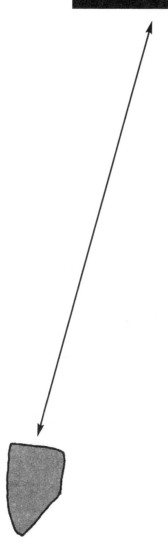

PART 2: HOW I GOT THERE

seven

So why am I depressed? That's the million-dollar question, baby, the Tootsie Roll question; not even the owl knows the answer to that one. I don't know either. All I know is the chronology.

Two years ago I got into one of the best high schools in Manhattan: Executive Pre-Professional High School. It's a new school set up to create the leaders of tomorrow; corporate internships are mandatory; the higher-ups of Merrill Lynch come and speak to classes and distribute travel mugs and stuff. This billionaire philanthropist named Bernard Lutz set it up in conjunction with the public school system, like a school within a school—all you have to do to get in is pass a test. Then your whole high school is paid for and you have access to 800 of the smartest, most interesting students in the world—not to mention the teachers and visiting dignitaries. You can come out of Executive Pre-Professional High School and go right to Wall Street, although that's not what you *should* do; what you *should* do is come out and go to Harvard and then law school. That's how you end up being, like, President.

I'll admit it: I kind of want to be President.

So this test—they named it the Bernard Lutz Philanthropic Exam, in honor of his philanthropicness—became fairly important in my life. It became more important than, uh, food, for instance. I bought the book for it—Bernard Lutz puts out his own line of test-prep books for his own test—and started studying three hours a day.

I was in seventh grade, and I got comfortable with my room for the first time—I'd come home with my heavy backpack and toss it on the bed and watch it bounce toward the pillows as I sat down in my chair and pulled out my test-prep book. On my cell phone, I would go to TOOLS: ALARM and set myself up for a two-hour practice exam. There were five practice exams in the book, and after I did them all, I was thrilled to discover an ad at the back for twelve *more* Bernard Lutz test-prep books. I went to Barnes & Noble; they didn't have all of them in stock—they'd never had anyone ask for *all* of them—so they had to put in an order for me. But then it was *game on*. I started taking a practice exam every day. The questions covered the standard junk that they test you on to determine if you're not an idiot:

Reading comprehension. *Ooh. Can you read this selection and tell what kind of tree they're trying to save?*

Vocabulary. *Did you buy a book full of weird words and learn them?*

Math. *Are you able to turn off your mind to the world and fill it with symbols that follow rules?*

I made that test my bitch. I mauled the practice exams and slept with the books under my pillow and turned my brain into a fierce machine, a buzz saw that could handle anything. I could feel myself getting smarter, under the light at my desk. I could feel me filling myself.

Now, I stopped hanging out with a lot of friends when I got into Executive Pre-Professional mode. I didn't have many friends to begin with—I had the kids who I sat with during lunch, the bare minimum—but once I started carrying flash cards around they sort of avoided me. I don't know what their problem was; I just wanted to maximize my time. When all of my test-prep books were done, I got a personal tutor to shore me up for the exam. She told me halfway through the sessions that I didn't need her, but kept my mom's $700.

I got an 800 on the test, out of 800.

The day I got those test results, a cold, plaintive, late-fall New York day, was my last good day. I've had good moments scattered since then, times when I thought I was better, but that was the last day I felt *triumphant*. The letter from Executive Pre-Professional High School came in the mail, and Mom had saved it on the kitchen table for me when I got home from Tae Bo class after school, which was something I intended to keep doing in high school, to have on my extracurricular activity sheet when I applied for college, which would be the next hurdle, the next step.

"Craig, guess what's here?"

I threw down my backpack and ran past the Vampire Mirror to the kitchen. There it was: a manila envelope. The good kind of envelope. If you failed the test, you got a small envelope; if you got in, you got a big one.

"*Yeesssss!*" I screamed. I tore it open. I took out the purple-and-gold welcome packet and held it up like the holy grail. I could have used it to start my own religion. I could have made, y'know, love to it. I kissed it and hugged it until Mom said, "Craig, stop that. That's very sick. How about you call your friends?"

She didn't know, because I never told her, that my friends were a bit estranged. They're sort of ancillary anyway, friends. I mean, they're *important*—everybody knows that; the TV tells you so—but they come and go. You lose one friend, you pick up another. All you have to do is talk to people, and this was back when I could talk to anybody. My friends, when I had them, pretty much just ragged on me and took my seat when I left the room anyway. Why did I need to call them up?

Except Aaron. Aaron was a real friend; I guess I'd call him my best friend. He was one of the oldest guys in my class, born on that cusp where you can be the youngest person in an older class or the oldest in a younger class, and his parents did the right thing and went with the latter. He was smart and fearless, with a flop of brown curly hair and the sort of glasses that made girls like him, square black ones. He had freckles and he talked a lot. When we got together we would start projects: an alarm clock torn apart and distributed over a wall, a stop-motion video of Lego people having sex, a Web site for pictures of toilets.

I had met him by wandering over to the table during lunch with my head buried in flash cards, sitting down, having one of his friends ask me what I was doing there, and having him come by, flush with tacos, to rescue me, ask what I was studying. It turned out that he and I were taking the same exam, but he wasn't studying at all—didn't believe in it. He introduced me to the table conversation about what Princess Zelda would be like in bed—I said she'd be terrible, because she'd been locked up in dungeons since puberty, but Aaron said that'd make her *super hot.*

Aaron called me that Friday night.

"Want to come over and watch movies?"

"Sure." I was done with my practice test for the day.

Aaron lived in a small apartment in a big building in downtown Manhattan by City Hall. I took the subway in (my mom had to okay it with Aaron's mom, which was horrifying), identified myself to Aaron's paunchy doorman, and took the elevator up to his floor. Aaron's mom greeted me and brought me into his ventilated chamber (past his dad, who wrote in a room that resembled a prison cell, occasionally beating his head against his desk, while Aaron's mom brought him tea) and flopped on his bed, which wasn't yet covered with the sort of stains that would define it in the future. I'm good at *flopping* on things.

"Hey," Aaron was like. "You want to smoke some pot?"

Oh. So *this* was what watching movies meant. Quick recap of what I knew about drugs: my mom told me never to do them; my dad told me not to do them until after the SATs. Mom trumped Dad, so I vowed to never do them—but what if someone *made* me? I thought drugs might be something people did *to* you, like jabbing you with a needle while you were trying to mind your business.

"What if someone makes me, Mom?" I had asked her; we were having the drug conversation in a playground. I was ten. "What if they hold a gun to my head and force me to take the drugs?"

"That's not really how it works, honey," she answered. "People take drugs because they *want* to. You just have to not want to."

And now here I was with Aaron, wanting to. His room smelled like certain areas of Central Park, down by the lake, where white guys with dreadlocks played bongos.

My mom hovered in my head.

"Nah," I was like.

"No problem." He opened a pungent bag and put a chunk of the contents of the bag in a very fascinating little device that looked like a cigarette but was made of metal. He lit it up with a butane lighter that made a flame approximately as large as my middle finger. He puffed right up against his wall.

"Don't you have to open a window?"

"Nah, it's my room; I can do what I want."

"Doesn't your mom care?"

"She has her hands full with Dad."

The section of wall he smoked against would get

discolored over the next two years. Eventually, like the rest of the room, it would get covered up with posters of rappers with gold teeth.

Aaron took three or four breaths of his metal cigarette and made the room smell musty and hot, then announced:

"Let's motivate, son! What do you want to get?"

"Action." *Duh.* I was in seventh grade.

"All right! You know what I want?" Aaron's eyes lit up. "I want a movie with a cliff."

"A mountain-climbing one?"

"Doesn't have to be *about* mountain climbing. Just needs at least one scene where some dudes are fighting and somebody gets thrown off a cliff."

"Did you hear about Paul Stojanovich?"

"Who's that?"

"He's the producer who invented *World's Scariest Police Chases* and *Cops*."

"No kidding? The host?"

"No, the producer. The host kicks ass, though."

Aaron led the way out of his room and past his father—typing away, wiping sweat, for all intents and purposes a part of the computer—to his front door, where his mom, who had long dirty-blond hair and wore overalls, stopped us and gave us cookies and our coats.

"I love my life," Aaron said. "Bye, Mom." We

entered the elevator with our mouths full of cookies.

"Okay, so what were you saying? I love *World's Scariest Police Chases.*" Aaron swallowed. "I love it when the guy is like"—Aaron put on a stern over-annunciated brogue—"'These two-bit bandits thought they could turn a blind eye to the law, but the Broward County Sherrif's office showed them the light—and it *led them straight to jail.*'"

I cracked up, spitting cookie bits everywhere.

"I'm good at voices. You want to hear Jay Leno blowing the devil? I got it from this comedian Bill Hicks."

"You never let me finish about Paul Stojanovich!" I said.

"Who?"

The elevator arrived in Aaron's lobby. "The producer of *World's Scariest Police Chases.*"

"Oh, right." Aaron threw open the glass lobby door. I followed him into the street, tossed up my hood, and bundled myself in it.

"He was posing with his fiancée, for like a wedding picture? And they were doing it in Oregon, right next to this big cliff. And the photographer was like 'Move back, move a little to the left.' And they moved, and he *fell off the cliff.*"

"Oh my God!" Aaron shook his head. "How do you learn this stuff?"

"The Internet." I smiled.

"That is too good. What happened to the girl?"

"She was fine."

"She should sue the photographer. Did they sue him?"

"I don't know."

"They better. I would sue. You know, Craig"—Aaron looked at me steadily, his eyes red but so alive and bright—"I'm going to be a lawyer."

"Oh, yeah?"

"Yeah. Screw my dad. He doesn't make any money. He's miserable. The only reason we even live where we do is because my mom's brother is a lawyer and they got the apartment way back when. It used to be my uncle's apartment. Now he does work for the building, so they cut Mom a deal. Everything good I have is due to lawyers."

"I think I might want to be one too," I said.

"Why not? You make money!"

"Yeah." I looked up. We were on a bright, cold, gray Manhattan sidewalk. Everything cost so much money. I looked at the hot dog man, the cheapest thing around—you wouldn't get away from him without forking over three or four bucks.

"We should be lawyers together," Aaron said. "Pardis and . . . what's your last name?"

"Gilner."

"Pardis and Gilner."

"Okay."

We shook hands, maintaining our stride, nearly clothesline-ing a frilled-up little girl walking in the other direction. Then we turned up Church Street and rented this reality DVD, *Life Against Death*, which had a *lot* of cliffs, as well as fires, animal attacks, and skydiving accidents. I sat propped in Aaron's bed, him smoking pot and me refusing, feeding off him, telling him that I thought I was getting a contact high when really I was just feeling like I had stepped into a new groove. At cool parts of *Life Against Death* we paused and zoomed in: on the hearts of explosions, spinning wheels after truck crashes, and one guy freaking out in a gorilla cage and getting a rock thrown at him. We talked about making our own movie someday.

I didn't go to sleep until four, but I was in someone else's house, so I woke up early—at eight—with that crazy sleeping-at-someone-else's-house energy. I passed Aaron's father at his computer and grabbed a book off their shelf in the living room—*Latin Roots*. I studied *Latin Roots* all morning, for the test.

We kept doing it. It became a regular thing. We never formalized it, never named it . . . but on Fridays Aaron would call and ask me to watch movies. I think he was lonely. Whatever he was, he became the one person I wanted to stay in touch with after junior high. And now, a year later, I was in my kitchen holding my acceptance letter and wondering if he had one too.

"I'll call Aaron," I told Mom.

eight

"What *up*, son? Did you get in?!"

"Yeah."

"*Allriiiiiiight!*"

"*Hoooooooo—ee!*"

"*Biyatch!*"

"That's right!"

"But you studied. I didn't study at all," he was like.

"True. I should feel lucky to talk to you. You're kind of like Hercules."

"Yeah, cleaning the stables. I'm having a party."

"When? Tonight?"

"Yup. My parents are away. I have the whole house. You're coming, right?"

"A real party? Without a cake?"

"Absolutely."

"Sure!" I was in eighth grade and I had gotten into high school and I was going to a party? I was set for life!

"Can you bring any booze?"

"Like drinks?"

"Craig, c'mon. Yes. Can you bring?"

"I don't have ID."

"Craig, *none* of us have ID! I mean, can you take some off your parents?"

"I don't think they have any . . ." But I knew that wasn't true.

"They have *something*."

I held my hand over my cell so Mom wouldn't hear. "Scotch. They have a bottle of scotch."

"What kind?"

"Jeez, dude, I don't know."

"Well, bring it. Can you call any girls?"

I had been in my room studying for a year. "No."

"That's all right, I'll bring the girls. You want to at least help me set up?"

"Sure!"

"Get over here."

"I'm going to Aaron's house!" I announced to Mom, flipping my phone shut. I still had the welcome packet in my hand; I gave it to her to put in my room.

"What are you going to do over there?" she asked, beaming at the packet, then at me.

"Um . . . sleep over."

"Are you going to celebrate? Because you should celebrate."

"Heh. Yeah."

"Craig, I'm being honest, I've never seen someone work as hard as you did getting into this school. You deserve a little break and you deserve to feel proud of yourself. You're gifted, and the world is taking notice. This is the first step in an amazing journey—"

"Okay, Mom, please." I hugged her.

I grabbed my coat and sat at the kitchen table, pretending to text on the phone. When Mom left the room, I invaded the cabinet above the sink, took out the one bottle of scotch (Glenlivet), and fetched from the back of the cupboard the thermos that I used to use for grade-school lunches. That would seem really cool at the party. I poured some scotch in and I put a little water back in the scotch, in case they checked levels, and stuffed the thermos in my big jacket pocket before leaving the house and calling back to Mom that I would call her later.

I took the subway to Aaron's without a book to study on my lap—first time in a year. At his stop, I bounded up the stairs into the gray streets, slipped into his building, nodded to the doorman to call up, and squished my thumb on the elevator button, giving it a twist and some flair. At the sixteenth floor was Aaron, holding his front door open, rap music about killing people on in the background, holding his metal cigarette out for me.

"Smoke. Celebrate."

I stopped.

"If anytime's the time, it's now."

I nodded.

"Come in, I'll show you." Aaron brought me into his house and sat me on his couch and demonstrated how to hold the cigarette so the metal wouldn't burn me. He explained how you have to take the smoke into your lungs, not your stomach—"Don't swallow it, Craig, that's how hits get lost"—and how to let it go as slowly as you could through your mouth or nose. The key was to hold it in as long as possible. But you didn't want to hold it *too long*. Then you *coughed*.

"How do I light it?" I asked.

"I'll light it for you," Aaron was like. He knelt in front of me on the couch—I took a look at his living room, fenced in with floor-to-ceiling bookshelves, filled up with a coffee table, a tall fluted ash tray, a porcelain dog, and a small electric piano—trying to remember how it all looked in case it changed later. The only thing I had done that people said was *kind of* like smoking pot was go really hard on the swings, and Aaron had told me that anyone who said that was probably high when they were on the swings.

The butane flame went up.

I sucked in on the metal cigarette as if a doctor were telling me to.

My mouth filled up with the taste that I knew so well from Aaron's room—a chemical taste, buzzy and light. I looked him in the eyes with my cheeks puffed out. He clipped the flame, smiling.

"Not in your cheeks!" he said. "You look like Dizzy Gillespie! In your lungs! Put it in your lungs."

I worked with new muscles. The smoke in me felt like a blob of clay.

"That's it, hold it, hold it . . ."

My eyes started watering, getting hot.

"Hold it. Hold it. You want more?"

I shook my head, terrified. Aaron laughed.

"Okay. Dude, you're good. You're good, dude!"

Pfffffffffffft. I blew it all in Aaron's face.

"Jesus! Man, that was *big!*" Aaron swatted at the cloud that came out of me. "You sure you haven't done this before?"

I panted, breathing in air that still had the smoke in it. "What's going to happen?" I asked.

"Probably nothing." Aaron stood up, took his cigarette back, put it in the stand-up ash tray. Then he reached down with his hand out—I expected a handshake, but he pulled me off the couch. *"Congratulations."*

We hugged, mouth to ear. It was a guy hug,

complete with slapping. I leaned back and smiled at him as I clasped his arms.

"You too, man. It's going to be great."

"I'm-a tell you what's going to be great: this *party*," Aaron said, and he began pacing, counting on his fingers. "I need for you to go and get some seltzer, for spritzers. Also we gotta put away all of my dad's books and writing so it doesn't get damaged. Also, call this girl; her dad threatened to call the cops if I called again; say you're with Greenpeace."

"I'm not going to remember this; hold on," I said, taking an index card from Aaron's coffee table. I was numbering it with a Sharpie, from one, when the weed hit me.

"Whoa. Wow."

"Uh-oh," Aaron said. He looked up.

"*Whoa.*"

"You feeling it?"

Is my brain falling out of my head? I thought.

I looked down at the index card that said *1)get seltzer,* and *1) get seltzer* twisted back, as if it had decided to fall off the card. I looked up at Aaron's bookshelves and they looked the same, but as I turned, they moved in frames. It wasn't like the slowness that came from being underwater; it was like I was under *air*—thick and heavy air that had decided to follow me. For being *high*, it felt pretty heavy.

"You feeling it?" Aaron repeated.

I looked at his stand-up ashtray, filled with crumpled cigarettes and the one clear, shining metal cigarette.

"It's like the king of the cigarette butts!" I said.

"Oh, boy," Aaron was like. "Craig. Are you going to be able to do the stuff for the party?"

Was I? I was able to do *anything*. Here I was making clever statements like "king of the cigarette butts"; if I went outside, there was no *telling* what I would be capable of.

"What's first?" I asked.

Aaron gave me a few bucks to get the seltzer, but just as I was opening the door to go out into the world, his buzzer rang.

"It's Nia," Aaron said, leaping to the closed-circuit phone in his kitchen, which was full of grapefruits and dark wood cabinets.

"*She's* coming?" I asked.

Nia was in our class; she was half Chinese and half Jewish; she dressed well. Every day she came in with something different—a chain of SpongeBob Burger King toys strung around her neck; one asymmetrical, giant, red-plastic hoop earring; black clown circles on her cheeks. I think her accessories were a courtesy meant to distract from her small, lucrative body and baby-doll face. If she let it all go natural, if she just let her hair swing down the way it would have if she'd grown up in a field with the wind, she'd make all us boys explode.

"Nia's pretty hot, huh," Aaron said, hanging up the phone.

"She's okay."

We sat watching the door like we were waiting for the mama bird to bring us food. She knocked.

"*Heyyyy,*" Aaron called, beating me.

"Hi!" I said. We rushed to the doorknob; Aaron gave a look, pulled it toward him, and there she was—in a green dress with a rainbow of fuzzy anklets on one leg. Her eyes were so big and dark that she seemed even more tiny and spindly, on high-heeled shoes that threw her forward at us and made her dress outline her little breasts.

"Boys," she said. "I think someone has been smoking *pah*-aht."

"No way," Aaron said.

"My friends are coming. When's the party starting?"

"Five minutes ago," Aaron said. "You want to play Scrabble?"

"Scrabble!" Nia put her bag down—it was shaped like a hippo. "Who plays Scrabble?"

"Well, I do, duh, and Craig does, too"—I didn't,

actually—"and we're some smart guys, seeing as we got in."

"I *heard!*" Nia grabbed her hippo bag and hit Aaron with it. "I did too!" As an afterthought, she hit me. "Congratulations!"

"Group hug!" Aaron announced, and we got together, a tiered threesome—Nia's head came up to my chin; my head came up to Aaron's chin. I put my hand around Nia's waist and felt her warmth and how narrow she was. Her palm curled around my shoulder. We pushed our torsos together in a sort of ballet. I could feel Nia's breath between us. I turned to look—

"Scrabble," Aaron said. He went across the living room, took it out of one of the bookshelves. He put it on the floor and we sat, Aaron between me and Nia, the ashtray taking up the fourth spot.

"House rules," Aaron said as he flipped over the tiles. "If you don't have any words to put on the board, you can make a word up, as long as you have an actual definition for that word in your head. If your definition makes the other people laugh, you get the points, but otherwise, you *lose* that many points."

"We can make up words?" I asked. This was brimming with possibilities. I could make up *Niaed*—what happens when Nia touches you, you get *Niaed*. That would make her laugh. Or not.

"What about Chinese words?" Nia asked.

"You have to know what they mean and be able to explain them."

"Oh. *That* shouldn't be a problem." She smiled wickedly.

"Who's going first?"

"Can we smoke?"

"So demanding." Aaron gave her the metal cigarette—I said no this time; I'd had enough.

For her first word, Nia put down M-U-W-L-I.

"What is that?" I asked.

"Chinese word."

"What's it mean?"

"Uh, cat."

"That's ridiculous. How do we know if *muwli* is real?" I turned to Aaron.

He shrugged. "Benefit of the doubt?"

Nia stuck out her tongue at me and *damn* it was a cute tongue. Is that a ring? I thought. Can't be. Wait—it's gone.

"I *swear*." she said. "'Come here, little *muwli*!' See?"

"I'm checking you on your next one," I said.

"The Internet's over there." Aaron was like.

"But while you're gone, we're going to give you all consonants." Nia smiled.

"Is it my go?" I put down M-O-P off M-U-W-L-I. Ten points.

Aaron put down S-M-A-P off M-O-P. "That's a cross between a smack and a slap. Like, 'I'm-a *smap* you.'"

Nia laughed and laughed. I chuckled even though I didn't want to. Aaron got the points.

Nia put down T-R-I-I-L.

"What is that?" I asked.

"It's a trill, you know, like a trill on the flute, except the first L is lowercase and the second is uppercase!"

"That's not trill, that's 'tree-eel'!"

"Okay, fine." She switched the letters. Now it said T-R-I-L-I.

"Trill-ee! What is a trill-ee?"

"An unmentionable act."

Aaron laughed so hard that he just *had* to ease his body into Nia's, leaning on her shoulder. She pushed back, tilting her flank into him.

I saw where this was going. I made eye contact with Nia and here's what her eyes said:

Craig, we're all headed to the same school. I'm going to need a boyfriend going in, to give me some stability, a little bit of backup, you know? Nothing serious. You're cool, but you're not as cool as Aaron. He has pot and he's so much more laid back than you; you spent the last

*year studying for this test; he didn't lift a finger for it.
That means he's smarter than you. Not that you're not
smart, but intelligence is very important in a guy—it
really is the most important thing, up there with sense of
humor. And he has a better sense of humor than you,
too. It doesn't hurt that he's taller. So I'll be your friend,
but right now let's let this develop. And don't be jealous.
That would be a waste of everybody's time.*

We kept playing. Aaron and Nia moved closer
until their knees touched, and I could only imagine
the energy that was going through those knees. I
thought maybe they were going to lean in for a
first kiss (or a second? No, Aaron would have told
me) right in front of me, when the buzzer rang
again.

It was Nia's friend Cookie. She had brought bottles of beer. We took ten minutes to open them,
eventually hitting them against Aaron's kitchen
countertop edge, to work the tops off. Then Nia
said Cookie should've gotten twist-offs, and she
asked what *twist*-offs were, and we all laughed.
Cookie had blond hair and glitter all over her neck.
She hadn't gotten into Executive Pre-Professional,
but that was okay because she was going to high
school in Canada. The guy down at the local
bodega let her buy beer if she leaned over the
counter—she had developed early and had the kind

of massive alluring breasts that moved in reverse rhythm when she walked.

We put Scrabble away—nobody won. The rap music seemed to be hooked up to some sort of Internet-capable playlist and kept going, never repeating, as more and more guests arrived. There was Anna—she was on Ritalin and snorted it off her little cosmetic mirror before tests; Paul—he was nationally ranked in *Halo 2* and trained five hours a day with his "team" in Seattle (he was going to put it on his college applications); Mika—his dad was a higher-up in the Taxi and Limousine Commission and he had some sort of badge that allowed him to get free cab rides anywhere, anytime. People started showing up who I had no idea who they were, like a stocky white kid in an Eight Ball jacket, which he announced, coming in, was so popular back in the '90s that you would get knived just for having it and *nobody* had vintage like *him.*

Inexplicably, someone came in a Batman mask. His name was Race.

A short, pugnacious, mustached kid named Ronny came with a backpack full of pot and set up shop in the living room.

A girl with hemp bracelets in different subtle shades proclaimed that we *had* to listen to Sublime's *40oz to Freedom,* and when Aaron refused to put it on, she started gyrating and put what she claimed was a Devil curse on him, saying, *"Diablo Tantunka"* and pointing her fingers in mock horns: *"Ffffffft! Ffffffft!"*

I smoked more pot. The party was like a movie—it should have *been* a movie. It was the best movie I'd ever seen—where else did you get shattering glasses, a kid trying to break-dance in the living room, a dictionary being thrown at a roach, a kid holding his head in the freezer and saying it could get you high, orange vomit spread out in a semicircle in the kitchen sink, people yelling out the windows that "school sucks," rap music declaring "I want to drink beers and smoke some shit," and one poor soul snorting a Pixie Stik, then hacking purple dust into the toilet . . . ? Nowhere.

nine

Aaron and Nia talked on the couch. I took my thermos of scotch—just to have something in my hand; I didn't open it—and watched how they moved, swaying toward and away from each other in increments that I doubt they even recognized. They stopped becoming people in my eyes; they morphed right into male and female sex organs on a collision course.

"What's going on, son?" Ronny asked. Ronny hadn't gotten his first piece of jewelry yet; he was in like a larval state. "You enjoying yourself?"

I was enjoying everything but Aaron and Nia. And the scotch. I wanted him to think I was enjoying the scotch, at least.

"Do you like this stuff?" I asked, opening my thermos.

"What is it?" He sniffed. "Yeah, dude, that's hard core. You gotta sip it."

I put it to my lips. I didn't even take any in, just

let it filter against me and felt how hot it was. It was cutting, evil, and bitter-smelling—

Ronny shoved the thermos at my mouth.

"*Sip* it!"

"Dude!" I backed off as scotch splashed on my shirt; it felt lighter, slicker, and warmer than water. "You're such a *dick!*"

"Pause!" He ran across the room and punched this kid Asen, told him he'd had sex with his mom, and threw a pillow at Aaron and Nia, who were now attached by the lips on the couch.

I wasn't that mad that it was happening. I was just mad that I'd missed *how* it happened. I hadn't seen him lean in, or her; I wanted to know for the future, for some girl who wasn't as desirable. But now at least I got a show; I got to see how Aaron moved his hands. He put his right hand on her face over and over, gently, while his left slid around her side and gripped the small of her back more firmly. His hands were playing good-cop–bad-cop.

There was still some scotch in the thermos. I drank from it. The taste didn't bother me since Ronny's shove.

"I didn't know you drank, Craig!" a voice was like behind me. Julie, who always wore sweatpants that said *Nice Try* in an arc on her butt cheeks, clanked a beer against my thermos.

"I don't, really," I was like.

"I thought you'd be busy studying. I heard you got into the school. What are you going to do now?"

"Go there."

"No, I mean with your *time*."

I shrugged. "I'll work hard at school, get good grades, go to a good college, get a good job."

"It was crazy how much you studied. You always had those cards."

I looked at the scotch. My esophagus was scorched, but I took more.

"Did you see Aaron and Nia making out? They're so cute!"

"They're making *out*?" I was shocked.

"Yeah, haven't you seen?"

"I saw them *hooking up*," I explained, looking out the kitchen at them. "I didn't think they were *having sex*."

"They're not!"

"I thought making out was having sex."

"Jeez, Craig, no. Making out is making out."

"Is that the same as hooking up?"

"Well, hooking up can mean having sex. You got confused."

Aaron and Nia were fully occupied now. One of his hands was hidden, exploring magical beige places.

"You should put it on one of your cards."

"Heh." I smiled.

Julie took a step toward me. "I really want to make out with somebody right now."

"Oh, cool."

"I've been looking and looking for someone."

"Um . . ." I eyed her. Her short blond hair framed a face that was a little wide at the bottom, and toothy, and somewhat red all around. I didn't want to hook up with her or make out with her or whatever. The person I wanted was ten feet away. This would be my first kiss, *if* she were offering me. Girls loved to say that they wanted to hook up with "someone" when it was anyone but you. Julie tilted her head up, though, with her eyes closed. I looked at her lips, trying to make myself kiss them, but stopped. For my first kiss, I didn't want to settle. Julie opened her eyes.

"Are you okay, man?"

"Yeah, yeah, I just . . ." Whew. *I'm drunk and stoned, Julie. Give me a break.*

"It's okay." She left the room, and soon after, the party. I had hurt her feelings, I found out later; I didn't know I had that power.

I wandered over to the laptop that was supplying the music to the stereo. Next to it was Aaron's father's record collection, shelved in the bookshelf, of old vinyl records. I suddenly needed some discrete information to put in my brain, to push out what was there, so I pulled a record out.

Led Zeppelin III.

It was big—as big as the laptop—and the cover was a spiral of images: male heads with lots of hair, rainbows, blimps (I guessed those were the Zeppelins), flowers, teeth. The edge of the record stuck out a bit, like a tab on a five-subject notebook, and I grabbed it experimentally. It turned, and when it turned, the whole circle turned inside, and the images that showed through the little holes changed: rainbows into stars, blimps into planes, flowers into dragonflies. It was frickin' *awesome*. One of the symbols that popped up looked just like the levels of Q-Bert, one of the best old video games—I didn't realize Led Zeppelin had invented Q-Bert!

I looked up—Aaron and Nia were still at it. Now he had his hand in her hair and he was pulling her toward him like a gas mask. I held the album up to hide their heads. Heh.

I dropped the album. Aaron and Nia. I held it up. More images. It was like they were part of it.

The house filled up. People began getting in line to go into one of Aaron's book-filled closets. They weren't *making out* or anything—a kid named John had announced that he had sprayed pepper spray in there and people were going in to see if they could handle it. Boys and a few girls stumbled out going "Aggg, my eyes!" and tearing, and running for water, but that didn't stop the ones lined up after them. It seemed like everyone at the party went except me.

I looked at more albums, like the Beatles' *White Album*, which I never knew was actually white, and each time I looked up, Aaron and Nia were in a deeper state of entanglement. Suddenly I got really sleepy and warm, from the scotch I guess, and leaned against the album stack, just trying to rest my eyes for a minute. When I woke up I looked instinctively for Aaron and Nia; they had disappeared. I craned from behind my resting spot and looked at the clock above the TV; somehow it was 2:07 A.M.

ten

The house had thinned out.

Jeez. I got up. The laptop playlist had stopped. My night was over. All I had done was look at records and almost hook up with a girl, but somehow I felt accomplished.

"Uh, Ronny?" I asked.

Ronny was playing PlayStation on Aaron's couch. The PlayStation cord stretched across the room. He looked up.

"What?"

"Where is everybody?"

"Having sex with your mom."

Next to Ronny, a girl named Donna was balled up in a lump on one end of the couch. The guy with the Eight Ball jacket occupied a chair. Someone yelled to put on more music; Ronny yelled to *Shut up, son*. The house was full of cups—mugs and glasses everywhere, like they had been multiplying during the party.

"Does anyone know where Aaron is?"

"Pause," was all Ronny could manage.

"Aaron!"

"Shut up, man! He's with his chick."

"I'm here, I'm here!" Aaron strode out from his room, adjusting his pants. "Jeez." He surveyed the damage. "What's up? You have a good rest?"

"Shoot, yeah. Where's Nia?"

"Asleep."

"You did her good, huh?" Ronny asked. "Asian invasion."

"Shut up, Ronny."

"Asian contagion."

"Shut up."

"Asian persuasion."

Aaron yanked his controller out of the PlayStation.

"Suh-*uhn*!" Ronny scrambled for it.

"You want to go for a walk?" Aaron asked.

"Sure!" I got my jacket.

Aaron woke up Eight Ball jacket and Donna and got them out; he forced Ronny to leave too, over many protests. We all took the elevator down; Eight-Ball jacket and Ronny went uptown; Donna and two others slid into a cab; me and Aaron, instinctively, started toward the shimmering Brooklyn Bridge, which carved its way through the night about three blocks from his house.

"You want to walk across the bridge?" Aaron asked.

"Into Brooklyn?"

"Yeah. You can go home or we can take the subway back to my place."

"When will it be light?"

"In three, four hours."

"Let's do it. I'll walk home and get breakfast."

"Cool."

We walked in step. My feet weren't cold at all. My head swam. I looked at bare trees and thought they were beautiful. The only way it could have been better was if it were snowing. Then I'd have flakes dripping down on me and I'd be able to catch them in my mouth. I wouldn't be worried about Aaron seeing that.

"So, how do you feel?" I was like.

"About what?" he was like.

"You know," I was like.

"Hold on a second." Aaron spotted a Snapple bottle on the curb; it looked like it was filled with urine, which happens a lot in Manhattan—I don't know why but homeless people fill up bottles with piss and then don't even have the courtesy to throw them away—but then again it could be apple Snapple—did they have that? He lunged at it and sent it sailing across the street with a three-point kick; it landed on the opposite curb and shattered yellow under the streetlight.

"*Rrrragh!*" Aaron screamed. Then he looked around. "There aren't any cops, right?"

I laughed. "No." We came to the entrance to the bridge. "So seriously, what was it like?"

"She's awesome. I mean, she likes everything—she really likes it. She likes . . . *sex.*"

"You had sex with her?"

"No, but I can tell. She likes everything else."

"What'd you do?"

He told me.

"No way!" I pushed him as we climbed the bridge. Air from the frigid New York Harbor blew at us, and I put my hood up over my head and tightened the chewed cord. "What was it like?"

"It's the craziest thing," Aaron was like. "It feels just like the inside of your cheek."

"No kidding?" I pulled one hand out of my pocket. "Yeah."

I stuck a finger in my mouth and pushed to the side. "That's it?"

"Just like that," Aaron said. He had his finger in his cheek too. "I'm serious. It's hot."

"Huh."

We walked in silence with our fingers in our mouths.

"Did you hook up with anyone?" he asked.

"Nope. Julie wanted to, though."

"Nice one. Did she slip you something?"

"What? *No.*"

"Because you crashed out pretty hard in the corner over there."

"I was drinking my mom's scotch and checking out your dad's albums."

"You're a trip, Craig."

"It's cold out here."

"Looks pretty cool, though."

We weren't even a tenth of the way up the bridge, but it did look cool. Behind us the walkway extended to City Hall, where the city had sprung for some spotlights to illuminate the dome of the building. It looked like a white pearl nestled between giants like the Woolworth building, which I learned in English class Ayn Rand had described as a "finger of God," and that was about right—green and white at the top like the world's most decorated mint. To our left were the other bridges of Manhattan, arrayed against each other like alternating *sin* and *cos* waves, carrying a smattering of late-night trucks whose tops trailed mist.

But to the right was the best view: New York Harbor. Mostly black. The Statue of Liberty was lit up, but it always struck me as a little cheesy, standing out there being all cute. The real action was on the sides: Manhattan had its no-nonsense downtown, where people made *money*, and on the other side was Brooklyn, sleepy and dark but with a trump card—the container cranes, lit up not for show or government pride but because there was *work* going on, even at this hour—ships unloading stuff that was famously unchecked for terrorist threats but somehow hadn't blown us up yet. Brooklyn was a port. New York was a port. We got things done. I had gotten things done, too.

Between Brooklyn and Manhattan, miles across the water, we saw the final curtain of New York City—the Verrazano Narrows Bridge. It spanned the opening to the port, a steel-blue pair of upper lips greeting the blackness.

I could do anything anywhere, in all four directions.

"Craig?" Aaron was like.

"What's up."

"What's up with *you?* You okay?"

"I'm happy," I said.

"Why not?"

"No, I said I'm *happy.*"

"I know. Why not be?"

We came up to the first tower of the bridge, with a plaque proclaiming who had built it; I stopped to read. John Roebling. Aided by his wife, and then his son. He died during construction. But hey, the Brooklyn Bridge might be here for eight hundred years. I wanted to leave something like that behind. I didn't know how I was going to do it, but I felt like I had taken the first steps.

"The really cool thing about Nia . . ." Aaron was saying, and he started to go into anatomical details, things about her that I didn't need to hear; I tuned him out; I knew he was talking to himself. This was what he was happy about. I was happy about different stuff. I was happy because someday I'd be walking across this bridge looking at this city, owning some piece of it, being *valuable* here.

"Her butt is like—I think her butt shape is where they got the heart logo. . . ."

We came to the middle of the bridge. On either side of us the cars hissed past; red on the left and white on the right, the lanes encased by thin metal trussing that stretched out from the walkway.

I had a sudden urge to walk out over the trussing and lean over the water, to declare myself to the world. Once it came into my head, I couldn't push it away.

"I don't know if it was *real*—" Aaron was saying.

"I want to stand out over the water," I told him.

"*What?*"

"Come with me. You want to do it?"

He stopped.

"Yeah," he said. "Yeah, I see where you're coming from."

There were pathways built onto the top of the trussing, places for the bridge workers to get out to the cables and repair them. I clambered onto one on the harbor side, the side crowned by the Verrazano, and grabbed the handrails and balanced my feet one in front of the other on a piece of metal about four inches wide. Below me cabs and SUVs hummed by. In front of me was the black of the water and the black of the sky and the cold.

"You're crazy," Aaron said.

I took steps forward. It was easy. Stuff like this always is. The stuff adults tell you not to do is the easiest.

Below me there were three lanes of traffic; I cleared the first, got halfway over the second; then Aaron yelled:

"What are you going to do out there?!"

"I'm just going to think!" I called back.

"About what?"

I shook my head. I couldn't explain. "It'll only take a minute!"

Aaron turned back.

I moved past the second lane and kept my eyes

on the horizon. I didn't move my eyes from it for the last lane, shifting my hands in front of one another in a tight rhythm. I came to the edge of the bridge and was sort of surprised how there wasn't any fence. There wasn't anything to keep you from falling off, just your hands and your will. I gripped the bars at either side—they were freezing—and then sprung my hands open and spread my arms wide and felt the wind whip and tug at me as I leaned myself over the water like . . . well, like Christ, I guess.

I closed my eyes and opened them, and the only difference was the feel of the wind on my eyeballs, because when I closed them I could still see the dotted lights perfectly. I threw back my head and yelled. When I was a kid I read these books, the Redwall books, fantasy books about a bunch of warrior mice, and the mice had this war cry that I always thought was cool: "Eulalia."

And like an idiot, that's what I yelled off the Brooklyn Bridge:

"Eulaliaaaaaaaaaaaaaaaaa!"

And I could have died right then.

And considering how things went, I really should have.

eleven

Depression starts slow. After howling off the Brooklyn Bridge, I walked home and felt great. Aaron split and took a late-night subway back to Manhattan, where he had a hell of a time cleaning up his apartment and returning Nia to her parents; I went to a diner and got some eggs and wheat toast and came home at ten in the morning, telling Mom I had slept over at Aaron's, and pouring myself into bed. When I got up in the afternoon there were some forms to sign about accepting my admission to Executive Pre-Professional and a physical to schedule—how glorious. For once I was looking forward to the doctor holding my balls and telling me to cough, which I still don't understand why they do.

The rest of junior high was a joke. I didn't need to do anything except make sure I didn't fail a class and get "rescinded" from Executive Pre-Professional, so I started hanging out with Aaron every day. Now that we had the pot barrier broken, it became a magnificent haze of yelling back at the TV; we stopped calling it "watching movies"; we started calling it "chilling."

"Want to chill?" Aaron would ask, and I would pop on over.

Ronny was never far behind. His insults never stopped, although they became more lovable, but that didn't matter, because he grew into a reliable dealer. He wasn't going to high school with us—for all we knew, he wasn't going at all—but he was going to set up a jewelry shop, sell drugs, and make beats, *that* was for sure.

Nia was always around, too. She and Aaron spent about as much time apart as me and my right hand. I thought I was cool with it, but as I saw them—sitting with each other, sitting *on* each other, hugging each other, touching each other's butt, smiling and kissing, in Aaron's room or in public—I started to get more and more pissed off. It was like they were throwing it in my face, although I knew neither of them meant that, the way I had thrown my studying in people's faces and not meant it. Why else would they tell each other how much they wanted each other in whispers in front of me? Why else would Aaron tell me, in great detail, about the first time they had sex? One day Aaron announced to me and Ronny as we watched MTV,

"You know what, since I got with Nia, I've forgotten how to masturbate."

"Me too, since I found your mom," Ronny said.

"Huh," I said. My stomach hitched.

"I'm serious, I don't even know, anymore!" Aaron grinned.

Great, man. Wonderful. I learned *how* to masturbate the last few months of junior high, when I went on AOL and started talking to girls with names like "LittleLusciousLolita42." I don't know if they were really girls. I just knew that I was lonely, and I wanted to make it so that when I got with someone, I'd have some idea what to do.

Problem was, no matter what girl I was talking to online, when I came to the end of the whole process, I would run to the bathroom. And as I knelt down in front of the toilet, in the final few milliseconds, I would think about Nia.

I had homework for school even before school started. They gave me this insane reading list for the summer that included *Under the Volcano* and *David Copperfield*. I tried to read them; I really did, but it wasn't like flash cards. It took *days*. Mom actually read the letters that the school sent and told me that part of their mission was to make us *well-rounded, liberally educated bearers of tomorrow's vision,* so I had better be ready to do English as well as math; but I found myself jealous of the people who wrote the books. They were dead and they were still taking up my time. Who did they think they were? I would much rather chill at Aaron's, sit in my room, run to the Internet and then to the bathroom, rinse, cycle, repeat. I ended up not finishing any of the summer-reading-list books.

That wasn't good when it came time to start school. The first day, I was quizzed on what I was supposed to have read over the summer. I got a 70, something I'd never seen on a sheet of paper in my life. Where do you see the number 70? There are no $70 bills; there's no reason to get a $70 check. I looked at the 70 as if it had stolen from me.

Aaron, who ended up in eight out of my nine classes, got a 100 on the start-of-school reading quiz. He had read the books in Europe, where he got to go over the summer because *his* dad's books were popular there. He came back not just tan and full of knowledge and pictures, but ripe with stories of the European girls he had hooked up with. He said he and Nia had talked and she was totally cool with the other girls; he said he was busy turning her into a *freak*, someone who would be down for *anything*. When we hung out now, I didn't say half as much as I did that first night; I just listened and stayed impressed, tried to control my lower half while Nia was there, pictured her in different freeze-frames for later in the evening.

Executive Pre-Professional High School was *hard.*

The teachers all told me I was going to have four hours of homework a night, but I didn't believe it— plus I believed I could handle it. I had gotten into the school; I'd definitely be able to take anything it could dish out, right?

The first semester, in addition to the book list, I had this class called Intro to Wall Street that required me to pick up the *New York Times* and *Wall Street Journal* every day. It turned out I was supposed to have been picking them up over the summer as well—some kind of handout that I didn't get in the mail. I needed to create a portfolio of current events articles and show how they related to stock prices, and to get the back issues. I couldn't use the Internet; the teacher made me go to the *library* and use microfiche, which is like trying to read the U.S. Constitution off a postage stamp, and when I got two weeks behind on that, I had two more weeks of newspapers to pick up. The papers were so *long*; it was unbelievable how much news there was every day. And I was supposed to scan it all? How did any- one do it? The papers piled up in my room, and every day when I came home I looked at them and knew that I could handle them, that if I just opened that first one I'd be able to get through them all and get the assignment done.

Instead I lay in bed and waited for Aaron to call.

It was about this time that I started labeling things Tentacles. I had a lot of Tentacles. I needed to cut some of them. But I couldn't; they were all too strong and they had me wrapped too tight; and to cut them I'd have to do something crazy like admit that I wasn't equipped for school.

The other kids were geniuses. I thought I was a big deal for getting an 800 on the exam—like the entire entering class had gotten 800. It turned out the test had been "broken" in my year; they were tweaking it to make it less formulaic—i.e., less likely to let in people like me. There were kids from Uruguay and Korea who had just learned English but were doing extra credit for the current events stuff in Intro to Wall Street, reading *Barron's* and *Crain's Business Daily*. There were freshmen taking calculus, while I was stuck in the math that came after algebra, which the teacher announced on the first day was "ding-dong" math and there was no reason for us not to get a 100 in everything. I got an 85 on my first test and a small frowny face.

Plus there were extracurriculars. Other kids did *everything*: they were on student government; they played sports; they volunteered; they worked for the school newspaper; they had a film club; they had a literature club; they had a chess club; they entered nationwide competitions for building robots out of tongue depressors; they helped teachers out after school; they took classes at local colleges; they assisted on "orientation days." I didn't do anything but school and Tae Bo, where I hit a plateau. They humored me in class, letting me fake-fight and do my not-that-form-fitting pushups, but the teacher knew it was something that I didn't really enjoy. I quit. That was the only Tentacle I ever cut.

Why were the other kids doing better than me? Because they were *better*, that's why. That's what I knew every time I sat down online or got on the subway to Aaron's house. Other people weren't smoking and jerking off, and those that *were* were gifted—able to live and compete at the same time. I wasn't gifted. Mom was wrong. I was just smart and I worked hard. I had fooled myself into thinking that was something important to the rest of the world. Other people were complicit in this ruse. Nobody had told me I was common.

That's not to say I did terrible in high school—I got 93's. That looked good to my parents. Problem is, in the real world, 93 is the crap grade; colleges know what it means—you do just well enough to stay in the 90's. You're average. There are a lot of you. You aren't going over the top; if you're not doing any extracurriculars you're *done*. You can change things in later years, but with 93's your freshman year, you're going to have a lot of dead weight.

In December, three months into Executive Pre-Professional, I had stress vomiting for the first time. It happened with my parents at a restaurant; I was eating tuna steak with spinach. They had brought me out to celebrate the holidays and talk with me. They had no idea. I sat there looking at the food and thinking about the Tentacles waiting for me at home, and for the first time the man in my stomach appeared and said I wasn't getting any of it; I had better back down, buddy, because otherwise this was going to get ugly.

"How's biology class?" Mom asked.

Biology class was hell. I had to memorize these hormones and what they did and I hadn't been able to make flash cards because I was too busy clipping newspaper articles.

"Fine."

"How's Intro to Wall Street?" Dad asked.

A guy from Bear Stearns had visited our class, thin and bald with a gold watch. He told us that if we were interested in getting into finance, we had better work *hard* and *smart* because a lot of machines were able to make investment decisions now, and in the future, computer programs would run everything. He asked the class how many of us were taking computer science, and everybody but me and this one girl who didn't speak English raised their hands.

"Great, excellent," the guy had said. "You other people are out of a job! Heh heh. Learn comp sci."

Please die right now, I mumbled in my head, where more and more activity was taking place. The Cycling had begun to develop, although it hadn't hit hard, and I didn't know quite what it was yet.

"Wall Street is fine," I told Dad across the table. The restaurant we were at was one of the ones in Brooklyn that was featured in a *Times* article I had yet to read for current events. I didn't think we could really afford it, so I didn't get an appetizer.

The spinach and tuna mulled in my stomach. My whole body was tight. Why was I here? Why wasn't I off somewhere studying?

Soldier, what is the problem?

I can't eat this. I know I should be able to.

Get over it. Eat it.

I can't.

You know why that is?

Why?

Because you're wasting your time, soldier! There's a reason the U.S. Army isn't made up of potheads! You're spending all your time at your little horn-dog friend's house and when you get home you can't do what you have to do!

I know. I don't know how I can be so ambitious and so lazy at the same time.

I'll tell you how, soldier. It's because you're not ambitious. You're just lazy.

"I've got to be excused," I told my parents, and I walked through the restaurant with that fast-walking gonna-throw-up gait—a run aching to get out—that I learned to perfect over the next year. I came to the chrome bathroom and let it go in the toilet. Afterward I sat, turned the light off, and pissed. I didn't want to get up. What was wrong with me? Where did I lose it? I had to stop smoking pot. I had to stop hanging out with Aaron. I had to be a machine.

I didn't get out of the bathroom until someone came and knocked.

When I went back to my parents, I told them: "I think I might be, y'know, depressed."

twelve

The first doctor was Dr. Barney. He was fat and short and had a puckered and expressionless face like a very serious gnome.

"What's the problem?" He leaned back in his small gray chair. It sounded like a callous way to put things, but the way he phrased it, so soft and concerned, I liked him.

"I think I have a serious depression."

"Uh-huh."

"It started last fall."

"All right," he took shorthand on the pad on his desk. Next to the pad was a cup that read *Zyprexa*, which I thought was the craziest-sounding medical name I'd ever heard. (It turned out to be a drug for psychotics, I wondered if maybe a psychotic person had called a doctor a "zyprexa" and that's how they came up with the name.) Everything in Dr. Barney's office was branded—the Post-it notes said Paxil on them; his pens were all for Prozac; the desk calendar had Zoloft on each page.

"I got into this high school, and I had every reason to be the happiest guy in the world," I continued. "But I just started freaking out and feeling worse and worse."

"Uh-huh. You completed your sheet, I see."

"Yes." I held up the sheet that they had given me in the waiting room. It was a standard sheet, apparently, that they gave all the new recruits at the Anthem Mental Health Center, the building in downtown Brooklyn where this brain evaluation was taking place. The sheet had a bunch of questions about emotions you had felt over the past two weeks and four checkboxes for each one. For example, *Feelings of hopelessness and failure. Feeling difficulty with your appetite. Feeling that you are unable to cope with daily life.* For each one, you could check 1) Never, 2) Some days, 3) Nearly every day, or 4) All the time.

I had run down the list, checking mostly threes and fours.

"They like to collect these sheets every time you come in, to see how you're doing," Dr. Barney continued, "but on yours right now there's one item of concern that we should discuss."

"Uh-huh?"

"'Feeling suicidal or that you want to hurt yourself.' You checked '3) Nearly every day.'"

"Right, well, not trying to *hurt* myself. I wouldn't cut myself or anything stupid. If I wanted to do it, I would just do it."

"Suicide."

It felt strange to hear. "Right."

"Do you have a plan?"

"Brooklyn Bridge."

"You'd jump off the Brooklyn Bridge."

I nodded. "I'm familiar with it."

"How long have you had feelings like that, Craig?"

"Since last year, mostly."

"What about before then?"

"Well . . . I've *had* them for years. Just less intense. I thought they were, you know, just part of growing up."

"Suicidal feelings."

I nodded.

Dr. Barney stared at me, his lips puckered. What was he so serious about? Who *hasn't* thought about killing themselves, as a kid? How can you grow up in this world and *not* think about it? It's an option taken by a *lot* of successful people: Ernest Hemingway, Socrates, Jesus. Even before high school, I thought that it would be a cool thing to do if I ever got really famous. If I kept making my maps, for instance, and some art collector came across them and decided to make them worth hundreds of thousands of dollars, if I killed myself at the height of that, they'd be worth *millions* of dollars, and I wouldn't be responsible for them anymore. I'd have left behind something that spoke for itself, like the Brooklyn Bridge.

"I thought . . . you haven't really *lived* until you've contemplated suicide," I said. "I thought like it would be good to have a reset switch, like on the video games, to start again and see if you could go a different way."

Dr. Barney said, "It sounds as if you've been battling this depression for a long time."

I stopped. No I hadn't . . . *Yes I had.*

Dr. Barney said nothing.

Then he said, "You have a flat affect."

"What's that?"

"You're not expressing a lot of emotion about these things."

"Oh. Well. They're too big."

"I see. Let's talk a little about your family."

"Mom designs postcards; Dad works in health insurance," I said.

"They're together?"

"Yes."

"Any brothers or sisters?"

"One sister. Younger. Sarah. She's worried about me."

"How so?"

"She's always asking me whether I'm good or bad, and when I tell her I'm bad she says, 'Craig, please get better, everyone is trying.' Things like that. It breaks my heart."

"But she cares."

"Yeah."

"Your family supports you coming here?"

"When I told them about it they didn't waste any time. They say it's a chemical imbalance, and if I get the right drugs for it, I'll be fine." I looked around the office at the names of the right drugs. If I got prescribed every drug that Dr. Barney repped, I'd be like an old man counting out pills every morning.

"You're in high school, correct?"

"Yes."

"And your sister?"

"Fourth grade."

"You realize there are a lot of parental consent forms that need to be filled out for us to help you—"

"They'll sign everything. They want me to get better."

"Supportive family environment," Dr. Booth scratched on his pad. He turned and gave his version of a smile, which was a slight affirmative, the lips barely curled, the lower lip out in front.

"We're going to get through this, Craig. Now, from a personal standpoint, why do you think you have this depression?"

"I can't compete at school," I said. "All the other kids are too much smarter."

"What's the name of your high school?"

"Executive Pre-Professional High School."

"Right. I've heard of it. Lots of homework."

"Yeah. When I come home from school, I know I have all this work to do, but then my head starts the Cycling."

"'The Cycling.'"

"Going over the same thoughts over and over. When my thoughts race against each other in a circle."

"Suicidal thoughts?"

"No, just thoughts of what I have to do. Homework. And it comes up to my brain and I look at it and think 'I'm not going to be able to do that' and then it cycles back down and the next one comes up. And then things come up like 'You should be doing more extracurricular activities' because I *should*, I don't do near enough, and that gets pushed down and it's replaced with the big one: 'What college are you going to, Craig?' which is like the doomsday question because I'm not going to get into a good one."

"What would a good one be?"

"Harvard. Yale. Duh."

"Uh-huh."

"And then the thoughts keep turning and I lie down on my bed and think them. And I used to not be able to lie down anywhere; I used to always be up doing something, but once the Cycling starts I can waste hours, just lying and looking at the ceiling, and time goes slowly and really fast at the same time—and then it's midnight and I have to go to sleep because no matter what I do, I have to be at school the next day. I can't let them know what's happening to me."

"Do you have difficulty sleeping?"

"Sometimes not. When I do it's bad, though. I lie there thinking about how everything I've done is a failure, death and failure, and there's no hope for me except being homeless, because I'm never going to be able to hold a job because everyone else is so much smarter."

"But they're not *all*, are they, Craig? Some of them have to be not as smart as you."

"Well, those are the ones who I don't have to worry about! But plenty of people are, and they're going to kick my ass everywhere. Like my friend Aaron—"

"Who's that?"

"My best friend. He has a girlfriend too, who I'm friends with."

"How do you feel about her?"

"Not so much . . . one way or the other."

"Uh-huh." Dr. Barney wrote on his pad.

"Anyway . . ." I tried to sum up. I was lying to this guy; that meant we really knew each other. "It's all about living a sustainable life. I don't think I'm going to be able to have one."

"A sustainable life."

"That's right, with a real job and a real house and everything."

"And a family?"

"Of course! You have to have that. What kind of success are you if you don't have that?"

"Uh-huh."

"So to have that I have to start shaping up now, but I can't because of this crap that's going on in my head. And I *know* that these things I'm thinking don't make sense and I think 'Stop!'"

"But you can't stop."

"I can't stop."

"Well." He tapped his Prozac pen. "You know that your thoughts aren't thoughts you want to have. That's a good thing."

"Yeah."

"Do you ever hear voices?"

Uh-oh. Now we were getting into the real meat. Dr. Barney was cuddly enough, but I was sure that if you gave him a straitjacket he'd be able to handle it just fine, coaxing you into it and leading you to a *very comfortable* room with soft walls and a bench where you could sit looking at a one-way mirror and telling people you were Scrooge McDuck. (How did they make one-way mirrors, anyway?) I knew I had problems, but I also knew I wasn't crazy. I wasn't *schizo*. I didn't hear voices. Well, I heard that one voice, the army guy, but that was *my* voice, just me trying to motivate myself. I was not going to get thrown in the loony bin.

"No voices," I said. Lied, technically. Lied again.

"Craig, do you know about brain chemistry?"

I nodded. I'd skipped ahead in the bio textbook.

"Do you know how depression works?"

"Yeah." It was a simple explanation. "You have these chemicals in your brain that carry messages from each brain cell to the next brain cell. They're called neurotransmitters. And one of them is serotonin."

"Excellent."

"Which scientists think is the neurotransmitter related to depression . . . If you have a lack of this chemical in your system, you can start to get depressed."

Dr. Barney nodded.

"Now," I kept on, "after the serotonin passes a message from one brain cell to the next, it gets sucked back into the first brain cell to be used again. But the problem is sometimes your brain cells do too much sucking"—I chuckled—"and they don't leave enough serotonin in your system to carry the messages. So they have these drugs called selective serotonin reuptake inhibitors that keep your brain from taking too much serotonin back to get more of it in your system. So you feel better."

"Craig, excellent! You know a lot. We're going to put you on medication that is going to do just that."

"Great."

"Before I write a prescription, do you have any questions for *me*?"

Sure I did. Dr. Barney looked happy. He had a nice gold ring and shiny glasses.

"How'd you get started in this?" I asked. "I'm always interested to know how people got started."

He leaned forward, his paunch disappearing in his shadow. He had huge gray eyebrows and a somber face.

"After college, I went through my own shit and decided that all the physical suffering in the world couldn't compare to mental anguish," he said. "And when I got myself cleared up, I decided to help other people."

"You got yours cleared up?"

"I did."

"What did you have?"

He sighed. "What you have."

"Yeah?"

"To a tee."

I leaned forward—our faces were two feet away from one another. "How did you fix it?" I begged.

He tilted the side of his mouth up. "Same way you will. On my own."

What? What kind of answer was that? I scowled at him. I was here for *help*; I wasn't here to figure this out on my own; if I wanted to figure it out on my own I'd be taking a bus tour of Mexico—

"We're going to start you on Zoloft," Dr. Barney said.

O-ho?

"It's a great medication; helps a lot of people. It's an SSRI, it's going to affect the serotonin in your brain like you said, but you can't expect an instant effect because it takes weeks to get into your system."

"*Weeks?*"

"Three to four weeks."

"Isn't there a fast-acting version?"

"You take the Zoloft with food, once a day. We'll start you on fifty milligrams. The pills make you feel dizzy, but that's the only side effect, except for sexual side effects." Dr. Barney looked up from his pad. "Are you sexually active?"

Ha ha ha ha ha ha ha. "No."

"All right. Also, Craig: I think that you would benefit from seeing someone."

"I know! Don't think I haven't tried. I'm not really good at talking to girls."

"Girls? No. I meant *therapists*. You should start seeing a therapist."

"What about you?"

"I'm a psychopharmacologist. I refer you to the therapists."

What a racket. "Okay."

"Let's take a look for one." He opened up what looked like the white pages on his desk and started rattling off names and addresses to me as if they made a difference. Dr. Abrams in Brooklyn, Dr. Fieldstone in Manhattan, Dr. Bok in Manhattan . . . I thought Dr. Bok was a cool name, so we set up an appointment with him—I missed it, though, because later in the week I was doing a history assignment, and I was so embarrassed that I didn't call to cancel with Dr. Bok that I never went to see him again. The next time with Dr. Barney we had to pick another shrink, and then another, and then another, among them the little old lady who asked if I had been sexually abused and the beautiful red-head who asked why I had so many problems with women and the man with the handlebar mustache who suggested hypnosis. It was like I was dating, except I didn't get to make out with any of the girls—and I was also bi because I met up with guys.

"I like talking to you," I told Dr. Barney.

"Well, you'll be seeing me in a month, to check up on how the medication is treating you."

"You don't do therapy?"

"The other doctors are great, Craig; they'll help."

Dr. Barney stood up—he was about five-foot-five—and shook my hand with a soft, meaty grip. He handed me the Zoloft prescription and instructed me to get it right away, which I did, even before taking the subway home.

thirteen

The Zoloft worked, and it didn't take weeks—it worked as soon as I took it that first day. I don't know how, but suddenly I felt *good* about my life—what the hell? I was a kid; I had plenty more to do; I'd been through some crap but I was learning from it. These pills were going to bring me back to my old self, able to tackle everything, functional and efficient. I'd be talking to girls in school and telling them that I *was* messed up, that I had *had* problems but that I'd dealt with them, and they'd think I was brave and sexy and ask me to call them.

It must have been a placebo effect, but it was a great placebo effect. If placebo effects were this good, they should just make placebos the way to treat depression—maybe that's what they did; maybe Zoloft was cornstarch. My brain said *yes I am back* and I thought the whole thing was over.

This was my first experience with a Fake Shift.

Dastardly stuff—you do well on a test; you make a girl laugh; you have a particularly lower-body-simmering experience after talking online and rushing to the bathroom; you think it's all over. That just makes it worse when you wake up the next day and it's back with a vengeance to show you who's boss.

"I feel great!" I told Mom when I got home.

"What did the doctor say?"

"I'm on Zoloft!" I showed her the bottle.

"Huh. A lot of people at my office take this."

"I think it's working!"

"It can't be working already, honey. Calm down."

I took my Zoloft every day. Some days I woke up and got out of bed and brushed my teeth like any normal human being; some days I woke up and lay in bed and looked at the ceiling and wondered what the hell the point was of getting out of bed and brushing my teeth like any normal human being. But I always managed to take it. I never tried to take more than one, either; it wasn't that kind of drug. It didn't make you feel anything, but then after a month, just like they said, I started to feel that there was a buoy keeping me upright when I got bad. If the Cycling started there was a panic button attached to my good thoughts; I could click it and think about my family, my sister, my friends, my time online; the good teachers at school—the Anchors.

I even spent time with Sarah. She was so smart, smarter than me for sure. She'd be able to handle what I was going through without seeing any doctors. Her homework bordered on algebra even though it was only fourth grade, and I helped her with it, sometimes doodling spirals or patterns on the side of the pages while she worked. I didn't do maps anymore.

"Those are cool, Craig," she would say.

"Thanks."

"Why don't you do art more?"

"I don't have time."

"Silly. You always have time."

"Oh yeah."

"Yes. Time is a person-made concept."

"Really? Where'd you hear that?"

"I made it up."

"I don't know if that's true. We all live within time. It rules us."

"I use my time how I want, so I rule *it*."

"You should be a philosopher, Sarah."

"*Uggg*, no. What's that? Interior design."

My eating came back around: first coffee yogurt, then bagels, then chicken. Sleeping, meanwhile, was two-steps-forward, one-step-back. (That's one of the golden rules of psychology: the shrinks say that *everything* in our lives is two-steps-forward, one-step-back, to justify that time you, say, drank paint thinner and tried to throw yourself off a roof. That was just *taking a step back*.) Some nights I wouldn't sleep, but then for the next two I slept great. I even dreamed: flying dreams, dreams of meeting Nia on a bus and talking with her, looking at her, seeing her off a few stops down the line. (Never having sex with her, unfortunately.) Dreams that I was I jumping off a bridge and landing on giant fuzzy dice, bouncing across the Hudson River from Manhattan to New Jersey, laughing and looking back at which numbers I had landed on.

When I couldn't sleep, though, it sucked. I'd think about the fact that my parents weren't going to leave me much money and they might not have enough to send my sister to college and I had a history assignment to do and how come I didn't go to the library today and I hadn't checked my e-mail in days—what was I missing in there? Why did I fret so much about e-mail? Why was I sweating into the pillow? It wasn't hot. How come I had smoked pot *and* jerked off today?—I had developed a rule: on the days you jerk off you don't smoke pot and on the days you smoke pot you don't jerk off, because the days you do both are the ones that become truly wasted days, days where you take *three* steps back.

I started to work in phases a little bit. For three weeks I'd be cool, fine, functional. Even at my most functional, I wasn't someone you'd pay a lot of attention to; you wouldn't see me in the halls at school and go "There he goes, Craig Gilner—I wonder what *he's* up to." You'd see me and go, "What does that poster say behind that guy—is the anime club meeting today?" But I was there, that was the important thing. I was at school as opposed to home in my bed.

Then I'd get bad. Usually it happened after a chill session at Aaron's house, one of those glorious times when we got really high and watched a *really* bad movie, something with Will Smith where we could point out all the product placements and plot holes. I'd wake up on the couch in Aaron's living room (I would sleep there while he slept with Nia in the back) and I'd want to die. I'd feel wasted and burnt, having wasted my time and my body and my energy and my words and my soul. I'd feel like I had to get home right now to do work but didn't have the ability to get to the subway. I'd just lie here for five more minutes. Now five more. Now five more. Aaron would eventually get up and I'd pee and force myself to interact with him, to get breakfast and hold down a few bites. Nia would ask me "You all right, man?" and one Saturday morning, while Aaron was out getting coffee, I told her no.

"What's wrong?"

I sighed. "I got really depressed this year. I'm on medication."

"Craig. Oh my gosh. I'm so sorry." She came over and hugged me with her little body. "I know what it's like."

"You do?" I hugged back. I'm not a crier; I just look it; I'm a hugger. Cheesy, I know. I held the hug as long as I could before it got awkward.

"Yeah. I'm on Prozac."

"No way!" I pulled back from her. "You should have told me!"

"You should have told me! We're like partners in illness!"

"We're the illest!" I got up.

"What are you on?" she asked.

"Zoloft."

"That's for wimps." She stuck her tongue out. She had a ring. "The *really* messed-up people are on Prozac."

"Do you see a therapist?" I wanted to say "shrink," but it sounded funny out loud.

"Twice a week!" She smiled.

"Jesus. What is wrong with us?"

"I don't know." She started dancing. There

wasn't any music on, but when Nia wanted to dance, she danced. "We're just part of that messed-up generation of American kids who are on drugs all the time."

"I don't think so. I don't think we're any more messed up than anybody before."

"Craig, like eighty percent of the people I *know* are on medication. For ADD or whatever."

I knew too, but I didn't like to think about that. Maybe it was stupid and solipsistic, but I liked to think about *me*. I didn't want to be part of some trend. I wasn't doing this for a fashion statement.

"I don't know if they really need it," I said. "I really need it."

"You think you're the only one?"

"Not that I'm the only one . . . just that it's a personal thing."

"Okay, fine, Craig." She stopped dancing. "I won't mention it, then."

"What?"

"Jesus. You know why you're messed up? It's because you don't have a *connection* with other people."

"That's not true."

"Here I am, I just told you I have the same problem as you—"

"It might not be the same." I had no idea

what Nia had; she might have *manic*-depression. Manic-depression was much cooler than actual depression, because you got the manic parts. I read that they rocked. It was so unfair.

"See? This is what I mean. You put these *walls* up."

"What walls?"

"How many people have you told that you're depressed?"

"My mom. My dad. My sisters. Doctors."

"What about Aaron?"

"He doesn't need to know. How many people have *you* told?"

"Of *course* Aaron needs to know! He's your best friend!"

I looked at her.

"I think Aaron has a lot of problems too, Craig." Nia sat down next to me. "I think he could really benefit from going on some medication, but he'd never admit it. Maybe if you told him, he would."

"Have you told him?"

"No."

"See? Anyway, we know each other too well."

"Who? Me and you? Or you and Aaron?"

"Maybe all of us."

"I don't think so. I'm glad I know you, and I'm glad I know him. You can call me, you know, if you're feeling down."

"Thanks. I actually don't have your new number."

"Here."

And she gave it to me, a magical number: I put it with her name in all caps on my phone. *This is a girl who can save me*, I thought. The therapists told you that you needed to find happiness within yourself before you got it from another person, but I had a feeling that if Aaron were off the face of the earth and I was the one holding Nia at night and breathing on her, I'd be pretty happy. We both would be.

At home I got through the bad episodes by lying on the couch and drinking water brought from my parents, turning the electric blanket on to get warm and sweating it out. I wanted to tell people, "My depression is acting up today" as an excuse for not seeing them, but I never managed to pull it off. It would have been hilarious. After a few days I'd get up off the couch and return to the Craig who didn't need to make excuses for himself. Around those times, I would call Nia to tell her I was feeling better and she would tell me she was feeling good too; maybe we were in synch. And I told her not to tease me. And she would smile over the phone and say, "But I'm so *good* at it."

In March, as I had eight pills left of my final refill, I started thinking that I didn't need the Zoloft anymore.

I was better. Okay, maybe I wasn't better, but I was *okay*—it was a weird feeling, a lack of weight in my head. I had caught up in my classes. I had found Dr. Minerva—the sixth one that Dr. Barney and I tried—and found her quiet, no-nonsense attitude amenable to my issues. I was still getting 93's, but what the hell, someone had to get them.

What was I doing taking pills? I had just had a little problem and freaked out and needed some time to adjust. Anyone could have a problem starting a new school. I probably never needed to go to a doctor in the first place. What, because I threw up? I wasn't throwing up anymore. Some days I wouldn't eat, but back in Biblical times people did that all the time—fasting was a big part of religion, Mom told me. We were already so fat in America; did I need to be part of the problem?

So when I ran out of the final bottle of Zoloft, I didn't take any more. I didn't call Dr. Barney either. I just threw the bottle away and said *Okay, if I ever feel bad again, I'll remember how good I felt that night on the Brooklyn Bridge.* Pills were for wimps, and this was over; I was done; I was back to me.

But things come full circle, baby, and two months later I was back in my bathroom, bowing to the toilet in the dark.

PART 3: *BADOOM*

fourteen

My parents are outside hearing me retch up the dinner I just ate with them. I look at the door; I think I can hear Dad chewing the last bite he took when he got up from the table.

"Craig, should we call someone?" Mom asks. "Is it an emergency?"

"No," I say, getting up. "I'm going to be all right."

"Um, hey, yeah, I told your mom not to make the squash," Dad jokes.

"Heh," I say, climbing to the sink. I wash out my mouth with water and then mouthwash and then more water. My parents pepper me with questions.

"Do you want us to call Dr. Barney?"

"Do you want us to call Dr. Minerva?"

"Do you want some tea?"

"Tea? Give the man some water. You want water?"

I turn on the light—

"Oh. He had the light off. Are you okay, Craig? Did you slip?"

I look at myself in the bathroom light. Yes, I'm okay. I'm okay because I have a plan and a solution: I'm going to kill myself.

I'm going to do it tonight. This is such a farce, this whole thing. I thought I was better and I'm not better. I tried to get stable and I can't get stable. I tried to turn the corner and there aren't any corners; I can't eat; I can't sleep; I'm just wasting resources.

It's going to be tough on my parents. So tough. And my little sister. Such a beautiful, smart girl. Not a dud like me, that's for sure. It'll be hard to leave her. Not to mention it might mess her up. Plus my parents will think they're such failures. They'll blame themselves. It'll be the most important event in their lives, the thing that gets whispered by other parents at parties when their backs are turned:

Did you hear about their son?

Teen suicide.

They'll never get over it.

I don't know how anyone could.

They must not've known the warning signs.

But you know what, it's time for me to stop putting other people's emotions ahead of my own. It's time for me to be true to myself, like the pop stars say. And my true self wants to blast off this rock.

I'll do it tonight. Late tonight. In the morning,

specifically. I'll get up and bike to the Brooklyn Bridge and throw myself off it.

Before I go, though, I'll sleep in Mom's bed for one final night. She lets me sleep there when I'm feeling bad, even though I'm too old—Dad'll sleep in the living room. There's plenty of space by her, and it's not like we *touch* or anything; she's just available to bring me warm milk and cereal. Tonight is something I owe her; her only son spending time with her before he goes. I'd be heartless not to. I'll hug my dad too, and my sister. But I'm not leaving any notes. What kind of crap is that?

"I'm okay," I say, unlocking the bathroom door and stepping out. My parents corner me in a hug that mimics the one at Aaron's blowout party, when we were confirming that our futures were bright.

"We love you, Craig," Mom says.

"This is true," Dad says.

"Uh," I say.

With Dr. Minerva I talk about my Tentacles and Anchors. Here's something for you, Doctor: my parents are now part of the Tentacles, and my friends too. My Tentacles have Tentacles, and I'm never going to cut them off. But my Anchor, that's easy: it's killing myself. That's what gets me through the day. Knowing that I could do it. That I'm strong enough to do it and I can get it done.

"Can I sleep in your bed tonight?" I ask Mom.

"Sure, honey, of course."

Dad nods at me.

"I'm ready for bed, then." I go into my room and pull out clothes to sleep in, stash another pile to die in. I'll get them when I leave in the morning. Mom announces that she's making some warm milk and it'll help me sleep. I go to my sister's room. She's up, sketching a kitchen at her desk.

"I love ya, little girl," I tell her.

"Are you okay?" she responds.

"Yeah."

"You threw up."

"You heard?"

"It was like *eccccccchhhh reeccccccch blacccchhh,* of course I heard."

"I turned the water on!"

"I have good ears." She points to her ears.

"You do good throw-up impressions, too," I say.

"Yeah." She turns back to her sketch. "Maybe when I grow up I could be like a stand-up comedian, and just get onstage and make those noises."

"No," I say, "what you could do, or what *I* could do, since I'm so good at it, is get up onstage and *actually* throw up, and people would pay to watch, like I was a professional vomit-er."

"Craig, that is so *gross.*"

But I don't think it's gross. I think it's kind of a good idea. How does performance art get started, after all?

Don't let that distract you, soldier.

Right, I won't.

You've made your decision and you're sticking to it, is that correct?

Yes, sir.

The point of you being in this room is to say good-bye to your sister, is that not right?

Absolutely, sir.

I'm sorry to see it come to this, soldier. I thought you had promise. But you gotta do what you gotta do, and sometimes you gotta commit hara-kiri, ya know?

Yes, sir.

I hug Sarah. "You're very sweet and smart, and you have great ideas. Stick with them."

"Of course." She looks at me. "What's wrong with you?"

"I'm okay."

"You're bad. Don't try and fool me."

"I'll be all right tomorrow."

"Okay. You like my kitchen?"

She holds it up. It's practically a blueprint, with the swinging quarter-circles for doors and the sink and refrigerator outlined in crisp, bird's-eye detail. It looks like something someone would pay for.

"It's amazing, Sarah."

"Thanks. What are you doing now?"

"I'm going to sleep early."

"Feel better."

I leave her room. Mom already has the warm milk for me and my place all set up in her bed.

"You feeling better?"

"Sure."

"Are you *really*, Craig?"

"Yes, jeez, sure."

"Lean back on the pillows." I get in her bed—the mattress is firm and real. I scrunch my feet under the covers and savor that feeling—fresh linen over your feet, bunching up in little mountain ranges. That's a feeling everyone can enjoy. Mom hands me the milk.

"It's only nine o'clock, Craig; you're not going to be able to go to sleep."

"I'll read."

"Good. Tomorrow we'll schedule something with Dr. Barney to help you. Maybe you need new medicine."

"Maybe."

I sit and drink the warm milk and think nothing. It's a talent I've developed—one thing I've learned recently. How to think nothing. Here's the trick: don't have any interest in the world around you, don't have any hope for the future, and be warm.

Damn, though. There's someone else I should call. I pick the cell out of my pocket and flip it open to the name that's all caps. I hit SEND.

"Nia?" I ask when she picks up.

"Hi, yeah, what's up?"

"I wanted to talk to you."

"What about?"

I sigh.

"*Ohhhh.* Are you okay, man?"

"No."

"Where are you?"

"At home. I'm in my mom's bed, actually."

"Whoa, we have bigger problems than we thought, Craig."

"No! I'm just here because it helps me sleep. Don't you remember when you were a little kid, sleeping in your parents bed was like, such a treat?"

"Well, my dad died when I was three."

Shoot. That's right. Some of us have actual things to complain about.

"Right, sorry, um, I—"

"It's okay. I slept with my mom sometimes."

"But you probably don't anymore."

"No, I do. Same situations as you, I bet."

"Huh. What are you up to now?"

"Home on the computer."

"Where's Aaron?"

"Home on his computer. What do you want, Craig?"

I take a breath. "Nia, you remember the party that we had when we all figured out we got into Executive Pre-Professional?"

"Yeahhhh . . ."

"When you came to that party, did you know you were going to hook up with Aaron?"

"Craig, we're not talking about this."

"Please, c'mon, I have to know if I had a shot."

"We're not."

"Please. Pretend I'm dying."

"God. You are *so* melodramatic."

"Heh. Yeah."

"I wore my green dress to that party, I remember that."

"I remember too!"

"And Aaron was very nice to me."

"He sat next to you in Scrabble."

"And I already knew he liked me. But I had been putting off getting involved with anyone until I knew about high school, because I didn't want it to distract me. And you and Aaron, you were like, in the running. You both talked to me. But you had that mole on your chin."

"*What?*"

"Remember, the big hairy one? It was all pock-marked and gross."

"I didn't have any mole!"

"Craig, I'm joking."

"Oh, right, duh." We both laugh. Hers is full, mine empty.

"You promise not to take this the wrong way, Craig?"

"Sure," I lie.

"If you had made a move, I would probably have, you know, gone along. But you didn't."

Death.

"See, it works out, though. Now we're friends, and we can talk about stuff like this."

"Sure, we can talk."

Death.

"Believe me, I get sick of talking with Aaron."

"Why?"

"He's always talking about himself and his problems. Like you. You're both self-centered. Only, you have a low opinion of yourself, so it's tolerable. He has a really *high* opinion of himself. It's a pain."

"Thanks, Nia, you're very sweet."

"You know I try."

"What if I tried now?" I ask. Nothing to lose.

"To what?"

"You know. What if I just came over and said screw it and stayed outside until you came out and grabbed you and kissed you?"

"Ha! You'd never do it."

"What if I did?"

"I'd smap you."

"You'd *smap* me."

"Yeah. Remember that? That was so funny."

I switch phones from ear to ear.

"Well, I just wanted to clear that up." I smile. And that's true. I don't want to leave loose ends. I want to know where I stand. I don't stand anywhere with Nia, really, not more than friends. I missed an opportunity with her, but that's okay, I've missed many. I have a lot of regrets.

"I'm worried about you, Craig," she says.

"What?"

"Don't do anything stupid, okay?"

"I won't," I tell her, and that's not a lie. What I'm doing makes a lot of sense.

"Call me if you think you're going to do anything stupid."

"Bye, Nia," I say. And I mouth into the phone, *I love you,* in case some of her cells pick up on the vibrations and it serves me well in the next life. If there is one. If there is a next life, I hope it's in the past; I don't think the future will be any more handleable.

"Bye, Craig."

I click END. I think it's a little harsh how the END button is red.

fifteen

I'm pretty stupid for thinking I could get any sleep tonight. Once I turn off the lights and put the cup aside, I get the Not-Sleeping Feeling—it's kind of like feeling the Four Horsemen of the Apocalypse rear up in your brain and put some ropes around it and pull it toward the front of your skull. They say, *No way, dude! Who did you think you were fooling! You think you were going to wake up at three in the morning and throw yourself off the Brooklyn Bridge without staying up all night? Give us a little credit!*

My mind starts the Cycling. I know it's going to be the worst that it's ever been. Over and over again, a cycling of tasks, of failures, of problems. I'm young, but I'm already screwing up my life. I'm smart but not enough—just smart enough to have problems. Not smart enough to get good grades. Not smart enough to have a girlfriend. Girls think I'm weird. I don't like to spend money. Every time I spend it, I feel as if I'm being raped. I don't like to smoke pot, but then I do smoke it and I get depressed. I haven't done enough with my life. I don't play sports. I quit Tae Bo. I'm not involved in any social causes. My one friend is a screwup—a genius blessed with the most beautiful girl in the world, and he doesn't even know it. There's so much more for me to be doing. I should be a success and I'm not and other people—younger people—are. Younger people than me are on TV and getting paid and winning scholarships and getting their lives in order. I'm still a nobody. When am I going to not be a nobody?

The thoughts trail one another in my brain, running from the back up to the front and dripping down again under my chin: I'm no one; I'll never make it in my life; I'm about to get revealed as a fake, I've already been revealed as a fake but I don't know it yet; I know I'm a fake and pretend not to. All the good thoughts—the normal ones, the ones that have occasionally surfaced since last fall—scramble out the front of my brain in terror of what lives in my neck and spine. This is the worst it'll ever be.

My homework swims in front of my closed eyes—the Intro to Wall Street stock-picking game, the Inca history paper, the ding-dong math test—they appear as if on a gravestone. They'll all be over soon.

Mom climbs into bed next to me. That means it's still early. Not even eleven. It's going to be such a long night. Jordan, the dog who should be dead, climbs into bed with her and I put my hand on him, try to feel his warmth and take comfort from it. He barks at me.

I turn on my stomach. My sweat drenches my pillow. I turn over on my back. It drenches it in the other direction. I turn on my side like a baby. Do babies sweat? How about in the womb, do you sweat in there? This night will never end. Mom stirs.

"Craig, are you still up?"

"Yes."

"It's twelve-thirty. Do you want cereal? Sometimes a bowl of cereal will just knock you out."

"Sure."

"Cheerios?"

I think I can handle Cheerios. Mom gets up and gets them for me. The bowl is heaping and I tackle it with the ferocity that I think a last meal deserves—shoving it all in me as if it owes me loot. I'm not going to throw this up.

Mom starts breathing regularly next to me. I start to think practically about how I'm going to handle this. I'm taking my bike, I know that. That's one thing I'll miss: riding around Brooklyn on the weekends like a maniac, dodging cars and trucks and vans with pipes sticking out of them, meeting Ronny and then locking the bikes up by the subway station to go to Aaron's house. Riding a bike is pure and simple—Ronny says he thinks it's mankind's greatest invention, and although I thought that was stupid at first, these days I'm not so sure. Mom won't let me take the bike to school so I've never ridden over a bridge—this'll be the first time. I don't think I'll wear my helmet.

I'll take the bike, and it'll be a warm spring night. I'll speed up Flatbush Avenue—the artery of fat Brooklyn—right to the Brooklyn entrance of the bridge, with the potholes and cops stationed all night. They won't look at me twice—what, it's illegal, a kid biking over a bridge? I'll go up the ramp and get right to the middle, where I was before, and then I'll walk out over the roadway and take one last look at the Verrazano Bridge.

What am I going to do about my bike, though? If I lock it up, it'll just stay there at the side of the bridge, as evidence, and they'll clip the lock or saw through the chain after a while. It's an expensive chain! But if I *don't* lock it up, someone'll take it quickly—it's a good bike, a Raleigh—and there won't be any evidence that I was ever even there.

I can't lose the bike, I decide. I'll take the key with me when I go down, and Mom and Dad will know, then, where I've gone. The cops will find the bike and tell them. It'll be harsh, but at least they'll know. It'll be better than not leaving anything.

What time is it? Time has stopped for me. Since I can't sleep and I'm still sweating, I decide I can try something to knock myself out: push-ups. I don't want to go to sleep, I just want to exhaust myself and rest a little bit so I can make the trip at the appropriate time, in an hour or so. I prop myself up in bed in proper push-up position, which is also proper sex position, I realize, and I haven't even had sex—I'm going to die a virgin. Does that mean I go to heaven? No, according to the Bible, suicide is a sin and I go straight to hell, what a gyp.

I learned push-ups in Tae Bo. I'm good at them. I can do them on my fingers and my fists, as well as my palms. Here, next to my mom, in a scene that would look *very* weird if you filmed it from the side, I start to do them up and down—one, two, three . . . I move very, very slowly so as not to wake Mom up—she's a heavy sleeper and doesn't notice my exercises; her head is turned in the opposite direction. When I get to ten push-ups I start counting down: Five, four, three . . . until I finish at fifteen. I collapse in bed.

I'm so weak from holding down nothing but Cheerios in the last twenty-four hours, I'm beat. I'm cracked from fifteen push-ups. But I feel something in the bed. I feel my heart beating. It's beating against the mattress, amplified, resounding not only in the bed but in my body. I feel it in my feet, my legs, my stomach, my arms. Beating everywhere.

I get on my palms again. One, two, three . . . My arms burn. My neck crinks; a bed isn't the best place to do push-ups; you tend to sink in. This set is tougher than the last. But when I get to fifteen I keep going, to twenty. I strain and hold back a grunt on the final one and discharge myself to the mattress.

Badoom. Badoom. Badoom.

My heart is ramming now. It's beating everywhere. It hits all the spots in my body, and I feel the blood pressuring through me, my wrists, my fingers, my neck. It wants to do this, to *badoom* away all the time. It's such a silly little thing, the heart.

Badoom.

It feels good, the way it cleans me.

Badoom.

Screw it. I want my heart.

I want my heart but my brain is acting up.

I want to live but I want to die. What do I do?

I get out of bed, glance at the clock. It's 5:07. I don't know how I got through the night. My heart radiates *badoom*, so I stand and shuffle into the living room and pick a book off my parents' shelf.

It's called *How to Survive the Loss of a Love*; it has a pink and green cover. It's sold like two million copies; it's one of these psychology books that people everywhere buy to get through break-ups. My mom bought it when her dad died and raved about how good it was. She showed the cover to me.

I looked at it just to see what it was about, and the first chapter said, "If you feel like harming yourself right now, turn to page 20." And I thought that was pretty silly, like a Choose Your Own Adventure book, so I turned to page 20, and right there it said to call your local suicide hotline, because suicidal thoughts were a medical situation and you needed medical help right away.

Now, in the dark, I open *How to Survive the Loss of a Love* to page 20.

"Every municipality has a suicide hotline, and they're listed right in the government services section of the yellow pages," it says.

Okay. I go into the kitchen and open up the yellow pages.

It's a pain in the ass to find those government listings. I thought they were marked with green pages, but the green pages turn out to be a restaurant guide. The government listings are in blue at the front, but it's all phone numbers for where to get your car if it's towed, what to do if your block has a rat problem . . . Ah, here, *health*. Posion control, emergency, *mental health*. There are a bunch of numbers. The first one says "suicide" near it. It's a local number, and I call.

I stand in the living room with my hand in my pants as the phone rings.

sixteen

"Hello."

"Hi, is this the Suicide Hotline?"

"This is the Brooklyn Anxiety Management Center."

"Oh, um . . ."

"We work with the Samaritans. We handle New York Suicide Hotline calls when they overflow. This is Keith speaking."

"So the Suicide Hotline is too *busy* right now?"

"Yes—it's Friday night. This is our busiest time."

Great. I'm common even in suicide.

"What seems to, ah, be the problem?"

"I really, just . . . I'm very depressed and I want to kill myself."

"Uh-huh. What's your name?"

"Ah . . ." *Need-a-fake-name, need-a-fake-name:* "Scott."

"And how old are you, Scott?"

"Fifteen."

"And why do you want to kill yourself?"

"I'm clinically depressed, you know. I mean, I'm not just . . . down or whatever. I started this new school and I can't handle it. It's gotten to a point where it's the worst it's ever been and I just don't want to deal with it anymore."

"You say you're clinically depressed. Are you taking medication?"

"I was taking Zoloft."

"And what happened?"

"I stopped taking it."

"Ah. That's probably, you know, a bad idea."

Keith sounds like he's just getting started with this whole counseling thing. I picture a thin college-age guy with wire-rim glasses at a desk lit up with a small reading lamp, looking out the window, nodding at the good deeds he's doing.

"A lot of people run into problems when they, y'know, stop taking their medication."

"Well, whatever the reason, I just really can't handle it right now."

"Do you have a plan for how you would kill yourself?"

"Yes. I'd jump off the Brooklyn Bridge."

I hear Keith typing something.

"Well, Scott, we aren't the suicide hotline, but if

you like, we have a five-step exercise for managing anxiety. Would you like to try it?"

"Um . . . sure."

"Can you get a pen and a piece of paper?"

I go to the drawers in the dining room and get a pencil and paper. I take it to the bathroom and sit on the toilet with Keith. The light's on.

"First, okay? Write down an event that happened to you. That you experienced."

"Any event?"

"That's right."

"Okay . . ." I write on the piece of paper *Ate pizza last week.*

"Do you have it?" Keith asks.

"Yes."

"Now, write down, ah, how you *felt* about that event."

"Okay." I write: *Felt good, full.*

"Now write down any 'shoulds' or 'woulds' that you felt about the event."

"Like what?"

"Things that you regret about it, things that you feel would have made it go better."

"Wait, uh, I don't think I have the right kind of event." I furiously erase my first statement, which is marked *1*. Instead of *Ate pizza*, I put down *Threw up Mom's squash* and then for *2*, I write *Felt like I wanted to kill myself*, all the while telling Keith to hold on, I messed up.

"Just put down 'shoulds' and 'woulds,'" he reassures me.

Well, I *should* have held down the squash and I *would* have been full if I had. I put that down.

"Now put down *only what you actually had to do* in the event."

"What I *had* to do?"

"Right. Because there are no such things as shoulds and woulds in the universe."

"There aren't?" I'm starting to suspect Keith a bit. For someone in Anxiety Management, he's giving me an exercise that is fairly confusing and anxiety-provoking.

"No," he says. "There are only things that *could have turned out differently*. You don't have any shoulds or woulds in your life, see? You only have things that could have gone a different way."

"Ah."

"You never know what truly would have happened if you had done your shoulds and woulds. Your life might have turned out worse, isn't that possible?"

"I don't see how it's really possible, seeing as I'm on the phone with you."

"What you really have in life are *needs*, and you

only have three needs: food, water, and shelter."

And *air*, I think. *And friends. And money. And your mind.*

"So the next step in the process is to put down only what you actually *had* to do in your event, and then compare it to the shoulds and woulds you assigned yourself."

"How many steps are in this thing?"

"Five. The fifth is the most important. We're at four."

"You know, I really, um—" I look at the piece of paper, covered with half-erased scribblings about pizza and squash. "—I think I should talk to the Suicide Hotline people because I still feel really . . . bad."

"All right," Keith sighs.

I'm worried that he thinks he's done a bad job, so I tell him: "It's okay. You've been really helpful."

"It's tough with young people," he says. "It's just tough. Have you called 1-800-SUICIDE?"

1-800-SUICIDE! Of course! I should've known. This is America. Everyone has a 1-800 number.

"That's Helpline, they're national. Then there's Local Suicide Watch . . ." Keith gives another number.

"Thanks." I write them both down. "Thanks so much."

"You're welcome, Scott," he says. I hit OFF—

these are the first calls I've made not on the cell phone in a long time—and type in 1-800-SUICIDE.

It's really convenient that suicide has seven letters, I think.

"Hello," a woman answers.

"Hi, I . . ." I give her the rap, just like I gave Keith. This woman's name is Maritsa.

"So you stopped taking your Zoloft?" she asks.

"Yes."

"You know, you should be on that for . . . a couple months, really."

"I *was* on it for a couple months."

"Some people stay on it for years. At least four to nine months."

"Well, I know, but I felt better."

"Okay, so how do you feel right now?"

"I want to kill myself."

"Okay, Scott, now, you know you're very young and you sound very accomplished."

"Thanks."

"I know high school can be tough."

"It's not that tough. I just can't handle it."

"Are your parents aware of how you're feeling?"

"They know I'm bad. They're asleep right now."

"Where are you?"

"I'm in the bathroom."

"At your house?"

"Yes."

"You live with them?"

"Yeah."

"You know, when you want to commit suicide, we consider that a medical emergency. Did you know that?"

"Ah, an emergency."

"If you feel like that, you need to go to the hospital, okay?"

"I do?"

"Yes, you go right to the emergency room and they'll take care of you. They know just how to handle it."

The emergency room? I haven't been in the emergency room since I got clipped by a sled and knocked myself out in the park in grade school. Blood was coming out of one ear, and when I woke up it was like I'd slept for three days and I wasn't quite sure what year it was. They kept me overnight, sent me through an MRI to make sure my brain wasn't dented, and sent me home.

"Are you going to go to the emergency room, Scott?"

"Ah . . ."

"Would you like us to call 911 for you? If you're unable to get to the emergency room, we can send an ambulance for you."

"No, no! That's not necessary." I do *not* need the neighbors seeing me carted off. Besides, I never realized, but I'm *right* next to a hospital. It's two blocks away—a tall gray building with big tanks of frozen oxygen out front and construction vehicles constantly adding new wings. Argenon Hospital. I can walk there from here. It might even feel good. And once I get there, I won't have to do anything. I'll just tell them what's wrong with me and they'll give me medicine. Probably they'll give me some kind of new pill—maybe they've invented that fast-acting Zoloft by now—and I'll come right back home. Mom and Dad won't even know.

"Scott?"

"I'm going. I have to . . ."

"You have to put on your clothes?"

"Right."

"That's great. That's wonderful. You're doing the right thing."

"Okay."

"You're very young. We don't want to lose you. You're being very strong right now."

"Thanks." I find my shoes. No, pants first. I put on my khaki pants. The only shoes I can find are my dress shoes, worn to Dr. Minerva's office this afternoon, a lifetime ago. They're Rockports, shiny and beveled.

"Are you still there?"

"Yeah, I'm just getting my hoodie." I pull it off the hook and flip it on. I grab the phone again. "Okay."

"You're very brave, Scott."

"Thanks."

"You're going to the hospital, right? What hospital?"

"Argenon."

"They're wonderful there. I'm proud of you, Scott. This is the right thing to do."

"Thank you, Maritsa. Thank you."

I hang up the phone and walk out the door. Jordan comes toddling out just as I'm leaving, cocks his head at me. He doesn't bark.

PART 4: HOSPITAL

seventeen

The emergency room is nearly abandoned at five-thirty in the morning—I don't know how I caught that lucky break. There's a long black metal bench sprinkled with people. A Hispanic couple walks around, the woman howling about her knee. An old white lady and her gigantic son fill out forms next to each other. A black guy with glasses sits at the end of the bench, opening peanuts and putting the shells in his left vest pocket, the peanuts in his right. It could be a plain-old doctor's office, really. Except for the peanut guy.

I walk up to the main desk: REGISTRATION. There are two registrat-ors, one sitting, and one standing behind. The one behind looks about my age—she's probably getting school credit.

"I need to be, uh, admitted. Registered," I say.

"Fill out a form and the nurse will see you shortly," the sitting one says. The standing one stuffs envelopes, eyes me. Do I know her from somewhere? I sniff my armpit to hide my face.

I take the Xeroxed form that's handed to me. It asks my birthdate and address, my parents' names and phone numbers, my health insurance. I don't know much about health insurance, but I know that my Social Security number is my ID number, so I put that down. I feel kind of good filling out the form, like I'm applying to a special academy.

I put the form, completed, in a small black tray hanging off the side of the registration desk. There's only one piece of paper in front of mine; I sit back down next to Peanut Man. I stare at the floor; it's made up of foot-long tiles in red and white, like a chessboard, and I imagine how a knight would move across it. I'm so crazy. I've lost it. This isn't going to help. I should leave. Is it too late? My bike is back at home in my hallway. I can do it. I'm strong enough.

"Craig?" a woman pops her head out from a door at the end of Registration.

I stand up. The Hispanic couple howls that they were here first and someone comes out to talk to them in Spanish. Sorry, people.

"Come," she beckons. "I'm the nurse."

I shake her hand.

"Have a seat." I enter her long, thin chamber, which has a computer and two chairs and an array of tubes and robes on hooks on the wall. The sun is rising through a window at the end of the room. Across from me is a poster about domestic violence: *If your man beats you, forces you to have sex, controls your money, or threatens you about immigration papers, you are a victim!*

The nurse—short with curly hair and a clownish face—reaches to the hooks behind her and unfurls a blood pressure gauge. I always liked these. Not that they're pleasant, but they always feel like they *could* be so much worse. She attaches it to some readout device and pumps me up.

"So what's wrong, ishkabibbles?" she asks.

Ishkabibbles? I give her the rap.

"Did you do anything to yourself? Did you try and cut yourself; did you try and hurt yourself; did you actually go anywhere?"

"No. I called 1-800-SUICIDE and they sent me here."

"Good. Wonderful. You did the right thing. They're so great."

She unwraps me, turns, and types information into the computer. She reads off my sheet in a tray to the right of the monitor, where I wrote "want to kill myself" as my reason for admission.

"Now, were you on medicine?"

"Zoloft. I stopped taking it."

"You stopped?" She opens her eyes wide. "We get that a lot." She types. "You really can't do that."

"I know." I'm glad I have a concrete thing to blame this on, something everyone can point a finger at.

"You really have to stop, right now, and think about how you feel. I want you to remember how you feel the next time you decide to stop taking your medicine."

"Okay." I commit it to memory; I feel dead, wasted, awful, broken, and useless. It's not the kind of feeling you forget.

"You're going to be *fine*, ishkabibbles," she says.

I look at what she's typing on the screen. Under "reason for admission," she puts SUICIDAL IDEATION.

That would be a good band name, I think.

"Come on," she says, getting up from the computer. Behind it, a printer is producing something, whining and clicking. She reaches back and pulls two stickers out, puts them on plastic bracelets that she has attached to her belt, which is like a nurse utility belt, and affixes them to my right wrist.

I look down. They both say *Craig Gilner*, and have my Social Security number and a bar code on them.

"Why do I get two?" I ask.

"Because you're *too* special."

She leads me out of the room into the ER

proper, past curtains that are alternately drawn and undrawn to show the cast of characters here on an early Saturday morning. The vast majority are old people—specifically, old white women with tubes in them, yelling and moaning. What they're yelling for is water—"*Waaa-taaa, waaa-taa*"—and what they're getting is totally ignored. Doctors—I think the doctors are in white coats and the nurses are in blue, right?—stride by holding clipboards. One has a young scruffy blond beard that I would never expect to see on a doctor—his name is Dr. Kepler. It says RESIDENT, so he's a college guy. That's one of the things I could be someday if I hadn't messed up and gotten myself in here.

"This way," the nurse says.

Beeping serenades us. It's coming from everywhere, a dozen different kind of beeps—loud ones, scary ones, *ding*-y ones, random ones. I wonder if they ever sync up as we pass by two giant metal racks on wheels—inside are pale yellow trays wrapped in plastic. Hospital breakfast. A nurse pushes them through a door marked FOOD PREP.

We move by a group of Hispanic guys lounging on stretchers who all look like they were in the same bar fight. One has a bandage on his face, one is pointing to his chest for a doctor, and one is rolling up his pants to show off what looks like a shark bite. The doctor hisses at him in Spanish, and he rolls his pants back down. We go by a bank of computers and there the nurse tells me to wait—she flags down an Indian doctor, and he takes a stretcher, which up close looks like a very complicated and expensive piece of machinery, with red and black levers sticking out everywhere, into a side room marked "22."

Room 22 is just big enough to accommodate the stretcher. It doesn't have a door, just a doorway. The walls are yellow. The nurse leads me in there.

"A doctor will be with you shortly," she says.

It's bright. Bright as hell. And I haven't slept. I sit on the stretcher. What am I supposed to do in here? There's nothing to do. There aren't even any hooks.

Outside of 22, a black guy with long dreads is on a stretcher next to a curtain. He's well dressed in dark brown—with black shoes like mine—and he's holding his hip and *writhing* in pain. It's something I've never seen except in movies—a man clutching himself and grimacing and swaying and breathing in little huffs and bearing his teeth and going "Nurse, nurse, *please.*" It looks like he's dislocated his hip. He rolls over on his side and then back on his back, but nothing seems to help.

Who's worse, soldier, you or him?

Dunno, sir!

It's a trick question, soldier.

Well, him, obviously. I mean I'm sitting here loung-ing; he's practically dying out there.

I expected more from you, son.

How?

You're a smart kid. You should be able to see when somebody's faking. And soldier—

Yes.

—Good job out there. I'm glad you're still on board.

I don't feel any better.

Life's not about feeling better; it's about getting the job done.

I look again at the black guy; as I do, a big police officer with closely cropped hair and those weird little fat bumps on the back of his neck saunters onto the scene with a newspaper and a cup of coffee. He takes an orange plastic seat and sits down right outside from me, between Room 22 and Room 21, another open-style, closet-sized space.

"Hey, how ya doin'," he says. He speaks slowly and calmly. "I'm Chris. If you need anything, let me know." He sits down and opens up his paper.

The black guy is really moaning now, bugging out his eyes at every nurse that passes by. He grabs his hip with both hands. Maybe he's a heroin addict. They come to the hospital and pretend they're hurt to get morphine. I watch him for minutes, trying to figure out if he's real or fake. There aren't any clocks. There are only beeps.

Chris shakes his paper. Page two is "86 Stories Down: Man Plunges from Empire State."

"Jeez," I say. I can't believe it. "Is that about a guy jumping off the Empire State Building?"

"No." Chris smiles, glancing at me over his shoulder. "Not at all." He flips the paper back over. "You're not supposed to be looking at this."

I chuckle. "That is too much."

"He lived!" Chris says.

"Yeah, right."

"He did! And you will too."

Did someone tell this guy what I was in for? Or do all people with mental difficulties get shuttled to room 22?

"What'd he do? Hit a tree?"

But Chris has moved on to page four. "Not supposed to be looking at this."

Someone must have told him. He's a cop in charge of making sure things are okay in the ER and someone must have told him they had a depressed kid in 22, and now he's trying to be helpful.

I lie down on my stretcher, take my hoodie off, and throw it over my face. It's not dark enough. I'm not going to be able to sleep. I'm sweating. I want to do push-ups, but I can't on the stretcher, and it's probably a bad idea to do them on the tiled floor, which doesn't look recently mopped. I don't need to go into Argenon Hospital for depression and come out with diphtheria.

"Nurse! Nurse! *Please!*" the black man groans.

"*Waaa-taaa. Waaa-taaa,*" a woman croaks.

"Hey, what's up?" Chris answers his phone. "No, I'm on."

Beep, something beeps.

These are the sounds of the hospital, the hospital, the hospital.

"Hello, Craig?"

A doctor comes into 22. She has long, dark hair and a pudgy face and bright green eyes.

"Hey."

"I'm Dr. Data."

"Dr. *Data?*"

"Yes."

Huh. I want to ask her if she's an android, but that wouldn't be very respectful; and besides, I'm not up to it.

"What's going on?"

I give her the rap. It gets shorter every time. I wanted to kill myself; I called the number; I came here. *Blah blah blah.*

"You did the right thing," she says, "A lot of

people get off their medication and get into big trouble."

"That's what they tell me."

"Now, besides wanting to jump off the Brooklyn Bridge, have you had anything else going on? Have you been seeing things? Hearing things?"

"Nope." I'm *not* talking about the army guy. Same rules as with Dr. Barney.

"Do your parents know you're here?"

"No."

"Okay, well, let me tell you what we can do for you, Craig." She takes out her stethoscope, holds it in her hands, and folds her short arms. She's pretty. Her eyes are serious and beautiful. "It's Saturday, and on Saturday our best psychologists are here, the really good ones. I'm going to recommend that you see Dr. Mahmoud. He'll be in soon, and he'll be able to give you the help you need."

I have a sudden vision of Dr. Mahmoud taking me into his office, a special shrink's office within Argenon Hospital. It must be very pleasant and bare. There's probably a black couch and a wide window and some Picassos. He'll take me up there; we'll have some emergency therapy; he'll give me the kind of trick that Dr. Minerva has been unable to give me, effect the Shift, re-prescribe me Zoloft (maybe that fast-acting Zoloft!), and I'll be on my way.

"Sounds like a plan."

"Now, you have to inform your parents about where you are, because when Dr. Mahmoud comes down, he's going to need them to sign for you."

"*Ohhhhh.*"

"Is that going to be a problem?"

"No. I can do it."

"Where are your parents?"

"Like two blocks away."

"They're together? They're supportive?"

"Yeah."

"Are they going to be okay that you're in here?"

I sigh. "Yes. I'm the one who's . . . not."

"Don't worry, it happens to a *lot* of people. It tends to be related to stress. Breathe for me, Craig." She puts her stethoscope by my back and has me take deep breaths, cough, the whole deal. She doesn't have to hold my balls, which is cool, because there's no door.

I look out as she's examining me. The black guy has a nurse leaning over him.

"Dr. Mahmoud will be down soon. Call your parents, please, and make sure they're here within two hours."

Two hours. Jeez. I've got to wait two more hours? "Gotcha."

Dr. Data nods at me. "We will help you."

"Okay." I try to smile.

She heads out. I figure that, with the parents, I should get it over with as soon as possible. I flip open my cell phone. No service in the emergency room. I walk out of Room 22 to find a pay phone.

Chris rises from his chair.

"Buddy, hey, I told ya, ya gotta ask me for things. What do you need?"

I turn and look at him, eye his badge and nightstick. I realize what he is now. He's not there in general or for the ER; he's there for my *protection*. When you come into the hospital with a mental disability, *they put a cop next to you so you don't hurt yourself*. I'm on like, *suicide watch*. You want to commit suicide, you call 1-800-SUICIDE; you get suicide watch.

"Ahm, I have to call my mom."

"Not a problem. Phones are right there. Dial nine." He nods.

The phones are like, three feet away. But Chris puts his hands on his hips and keeps close watch as I pick up a receiver.

eighteen

Hi, Mom, I'm in the hospital? No.

Hey, mom, are you sitting down? Eh.

Mom, you're not going to believe where I'm calling you from! Nah.

"Hey, Mom," I say when I hear her groaned hello. "How are you?"

"Craig! *Where are you?!* I just—you just woke me up and you aren't in bed! Are you okay?"

"I'm okay."

"Are you at Aaron's?"

"Uh . . ." I suck air through my teeth. "No, Mom. I'm not at Aaron's."

"Where are you?"

"I, uh . . . I really freaked out last night, and I was feeling really bad, and I, um, I checked myself into Argenon Hospital."

"Oh, my goodness." She stops, hitches her breath. I hear her sit down, exhale. "You . . . are you okay?"

"Well, I mean—I wanted to kill myself."

"Oh, *Craig.*" There's no crying, but I hear her put her face in her hands.

"I'm sorry."

"No. No! *I'm* sorry. I was sleeping! I didn't know!"

"Please, Mom, how could you know?"

"I knew you were bad, but I didn't realize. What did you do? How did you get there?"

"Don't worry. I didn't do anything. I used your book."

"What, the Bible?"

"No, your *How to Deal with the Loss of a Love* book."

"Survive. *How to Survive the Loss of a Love.* Wonderful book."

"It recommended calling the suicide hotline number in there, and I did."

"Is that this sheet of paper by the phone?"

"Yeah, you can throw that away. They said, you know . . . if I was feeling like I was in an emergency, I should come to the emergency room, and I put on my shoes and came here."

"Oh, Craig, so you didn't do anything to yourself?" She pauses.

"No, I checked myself in."

I hear her breath catch and I think, in my house

a few blocks away, her hand is on her chest. "I am so proud of you."

"You are?"

"This is the bravest thing you've ever done."

"I . . . thank you."

"This is the most life-affirming thing you've ever done. You made the right decision. I love you. You're my only son and I love you. Please remember."

"I love you too, Mom."

"I thought I was a bad mother, but I'm a good mother if I taught you how to handle yourself. You had the tools to know what to do. That is so important. And they're going to be *great* over there; it's an excellent hospital. I'm coming right down—you want me to bring your dad?"

"I don't know. It might be good to just have as few people as possible, if possible."

"Where are you now?"

"In the emergency room. They want you to sign some forms."

"Where are they taking you?"

"To talk with this doctor, Dr. Mahmoud."

"And how are you feeling?"

"I don't know. Like the whole thing is unreal. I didn't really get any sleep last night."

"Oh, *Craig*—if I had known . . . I didn't know . . ."

I smile. "I love you, Mom. I have to go." Chris is looking at me.

"I love you. I'm so proud of you."

I hang up. My mom seems happier about me getting into the hospital than she was about me getting into high school.

I turn to Chris and notice that the room next to him, Room 21, is now occupied. A black guy is in there, sitting up on a stretcher. He's bald, but not shaved-head bald—old bald with thin white hairs in a halo around him. His face is unshaven; his arms lie on his legs at cross-purposes. He's skinny, in sweatpants and a white T-shirt covered, from the neck down, with an unidentifiable dark stain. He turns his head toward the wall and I see a scar running from his ear down to his neck. Then he turns back to me. The only thing you can say for him is that he has all his teeth, and they're white, and he's smiling.

I slink back into Room 22 and return to watching the guy with the dreads. He's not writhing anymore; apparently the nurse gave him what he needed, because he's sitting up, eyes closed, pants rolled up to his knee, scratching everything—his lower leg, chest, face—mumbling and swaying. His scratches are light and don't seem intended to actually relieve any sort of itch. He rocks back and forth at a slow rhythm that fits in with the beeps, and opens his eyes about a quarter of the way every minute.

Maybe that should be me. If I were on drugs that good, maybe I wouldn't have time to get depressed. It's heroin, right? That's what I need: some heroin.

But I reconsider. First of all, it'd be pretty tough to ask my friends: *Hey, who knows where I can get heroin?* They'd think it was a joke. Plus it has the worst nicknames: "horse," right? How could I ask for "horse" with a straight face? And, if I were doing heroin, then I'd be a depressed teenager *on heroin.* I didn't need to be that.cliché.

"Want some breakfast?" Chris asks, and before I can say no, one of the sad yellow trays is pushed in at me. The tray has a half pint of what appears to be oatmeal, a hardboiled egg squished into a lidded Styrofoam container, a coffee (I can tell, because the lid is stained with coffee), a foil-topped cuplet of orange juice, and a piece of wheat bread individually sealed from the elements. Also a fork, spoon, knife, salt, pepper, sugar. It disgusts me. I have no interest in any of it. But they might be monitoring me, so I open the bread and force myself to eat it strip by strip, chasing it with orange juice. I ask one of the nurses for a tea and she brings me another coffee. I sniff the coffee but it smells pretty dangerous, so, just to annoy him, I offer some to Chris.

"Got my own," he says, and holds up a popular worldwide brand of coffee. It's strange to see brand names in the hospital.

As Chris yaks on his cell phone (I'd like to know what company gives you service in here; they could like, use it on a commercial: a guy behind padded walls, "Can you hear me now?"), Dr. Data comes back with forms for me to sign about my age and residence. She also brings forms to the older man next to me, the one in Room 21.

"How're you doing, Jimmy?" she asks in there. She has to talk very loud.

"I toldja: it come *to* ya!" he yells back in a succinct Southern voice.

She makes a *tsk tsk* noise. "How'd you get back in here, Jimmy? We didn't think we would see you for a long time."

"I, I, I woke up, and the bed was on *fire*."

It's pretty clear at this point that Mom is going to be late. She's probably trying to pack me an activity bag. I should really get some sleep. I crash on the stretcher with my hoodie draped dejectedly over my head, but there are way too many thoughts in my brain. What am I going to do? It's starting to hit me under there. I'm in the *hospital*. I'm supposed to *do stuff* tonight. There's a party—a big one—at

Aaron's house. Am I going to be able to go? And if I don't go, what will I say? And what's the alternative? Will I stay home and try to work but not be able to and end up with another sleepless night? I can't have another sleepless night.

How do you know when you've hit bottom? Real bottom involves being on the street, I think, not in a hospital. But the Cycling is starting and I can't deal with it and it feels like bottom. I sit up, throw the hoodie off.

"Can I use the bathroom?" I ask Chris.

He leads me past the chatty Hispanic patients to a chrome-and-tile bathroom that's probably seen some bad action. He stays outside. I look around and muse at how I would kill myself in here if I really needed to—I'd have to crush my head in the toilet seat. *Ouch.* I haven't even seen that in a horror movie. I look at the toilet and decide to stand. I'm not going to sit down like the world's beaten pup anymore. I stand, push hard, wash my hands, and step out.

"Wow, that was quick," says Chris.

We pass Jimmy in Room 21 on my way back. His hands are still crossed in his lap as Dr. Data tries to ask him questions.

"I tell you once: *it the truth.* You play that number, *that number will come to you!*"

The guy with the dreads is still tripping out.

I lie down. A nurse comes with a cart that threatens to have more food on it. She knocks—as if there were a door—and says she has to take my heart rate. This involves the placement, all over my body, of sticky tabs attached to wires. They don't hurt; I have a feeling they will when they come off, though. I turn to the cart as she puts them on, and a metal arm like a record needle is reading out my pulses. I watch it: a spike, then a flatter spike, then a dip and a repeat. *That's you. That's your heart.*

"All right," the nurse says. She pulls the tabs off my skin. They don't hurt—the adhesive is kind and soft. My tabs hang off the cart like a tangle of roots as it rolls away. I lie doing nothing for a second, then put my shirt back on, then my hoodie. How long have I been here? I open my phone. Two-and-a-half hours.

"Mr. Gilner?"

A man in a dark suit and a gray tie stands at the entrance to my room. He almost completely occupies it; he's large and barrel-shaped with a stately, pockmarked face, gray hair, big eyebrows, and a firm handshake.

"I am Dr. Mahmoud, yes? You are feeling how? Why are you here?"

I give him the rap.

"Are your parents here?"

"Um, I called them but . . ."

"Here, okay, thanks!" I hear Mom's voice out in the ER. I put my head in my hands.

"He's here? Twenty-two?"

Dr. Mahmoud steps aside, and there's Mom, trailed by the nurse who let me in, with an over-stuffed tote bag on her left arm and Jordan in her right.

"Miss!" the nurse is yelling. "You really can't have dogs in here!"

"What dog?" Mom asks, slipping Jordan into the tote bag. He pokes his head up at me and barks, then dips down.

Everyone in the ER is silent all of a sudden. Even the cracked-out guy with dreads looks at my mom. Chris approaches her; the nurse who let me in points to me—

"Wait a second," says Dr. Mahmoud. "Mrs. Gilner?"

"Yes? Craig! Oh my gosh!"

Everyone lets her into Room 22. They fan out in a three-person semicircle as she hugs me tight, the kind of hug she used to give me when I was a five-year-old, complete with swaying. Jordan *grrrs* at me.

"He had to come; he was making a fuss. I love you so much," Mom whispers into my ear, hot and full of spittle.

"I know." I hold her back.

"Mrs. Gilner—"

"She really needs to leave with the dog," the nurse says.

"She has a dog? Dogs are against policy," Chris says.

"Just one second," Dr. Mahmoud says.

We all look at him.

"All right, Mrs. Gilner, since you're here, your son has checked himself in due to suicidal ideation and acute depression, you understand?"

"Yes."

"He was on his Zoloft but he stopped taking it."

"You did?" Mom turns to me.

"I thought I was better." I shrug.

"Stubborn like your father. Yes, Doctor?"

"Well, the next question is for Craig. Craig, would you like to be admitted?"

Admitted. That probably means to the special room where I get to talk with Dr. Mahmoud. A quick visit and then I'm gone. It'll give me the feeling that I've accomplished something, that I haven't just languished in the ER.

"Yes," I say.

"Good decision," Mom says.

"Mrs. Gilner, you have to sign off for Craig on that decision," the doctor says. He swivels his clipboard, which he had been holding in front of me, toward her. There's a terrible amount of very small writing on the top half of the page and even more on the bottom half; in the middle, an equator of sorts marks where you're supposed to sign.

"There is one thing," the doctor says. "Right now the hospital is undergoing renovations and we're very tight for space, so your son will be admitted with the adults."

"I'm sorry, what?"

"He will be admitted along with our adult patients, not with the teenagers alone."

Oh, so I'll be waiting with old people to see Dr. Mahmoud? "That isn't a problem," I say.

"Good." The doctor smiles.

"Will he be safe?" Mom asks.

"Absolutely. We have the best care in Brooklyn here, Mrs. Gilner. The renovations are only a temporary situation."

"All right. Craig, you're okay with that?"

"Sure. Whatever."

Mom puts her loopy indecipherable signature on the sheet.

"Great. We'll get everything ready for you, Craig," Dr. Mahmoud says. "You're going to feel a lot better."

"Okay," I shake his hand. He turns and heads

out, a large suit greeting patients left and right in the ER.

The nurse touches Mom's shoulder. "I'm sorry, you really have to go with the dog, ma'am."

"Can I give my son a bag of clothes?"

"What am I going to need clothes for?" I ask. I look in the bag: not only are there clothes, and not only are they the clothes I hate, but Jordan is sitting on them.

"If you want to bring him items, you can bring them to the hospital later in the day," the nurse answers.

"Where is he going to be?" Mom asks, like I'm not there.

"In Six North," the nurse answers. "Just ask for him. Come on."

"I love you, Craig."

"Bye, Mom."

A quick hug, and she's on her way—Chris watches, with his hands on his hips. I'm really curious about his efficacy as a hospital security guard.

"What's Six North?" I ask him.

"Ah, uh, we're not supposed to be talking," he says, and sits back down with his paper. I look out the door for some news, but it's all the same. You know, this is a crappy place to be. I wish I wasn't depressed so I didn't have to be here.

"Mr. Gilner?" someone finally asks. A new guy walks up to the door, a thin, short-bearded, older hippie-looking guy—except without the long hair—with glasses. He's not wearing a white robe or a blue robe or a cop uniform. He's wearing jeans, a blue-collared shirt, and what appears to be a leather vest.

"I'm Smitty. We're ready to take you up now."

"There're two!" a doctor says as she passes by. "Twenty-one *and* twenty-two."

"Well, I don't have papers for Mr. Twenty-One." Smitty shakes his head. "So I'm going to be taking up Mr. Gilner, and I'll be back down, all right? Hey, is that *Jimmy?*"

"He's *back*," the doctor moans.

"Hey, it's Saturday, baby. Everything is going to be all right. Mr. Gilner?" He turns to me.

"Uh, yeah."

"You ready to get out of this crazy place?"

"Am I going to see Dr. Mahmoud?"

"Sure. Later in the day."

"You got this one, Smitty?" Chris asks.

"I don't think you're going to give me any trouble, are you, Mr. Gilner?"

"Um, no."

"Okay, do you have your stuff?"

I check my bracelets, my keys, my phone, my wallet. "Yep!"

"Let's walk."

I hop off the stretcher, nod at Chris, and follow Smitty at his slow pace through the ER. We open a door near the bathroom and pierce a seal into an entirely different biome of the hospital—red brick, indoor trees, posters of notable doctors who practiced there. Smitty leads me through an atrium to a bank of elevators.

He hits the up button, stands by me, and nods. I notice a plaque between the two elevators, showing us what's on each floor.

4 - Pediatrics.

5 - Delivery.

6 - Adult Psychiatric.

Oh, he'll be up in Six North.

"Going to adult psychiatric, huh?" I ask Smitty.

"Well"—he looks at me—"you're not quite old enough for geriatric psychiatric." And he smiles.

The elevator dings; we get in and turn around, each taking a corner. Smitty leads me left when we get to six. I pass a poster with a chubby Hispanic man in blue robes holding his hand over his mouth: SHHHHHHHH! HEALING IN PROGRESS. Then Smitty passes some kind of card in front of two double doors, and the doors open and we walk through them.

It's an empty hallway, wide enough for a grown

man to lie across with his arms stretched up. At the end are two big windows and a collection of couches. To the right is a small office with a glass window that has inch-wide squares of thin wire embedded in it; inside, nurses sit at computers. Just beyond the office, another hall branches off to the right. I follow Smitty forward, and when we come to the crossroads of the two halls, I glance down the one to my right.

A man stands there, leaning on the banisters that line the hall even though there are no steps. The man is short and stocky; he has bugged-out eyes and a squashed face and an almost-but-not-quite harelip. There's fuzz coming out of his neck and a big swath of black hair on his little head. He looks at me with homeless-person eyes, like I just popped out of a manhole and offered him valuable paper clips from the moon.

Oh my God, it hits. I'm in the mental ward.

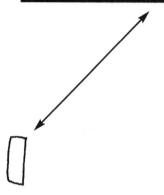

PART 5: SIX NORTH, SATURDAY

nineteen

"Come this way, we're going to take your vitals," Smitty says, seating me in the small office. He takes my blood pressure off a rolling cart and my pulse with delicate fingers. He writes down on a sheet in front of him: *120/80.*

"One-twenty-over-eighty, that's dead normal, isn't it?" I ask.

"Yeah." Smitty smiles. "But we prefer live normals." He wraps up the blood pressure gauge. "Stay right here, we'll send a nurse in to talk to you."

"A nurse? What are *you?*"

"I'm one of the daytime directors on the floor."

"And what is this floor, exactly . . . ?"

"It's a short-term facility for adult psychiatric."

"So like, a mental ward?"

"Not a ward, a hospital. Nurse'll answer any questions." He steps out of the office, leaving me with a form: name, address, Social Security number. Then—wait—I've seen this before! It's the questions from Dr. Barney's office:

Feeling that you are unable to cope with daily life. 1) Never, 2) Some days, 3) Nearly every day, 4) All the time.

What the hell, I'm in the hospital; I put 4's down the line—there are about twenty prompts—except for the lines about self-mutilation, drinking, and drug use (I am *not* putting anything about pot, that's just the rule, told to me by Aaron—you don't ever, *ever* admit to smoking pot, not to doctors, not to teachers, not to anyone in authority no matter how much you trust them; they can always report you to the FBI Pot-Smoking List). As I'm getting done, a squat black nurse with a kind wide smile and tightly braided hair steps in. She introduces herself with a thick West Indian accent.

"Craig, I am Monica, a nurse on the floor here. I am going to ask you a couple of questions about what you're feeling and find out how to help you."

"Yeah, uh . . ." It's time to state my case. "I came in because I was really freaked out, you know, and I checked in downstairs, but I wasn't totally sure where I was going, and now that I'm here, I don't know if I really—"

"Hold on, honey, let me show you something." Nurse Monica stands over me, although she's so short that we're almost the same height, and pulls out a photocopy of the form my mom signed downstairs only an hour before.

"You see that there? That signature says that you have been voluntarily admitted to psychiatric care at Argenon Hospital, yes?"

"Yeah . . ."

"And see? It says that you will be discharged at the discretion of the doctor once he has come up with your discharge *plan*."

"I'm not getting out of here until a doctor *lets* me out?!"

"Now, wait." She sits. "If you feel that this is *not* the place for you, after five days you can write a letter—we call it the Five-Day Letter—explaining why you feel that you do *not* belong here, and we will review that and allow you to leave if you qualify." She smiles.

"So I'm here for at least *five days?*"

"Sometimes people are just here for two. Definitely not more than thirty."

Ho-boy. Well, not much to say about it. That *is* my mom's signature. I sit back in my chair. This morning I was a pretty functional teenager. Now I'm a mental patient. But you know, I wasn't that functional. Is this better? No, this is worse. This is a *lot*—

"Let's talk about how you came to be here," Monica prompts.

I give her the rap.

"When was the last time you were hospitalized?"

"Like, four years ago. I was in a sledding accident."

"So you've never been hospitalized for mental difficulties before."

"Uh, nope."

"Good. Now I want you to look at this chart. Do you see here?"

There's a little scale of 0–10 on a sheet in front of her.

"This is the chart of physical pain. I want you to tell me, right now, from a scale of zero to ten, are you experiencing any physical pain?"

I look closer at the sheet. Below the zero it says *no pain* and below the ten it says *unbearable excruciating pain*. I have to bite my tongue.

"Zero," I manage.

"All right, now, here's a very important question"—she leans in—"did you actually try to do anything to hurt yourself before you came here?"

I sense that this *is* an important question. It might be the kind of question that determines whether I get a normal room with a TV or a special room with straps.

"No," I enunciate.

"You didn't take anything? You didn't try for the *good sleep?*"

"I'm sorry?"

"The good sleep, you know? That's what they call it. When you take many pills and drink alcohol and . . ."

"Ah, no," I say.

"Well, that's good," she says. "We don't want to lose you. Think of your talents. Think of all the tools you have. From your hands to your feet."

I do think about them. I think about my hands signing forms and my feet running, flexing up and down, as I sprint to some class I'm late for. I am good at certain things.

"So right now we are getting ready for lunch," Monica says. "Are you a Christian?"

"Uh, yes."

"Are you vegetarian?"

"No."

"So no specific diet restrictions, good. I need you to read these rules." She drops four sheets of paper in front of me. "They're about conduct on the floor." My eye falls on 6) *Patients are expected to remain clean-shaven. Shaving will be supervised by an attendant every day after breakfast.*

"I am not sure if you notice, but do you see what that first item is on the list?"

"Uh . . . 'No cell phones on the floor'?"

"That's right. Do you have one?"

I feel it in my pocket. I don't want to lose it. It's one of the only things that's making me me right now. Without my cell phone, who will I be? I won't have any friends because I don't have their numbers memorized. I'll barely have a family since I don't know their cell phone numbers, just their home line. I'll be like an animal.

"Please give it here," Monica says. "We will keep it in your locker until your discharge, or you can have visitors take care of it."

I put it on the table.

"Please turn it off."

I flip it open—two new voice mails, *who are they?*—and hold END. *Bye-bye, little phone.*

"Now, this is very important; do you have anything sharp on your person?"

"My keys?"

"Same as the phone. We keep those."

I plop them in a heap on the table; Monica sweeps them into a tray like an airport security worker.

"Wonderful—do you have anything else you can think of?"

Monica, I'm down to my wallet and the clothes on my back. I shake my head.

"Great, now hold on." She gets up. "We're going to have Bobby give you a tour." Monica nods at me, keeps my charts, leaves me to review the papers, and goes into the hall. She returns a minute later with a gaunt, hollow man with big circles under his eyes and a nose that looks like it's been broken in about three places. In contrast to floor policy, scruff lines his chin. He's older but still has all his hair, a stately gray mop, combed half-heartedly. And he carries himself a little weird, leaning back as if he were on a headrest.

"Jesus, you're a kid!" he says, curling his mouth. He reaches out a hand for me and his hand comes out sort of sideways, thumb crooked up.

"I'm Bobby," he says.

His sweatshirt has Marvin the Martian on it and says WORLD DOMINATOR.

"Craig." I stand up.

He nods, and his Adam's apple, which has some extra gray whiskers on it, bobs. "You ready for the grand tour?"

twenty

Bobby leads me into the bright hall with his odd gait.

"Everybody's in the dining room right now." He gestures as we go down the sideways hall, the one that branches off of the one I entered. I look left— there's the dining room, painted blue, overlooked by a television, full of circular tables, separated from the hall by that glass with the square wire mesh in it. Inside, the tables have been pushed aside, and a panoply of people sit in a loose circle.

I can't even process them: they're the motliest collection of people I've ever seen. An old man with a crazy beard (what happened to the shaving?) rocks back and forth; a gigantic black woman rests her chin on a cane; a burned-out-looking guy with long blond hair puts his hand through it; a stocky bald man with slitted eyes scratches his armpit and frowns; an older woman with glasses mimes what appears to be an eagle, talking, before turning and inspecting the back of her chair. The small man I saw in the hall twitches his leg. A girl with a streak of blue in her dark hair slumps over her chair like she's obviously more messed up than the others; a big girl with a wan frown leans back and twiddles her thumbs; a black kid with wire-rim glasses sits perfectly still, and hey—there's Jimmy from downstairs. He's still got his stained shirt on, and he's looking up at the lights. They must have processed him quick because he's a return visitor.

You can tell who the meeting leader is: a thin woman with short dark hair. Out of a dozen or so people, she's the only one in a suit. Some people aren't even in their clothes, but in dark blue robes, loose and V-necked at the top.

"Hey, man," Bobby says, pulling me down the hall. "If you're really interested you can just sit in on the meeting."

"No, I—"

"I'm doing the tour so I can get out."

"Heh."

"Now, smokes are at—wait, you don't smoke, do you?"

"Uh . . . I smoke *some* things—"

"Cigarettes, I'm talking about."

"No, I don't."

"Did they ask if you did?"

"No."

"That's probably because you're underage. How old are you?"

"Fifteen."

"Jesus! Okay, well, smokes are after breakfast, after lunch, at three in the afternoon, after dinner, and before lights out. Five times a day."

"All right."

"Most people smoke. And if you had told them you smoked, they might have given you cigarettes."

"Darn." I chuckle.

"It's one of the only hospitals left that lets you smoke." Bobby points behind us. "The smoking lounge is in the other hall."

We come across a third hall, perpendicular to the one we're in. I see that Six North is shaped like an H: where you enter is at the bottom of the left leg; the nurses' office is at the junction of the left leg and the center line; the dining room is at the junction of the center line and the right leg; and the rooms line the left and right legs. We're passing them now, going toward the top right of the H: they're simple doors with slots outside filled with slips of paper that say who's living in them and who their doctor is. The patients are listed by their first names; the doctors by their last. I see *Betty/Dr. Mahmoud, Peter/Dr. Mullens, Muqtada/Dr. Mahmoud.*

"Where's my room?"

"They probably don't have it set up yet; they'll have it after lunch for sure. Okay, so here's the shower—" He points to the right, to a door with a pink sliding plastic block on it between the words VACANT and OCCUPIED.

"When you're inside, you're supposed to put it to OCCUPIED, but people still don't pay any attention, and there's no lock on the door, so I like to keep real close to the door. It's tough, 'cause the water doesn't reach."

"How do I make it say 'Occupied'? From inside?"

"No, here." Bobby slides the block. It covers up VACANT and only OCCUPIED appears.

"That's pretty cool." I push it back. It's a simple system, but I wouldn't know if Bobby hadn't showed me.

"Is there a guys' bathroom and a girls' bathroom?"

"It's not a bathroom, it's a shower. You have your own bathroom in your room. But it's unisex, yeah. There's a shower in the other hall too"—we keep walking—"but I wouldn't use it. It bothers Solomon."

"Who's Solomon?"

We come to the end of the hall. The windows have two panes of glass with blinds, somehow, *between* them. Outside it's a cloud-spattered May Brooklyn day. Chairs line the dead end. As we approach, a wilted little girl with blond hair and cuts on her face looks up from a pad of something and scurries into a nearby room.

"They show movies here sometimes." Bobby shrugs. "Sometimes at the other end by the smoking lounge."

"Uh-huh. Who was that?"

"Noelle. They moved her in from teen." We turn around. "Medications are given out after breakfast, after lunch, and before bed. We take them over there." Bobby points to a desk across from the dining room, where Smitty sits, pouring soda. "That's the nurses' *station*; the other place is the nurses' *office*. All your lockers and stuff are behind the nurses' station."

"They took my cell phone."

"Yeah, they do that."

"What about e-mail?"

"What?" We're back by the dining room. I slow my pace. Inside, the stocky bald man with squinty eyes who was frowning is speaking slowly and plaintively:

". . . Some people here who treat you like they have no respect for you as a human being, which I take personal offense to, and just because I went to my doctor and told him, 'I'm not afraid of dying; I'm only afraid of living, and I want to put a bayonet through my stomach,' that doesn't mean I'm afraid of any of *you*."

"Let's concentrate on our discussion of things that make us happy, Humble," says the psychologist.

"And I know about psychologists, when they're writing down what you're saying they're really writing down how much money they're going to get when they sell their latest yacht, because they're all yuppies with no respect. . . ."

"C'mon," Bobby taps me.

"Is his name Humble?"

"Yeah. He's from Bensonhurst." Bensonhurst is a particularly retro section of Brooklyn, an Italian and Jewish neighborhood where a girl can walk down the street and have a car full of guys cruise up to her: *Hey baby, you wanna ride?*

"Where are you from?" I ask.

"Sheepshead Bay." That's another old-time Brooklyn 'hood. Russian. All these parts are far out.

"I'm from here," I say.

"What, this neighborhood? This neighborhood is nice."

"Yeah, I guess so."

"Man, I'd give my one remaining ball to live here, I tell you that. I'm trying to get into a home

around here, at the Y. Anyway—there's the phone."
He points to our left. There's a pay phone with a
yellow receiver. "It's on until ten at night," he says.
"The number to call back is written right on it, and
it's on your sheet too, if you need people to call
back. If someone calls for you, don't worry, someone'll find you."

Bobby stops a second.

"That's it."

It's really very simple.

"What do we *do* in here?" I ask.

"They have activities; a guy comes and plays guitar. Joanie comes in with arts and crafts. Other than
that, you know, just take phone calls; try and get
out, really."

"How long do people stay?"

"Kid like you, got money, got a family, you'll be
out in a few days."

I look at Bobby's deep-sunk eyes. I get the
feeling—I don't know how I know the rules of
mental-ward etiquette; maybe I was born with
them; maybe I knew I'd end up here—but I get the
feeling that one big no-no in this place is asking
people how they got here. It'd be a little like walking up to somebody in prison and going "So? So?
What's up, huh? Didja kill somebody? *Didja?*"

But I also get the impression that you can

volunteer the reasons you got here at any time and no one will judge; no one will think you're too crazy or not crazy enough, and that's how you make friends. After all, what else is there to talk about? So I tell Bobby: "I'm here because I suffer from serious depression."

"Me too." He nods. "Since I was fifteen." And his eyes shine with blackness and horror. We shake hands.

"Hey, Craig!" Smitty says from his desk. "We got your room ready; you want to meet your room-mate?"

twenty-one

My roommate is Muqtada.

He looks about like what you'd expect for a guy named Muqtada: big; straight gray beard; wide, wrinkled dark face; glasses with white plastic rims. He doesn't have any clothes, apparently, because he's in a dark blue robe, which smells intensely of body odor. Not that it's easy to notice any of this stuff at first, because when I go into the room, he's burrowed into bed.

Smitty flicks on the light. "Muqtada! It's almost lunch! Wake up. You have a new roommate!"

"Mm?" He peers out from his sheets. "Who is?"

"I'm Craig," I say, hands in my pockets.

"Mm. Is very cold here, Craig. You not like it."

"Muqtada, weren't the men in here to fix the heat?"

"Yes, they fix yesterday, very cold. Fix today, tonight very cold."

"It's spring, buddy; it doesn't get cold."

"Mm."

"Craig, that's you over there."

The bed in the far corner is made up for me, if you can call it that. It's the sparsest bed I've ever seen: small and pale yellow with a sheet, a topsheet, and one pillow. No blanket, no stuffed animals, no drawers below, no patterns, no candles, no headboard. This reflects the style of the room, which basically has a window (encased blinds again), a radiator under paneling, two beds, a table between the two beds with two funny-shaped hospital pitchers of water on top, lights, closet, and a bathroom. There aren't any patterns on the wall; only the ceiling has porous tiles that could be fun to look at. I check the closet. Muqtada has a tired pair of pants on the bottom shelf. The rest of the space is mine. I take off my hoodie and stuff it in there.

"Okay?" Smitty asks. "Lunch in five minutes." He leaves the door open.

I sit down on my bed.

"Please close door, please," Muqtada says. I close it, come back. He looks right through me. "Thank you."

"What do we have for lunch?" I ask.

"Hm."

I'm not sure how to respond to that. I asked him a *what* question. "Ah . . . Is the food good?"

"Mm."

"Ah . . . Where are you from?"

"Egypt," he says in a clipped voice, and it's the first word I've heard him say that he sounds happy with. "Where are *you* from? Your family?"

"White. German and Irish and Czech. A little Jewish, we think. But I'm Christian, I guess."

That reminds me: in this sparse room, is it possible that the Gideons have placed a Bible? They put one in *every* motel in the world; they should have gotten to this place. I check the drawers, under the pitchers of water: nope. Out of range of the Gideons. This is *serious*.

"Mm," Muqtada says. "What you look for? There is nothing." He keeps staring.

I want to lie down, to get the sleep I couldn't get last night, but something about the way my roommate is lying there makes me want to leave, to walk around. Maybe it'll be good to be with someone like him, someone who seems worse off than me. I never really considered it, but there are people worse off than me, right? I mean, there really are people who are homeless and can't get out of bed and are never going to be able to hold a job and, in Muqtada's case, have serious problems with temperature, all because their brains are broken. Compared to them I'm . . . well, I'm a spoiled rich kid. Which is another something to feel bad about. So, who's worse off?

I go out into the hall and almost bash headlong into one of the giant metal racks of trays. The rack gives off heat and smells of fresh cooked salty food and is being wheeled along by an attendant in a skullcap.

"Careful!" he yells at me.

Oh, no. Now I have to eat. This will be the first time that they'll see how bad things are with me— I couldn't eat that egg downstairs and can't eat anything now. What if I get stressed and the man pulls his rope in my stomach and I throw up in the dining room? That'll be a fine entrance.

"Lunch!" the little man with the almost harelip calls down the hall. He pops out of the dining room, walks down to the far window and back, and knocks on everyone's door, even if they're awake and right in his face. "Come on, Candace! Let's go, Bernie! C'mon, Kate! Time to eat! Come on, Muqtada!"

"That's Armelio," a voice says behind me. I turn; it's Bobby in his Martian sweatshirt. "They call him the President. He runs the whole floor."

"Hi, who're ya?" Armelio asks as he passes.

"Craig." I shake his hand.

"Great to meet you! All right! People! We have a new person here! Excellent, buddy! My new buddy. Tha's great! Time for lunch! Solomon, come out of your room, don't give any trouble, come and eat! Everybody's gotta eat!"

I move into the dining room with Armelio bellowing and cast myself at a seat next to the bald man, Humble, who is still talking about psychologists and yachts.

twenty-two

What are the chances, in picking a meal for me, that Argenon Hospital gets the one thing I can handle right now? Between fish nuggets and veal marsala and a Technicolor quiche and other items of disgust I see handed out on trays to other people (Armelio, the President, hands out all the trays, announcing people's names as he does so: "Gilner, Gilner, that's my new friend!"), I get curry-flavored chicken breast: it doesn't have real liquid curry, just a lovely infusion of yellow spices and a plastic knife and fork to cut it up. It also has broccoli, the vegetable I like best, and herbed carrots on the side. When I open the plastic lid, I grin, because I know something has shifted in my stomach—not the big Shift, but something concrete—and I am going to eat this. Besides the chicken and vegetables, the tray has coffee, hot water, a teabag, milk, sugar, salt, pepper, juice, yogurt, and a cookie. It's as good-looking a meal as I can remember. I start to slice the chicken.

"Does anyone have extra salt?" Humble, across my table, stretches his neck to the room.

"Here." I split him off my salt packet. "I would've hooked you up."

"See, you didn't speak to me," Humble says, pouring the salt on his chicken, looking at me through eyes surrounded by thin and purple-hued skin, as if he got punched in both a week ago. "So naturally I assumed you were one of those yuppies."

"I'm not." I put chicken in my mouth. It tastes good.

"There's a lot of yuppies in this place, and you have that look about you, you know—the yuppie look of people with money?"

"Yeah."

"People who don't *care* about other people. Unlike me. See, I genuinely care about other people. Does that mean that I sometimes won't be inclined to beat the hell out of somebody? No, but that's my environment. I'm like an animal."

"We're all like animals," I say. "Especially now, when we're all in a room eating. It reminds me of high school."

"You're smart, I see that. We're all animals, high school is animals, but some of us are more animal than others. Like in *Animal Farm*, which I read, all animals are created equal, but some are more equal than others? Here in the real world, all equals are created animal, but some are more animal than others. Hold on, let me write that down." Humble reaches behind him to the one window in the dining room, which has board games stacked up under it. He pulls Scrabble off the top of the stack, fishes out a pen from the box, removes the board, flips it over, and writes on the back of it, which is already covered with scribbling—

"Humble!" Smitty says from the door.

"Hey, hey, okay!" He throws his hands up. "I didn't do it!"

"How many times do we have to tell you, no writing on the Scrabble board! Do you need pencil and paper?"

"*Whatever*," he says. "It's all in here." He points to his head, then turns back to me as if absolutely nothing had interrupted our conversation. "Me and you, we might be equals, but I'm more animal."

"Uh-huh." I clearly picked the right place to sit.

"I need to be the alpha male in any given situation. That's why as soon as I noticed you I made a few judgments. I saw that you were very young. Now in the wild, the lion who sees new youngsters from another pride, another breed, he'll kill and eat those youngsters so he can breed his own offspring. But here"—he gestures around, as if you need to elucidate what "here" is, as if you don't just take it for granted once you're inside—"there unfortunately appears to be a distinct lack of women accepting of my breeding potential. So in your youth you are not a threat to me."

"I see." Across the room, Jimmy is trying to open his juice with one hand. The other hand stays at his side; I can't tell if he can't move it or just doesn't want to. Smitty comes over and helps him.

"It'll come *to ya!*" he says.

"Do you feel that I'm a threat to you?" Humble asks.

"No, you seem like a pretty cool guy." I munch.

Humble nods. His food, which was sitting on the plate in front of him, very innocent and oblivious, gets destroyed over the next twenty seconds as he eats half of it. I continue my slow and steady pace.

"When I was your age—you're fifteen, right?"

I nod. "How'd you know?"

"I'm good with ages. When I was fifteen, I had this chick who was twenty-eight. I don't know why, but she *loved* me. Now, I was doing a lot of pot back then, my whole life was pot . . ."

It's weird how your stomach can come back around. As I tune Humble out, I eat not because I want to, not because I have to overcome anything, not to prove myself to anyone, but *because it's there*.

I eat because *that's what people do*. And somehow when the food is put in front of you by an institution, when there's a large gray force behind it and you don't have to thank anyone for it, you have the animal instinct to make it disappear, before a rival like Humble comes along and snatches it away. I think, I think as I chew, my problem might be too much thinking.

That's why you need to join the Army, soldier.

I thought I was already in the Army, sir!

You're in the mental army, Gilner, not the U.S. Army.

So I should join?

I don't know: can you handle it?

I don't know.

Well, you seem to know that you like order and discipline. That's what the Army offers young men like you, Gilner, and that's what you're getting here.

But I don't want to be in the Army; I want to be normal.

You've got some considerin' to do, then, soldier, because normal ain't no job as far as I'm concerned.

"Do you have a girlfriend?" Humble asks.

"What?"

"Do you? Somewhere out there. You got a hot little fifteen-year-old?" He points his food-colored fork at me.

"No!" I smile, thinking of Nia.

"They got cute ones, though." Humble runs his hand through hair that is no longer there. He has hairy dark arms with tattoos of jokers, swords, bulldogs, and pirate ships. "They just keep making the girls cuter and cuter."

"It's all the hormones," I say.

"That's right. You're very smart. You got any sugar?"

I hand over a sugar packet. I've finished my chicken and I could eat more, frankly, but I don't know who to ask. Might as well make the tea. I open the teabag, which is labeled "Swee-Touch-Nee," a brand I have never heard of and am not convinced actually exists, and stain my water with a bunch of deep dips. As I'm finishing up, Smitty approaches with a second tray of food, identical to the first.

"You look like you could handle some seconds," he says.

"Thanks."

"Eat up."

I tackle the second chicken. I am a working machine. Part of me works that didn't before.

"The girls, they drink all this milk with cow hormones," I say between bites, "and they develop a lot younger."

"You're telling me!" Humble says. "The crazy thing is how the girls in my day were a lot better than my father's girls. I wonder what the next generation will be like."

"Sex robots."

"Heh heh. Where you from?"

"Around here."

"This neighborhood? Nice. Must've been a quick ride. *If* you came by ambulance. And I'm not assuming and I'm not judging. I'm just being curious." He eats two gigantic bites of his food, chews and continues, "How did you get here?"

He's broken the rule of Six North. But maybe it's not a rule. Or maybe eating with someone breaks it.

"I checked myself in."

"You did? *Why?*"

"I was feeling pretty bad; I wanted to kill myself."

"Buddy, that's what I told my doctor the other week. I told him, 'Doc, I'm not afraid of dying; I'm only afraid of living, and I want to put this bayonet through my stomach,' and then I stopped taking my blood-pressure medication. Because I have high blood pressure on top of everything else, on top of the drugs they have me on here that keep me *whacked out of my mind*; if I don't eat lots of salt to regulate my blood pressure I'll die, so when I told him I wasn't taking my medication he said 'What, are you crazy? Are you trying to *kill yourself?!*' And I looked him right in the eyes and said 'Yes.' And they carted me off here."

"Huh."

"The problem is I've been living in my car for the last year. I have nothing; I have the clothes on my back and that's it. The only thing I have is the car and now the car has been towed and all my stuff is inside. There's thirty-five hundred dollars' worth of film equipment in there."

"Wow."

"So over the next few days I have to call the police station, the tow yard, get myself into an adult home, and talk to my daughter. She's about your age. The mother I'm completely over but the daughter I love to death. The mother I'd like to love to death."

"Heh."

"Don't do me any favors; only laugh if it's funny."

"It is!"

"Good. Because right now I don't have you pegged as a yuppie. You're something else. I'm not sure what you are, but I'm going to find out."

"Cool."

"I'm gonna go get my medication so I can sit through this afternoon with my head completely *whacked.*" Humble slides away; I finish eating the chicken. When it's done—clean plate—I feel better than I have about anything I've done in a long time, maybe a year. *This* is all I need to do. Keith was hesitant at the Anxiety Management Center, but he was right—all you need is food, water, and shelter. And here I have all three. What next?

I look across the dining room, and three of the younger people—the big girl, the girl with dark hair and blue streak, and the blond girl with cuts—are all sitting together.

"C'mere." Blue Streak beckons.

twenty-three

It's been a while since a bunch of girls asked me over to their table. First time, really.

"Me?" I point at myself.

"No, the other new guy," Blue Streak says.

I'm not sure what to do with my tray. I get up, then turn back, then turn toward the girls, then swivel—

"On the cart," Blue Streak says. She turns to the big girl. "God, he's so *cute*."

Did she just say that? I put my tray on the cart and sit at the vacant seat with the girls.

"What's your name?" Blue Streak asks.

"Ah, Craig."

"So what's it like to be the hottest guy in here, Craig?"

My body hitches and jerks up as if on a pulley system. She's got it all wrong—*she's* the hot one. It's tough to tell whether her skin or teeth are the more perfect white. Her eyes are dark and her lips pouty and open; the blue streak accents the contrast of hair and face, and she smiles at me—that's definitely smiling. I don't know how I didn't notice her hotness before, when I looked into the dining room.

"Jenni*fer*," the big girl says. She leans toward me. "I'm Becca. Don't take advantage of Jennifer; she's a sex addict."

Jennifer smacks her lips: "Shut up!" She turns back. "I'm only here for one more day." She slithers forward. "You want to spend it with me?"

I think about what Humble would say. He would say *Yeah, absolutely*, because he's the alpha male. I try to develop and drop my words, keeping my voice deep and level: "Yeah, absolutely."

"Good," she says, and there's a heat on my knee and a hand moving up my leg. She leans in. "I think you're really *hottt*." The hand encloses my thigh. "I have my own private room because I'm so messed up they won't let me sleep with anybody else."

"You have your own private room because you're a slut!" Becca corrects, and Jennifer kicks her.

"Ow!"

Without warning, the blond girl with the cuts on her face gets up and speed-walks out of the room. I look through the window for her: nothing.

"Forget her," Jennifer says. "She's no good for you." Then, sparking an out-of-body experience that truly makes me question whether I'm dreaming this, or have died and gone to some kind of awesome hell, she flicks her tongue around her lips in a perfect O.

Something flashes out in the hall. The blond girl streaks to the window. I can't be sure it's her. I mean, it is *a* her—it has breasts. And I think I recognize her small body and wife-beater. But I can't see her face because she presses up a piece of paper against the glass:

BEWARE OF PENIS

The sign slides down as if on an elevator.

"What are you looking at?" Jennifer asks, turning back. I eye her body as she swivels; from the waist up she doesn't look like she has a penis. I keep my peripheral vision on the hall in case the messenger returns.

"Ha!" Becca is like. "Noelle did it to you again."

"She what?" Jennifer stands. She has a round and totally female shape. Her legs are encased with jeans that have frills around her butt.

"I can't be*lieve* her . . . *hey*." She turns back. "You looking at my pants?"

"Yeah," I gulp. I've lost all alpha maleness. Could I be like a theta male? They have to get lucky sometime. Being on top of the sexual food chain is a lot of pressure.

"I made them myself," she says. "I'm a fashion designer."

"Wow, really? That's like a real job." My mind spins; it's somehow fallen off the sex track into grade-school logic. "I thought you were *my* age; how'd you learn how to design clothes—"

"All right," Smitty strides in. "Playtime's over. C'mon, Charles."

"What the hell!" Jennifer jumps a few inches in the air and stomps her feet. Then, horror of horrors, her voice drops two octaves. "You guys won't let me have any fun!"

It's a bad voice, even for a guy, like a frog croaking. Becca laughs and laughs, doubling over on herself, and all I can do is catch my breath and stare goggle-eyed at Jennifer for signs. It can't be. She's flat, that's all. She has big hands; lots of girls have big hands. She doesn't have an Adam's apple—oh, wait, she's wearing a turtleneck.

"C'mon, don't bother Craig," Smitty says.

"But he's so cute!"

"He's not cute, he's a hospital patient like you. You're supposed to get out tomorrow; don't jeopardize it. Have you taken your medicine yet?"

"Hormone treatments." Jennifer/Charles winks at me.

"C'mon, enough."

Becca laughs, sighs. "Oh, she got you good. I'm getting my meds."

I look down at the table as they leave. *I need some meds.* I glance up and see patients lined up at the desk next to the phone, the nurses' station, eagerly passing the time in their own little ways—President Armelio bopping from foot to foot, Jimmy holding the hand that refuses to work—before getting pills in little plastic cups. Jennifer/Charles and Becca eventually appear at the end of the line, chatting and gesticulating, and Jennifer/Charles blows me a kiss. I don't think I need to be in line behind them right now. Besides, all I take is Zoloft in the morning; if they wanted me on something midday, they would have told me.

When Becca and J/C are gone and I'm still sitting shell-shocked at the table, another sign appears at the window, this one inching up from below as if hoisted by spider threads:

DON'T WORRY. HE/SHE/IT GETS EVERYBODY. WELCOME TO SIX NORTH!

When I go out to find her, she isn't there. I ask the nurse wrapping up her dispensing duties if I need any meds, and she says I'm not scheduled for any. I ask her if I *can* have some. She asks what I need them for. I tell her, to deal with this crazy place. She says if they had pills for that, they wouldn't need places like this in the first place, would they?

twenty-four

"So what's it like?" Mom asks, holding a tote bag of toiletries, with Dad and Sarah next to her. We're at the end of the right H leg, me in one chair facing the three of them. Visiting hours are from 12 to 8 on Saturday.

Sarah doesn't let me answer.

"It's like *One Flew Over the Cuckoo's Nest!*" she says, excited. She's dressed up in jeans and a fake suede jacket for Six North. "I mean, all these people look like . . . serious crazies!"

"*Shhh,*" I tell her. "Jimmy's right there." Jimmy is behind her at the window, sitting with his arms crossed as usual, out of his shirt and into a clean navy robe.

"Who's Jimmy?" Mom asks eagerly.

"The guy I came in with downstairs. I think he's schizophrenic."

"Doesn't that mean he has two personalities?" Sarah asks, turning. "Like, he's not just Jimmy; he's also Molly or something."

"No, you'd be surprised, that's a *different* one," I raise my eyebrows. "Jimmy's just a little . . . scattered."

Jimmy sees me looking at him and smiles. "I tell you, you play those numbers, it'll *come* to *ya!*" he chirps.

"I think he's talking about Lotto numbers," I explain. "I've been trying to figure it out."

"Oh my *gosh.*" My sister covers her face.

"No, Sarah, don't do that, watch," Mom says. She turns around. "Thank you very much, Jimmy."

"I tell you: it the *truth!*"

"I like this place," Mom turns back. "I think it's full of good people."

"I *really* like it." Dad leans in. "When can I join?" But when no one laughs, he leans back, clasps his hands, sighs.

"Is that a *transvestite?*" Sarah asks. J/C is down the hall, like forty feet away, and I don't know for the life of me how Sarah suspects something out there that I couldn't see at point-blank range.

"No, now listen—"

"Is it?" Dad squints.

"Guys!"

"Trans-*vestite!*" Jimmy shrieks. He does it at top range—I haven't heard him that loud before. The entire hall, which admittedly is just me, my family,

J/C, and the older professor-type woman with the glasses, stops and stares.

"I tell you once, it'll come: it come to ya!"

J/C starts walking toward us. "Are we talking about *me?*" he asks in his guy voice. He waves at Jimmy. "Hey, Jimmy." He comes right up between me and my sister. "Craig, your name is, right?"

"Yeah," I mumble.

"Wow, is this your family?"

"Yeah." I tip my palm at each of them—it's at the level of the frills on his pants. "My dad"—he juts his lip out—"my mom"—she nods, all smiles—"and my sister, Sarah"—she reaches out a hand.

"Oh my God, so lovely!" J/C says. "I'm Charles." He shakes with everyone. "They're going to take really good care of your son here. He's a good guy."

"How about you; what are you in for?" Dad asks. I kick him. Doesn't he know what not to ask?

"It's okay, Craig!" J/C touches my shoulder. "My gosh, did you just *kick* your dad? *I* never even did that." He addresses Dad: "I have bipolar, sir, and I had an episode, and they brought me here. I'm going back upstate today. But the doctors are very attentive here, and the turnaround time is great."

"Wonderful," Mom says.

"Of course"—J/C gestures to us—"it's a lot better when you have family support. They want to make sure they discharge you into a safe environment. I don't have that." He shakes his head. "Craig, you're very lucky."

I look at them: my safe environment. I frankly wouldn't be surprised to find any of them in Six North.

"Well, I'll leave you guys to your afternoon," J/C says. He walks away slowly.

Jimmy makes an indecipherable high-pitched whining noise.

"That's applause, isn't it?" Dad asks, throwing a thumb behind him. "I like that."

"Those are awesome *pants*," Sarah says.

"Okay, so let's get down to business, Craig," Mom is like. "What do you need?"

"I need a phone card. I need you guys to take my phone and leave it plugged in so the calls register. I need some clothes, like what you were bringing before, Mom. I don't need towels; they have those. Magazines would be good. And a pencil and paper, that would rock."

"Simple enough. What kind of magazines?"

"Science magazines! He loves those," Dad says.

"He might not be up for science magazines right now," Mom answers. "Do you want anything lighter?"

"Do you want *Star*?" Sarah asks.

"Sarah, why would I want *Star?*"

"Because it's *awesome.*" She reaches into her purse—her first one, black, a recent Mom purchase—and unrolls a glossy pink monstrosity, complete with pictures of the most recent spectacular outing of a celebrity breast in public.

I hold it up for Jimmy.

"*Mmmmmm-hmmmmmm!*" he says. "I tell you! I tell you! It *come to ya!*"

"That's very nice," says the professor woman with bugged-out eyes, who I somehow didn't realize had migrated right behind me. "Oh, excuse me," she looks up. "I wasn't listening to your conversation at all." She walks to her room.

"Um . . ." Sarah says.

"I'll take it," I say. I put it under my seat. "I think the floor will enjoy it."

"Is it just me, or are you starting to develop a sort of allegiance to the tribe?" Dad asks.

"*Shhh.*" I smile.

"Craig, the next order of business: have you called Dr. Barney?"

"No."

"Have you called Dr. Minerva?"

"No."

"Well, they both need to know where you are, for health insurance reasons and because they're your doctors and they care about you and this is going to be very important to them."

"Their numbers are in my phone."

"Well, let's call them; we picked up your phone from the front," Mom reaches into her bag—

"No!" Dad grabs her hands. "Don't take out the phone!"

"Don't be ridiculous, honey. Craig's the one who's not allowed to have it, not us."

"Well, uh, I don't think we want to be getting our son in trouble. This isn't the kind of place you want to be getting sent to a *time-out*."

I look at him. "That's really not that funny."

"What? Oh, sorry," he says.

"No, Dad, seriously. It's not . . . I mean, this is serious business."

"I'm just trying to lighten the mood, Craig—"

"Well, that's what you're always trying to do. Let's just, not do it here."

Dad nods, looks me dead in the eyes; slowly and regretfully, he banishes all the smiling and joking from his face, and for once he's just my dad, watching his son who has fallen so low. "All right, then."

We stay quiet.

"Is that the truth, Jimmy?" I ask without looking at him.

"It's the truth, and it *come to ya!*"

I smile.

"We'll handle the phone later," Dad sums up.

"Next order of business?" Mom asks.

"How long I'm going to be in here, I think."

"How long do you think?"

"A couple of days. But I haven't seen the doctor yet. Dr. Mahmoud."

"Right, how is he? Is he good?"

"I don't know, Mom. You met him for as long as I did. He makes rounds soon, and I'll get to talk with him."

"I think you need to stay here until you're better, Craig. You don't want to come out early and have to come back; that's how you get 'in the system.'"

"Right. I won't. I think that's actually a big part of places like this: they make them so you *don't want* to come back.

"How's the food?" Sarah asks.

"Oh, I almost forgot," I look at my family. "I'm . . . I know I shouldn't be proud about this; it's like really sad that this is my big accomplishment of the day . . . but I ate everything at lunch."

"You did?" Mom stands up, pulls me up and hugs me.

"Yeah." I pull away. "It was chicken. I actually ate two helpings of it."

"Son, that is a big one," Dad gets up and shakes my hand.

"No, it's not, it's really simple, everybody does it, but for me it's like a stupid triumph—"

"No," Mom says, looking me in the eyes. "What's a triumph is that you woke up this morning and decided to *live. That's* a triumph. That's what you did today."

I nod at her. Like I say, I'm not a crier.

"Yeah, cause if you had died . . ." Sarah is like, "that would have *sucked.*" She rolls her eyes and hugs my leg.

I sit back down. "Once the food is in front of you it's just like, *eat.* I mean, they're professionals here; they know how to take people and put them in a routine that gives them something to do."

"That's right," Mom says. "So what are you going to do now?"

"I think there are activities—"

"Hey, Craig, is this your family?" President Armelio steps on the scene. His half-harelip and hair shock my sister, but his relentless enthusiasm for just—I don't know—*living*—would knock the fear out of anybody. He shakes all the hands and says we're a beautiful family and I'm a good guy, he can tell.

"Craig's my buddy! Hey, buddy—you want to play cards?"

President Armelio holds up a deck of playing cards like he just fished it out of the sea.

"Yeah, absolutely!" I say. I stand up. When was the last time I played cards? Before the test, probably—before high school.

"All right!" Armelio says. "My kinda guy! Let's do it. I've been looking and looking: nobody here likes to play cards like I do! What do you want to play? Spades? I'll *crush* you, buddy; I'll *crush* you."

I look at my parents. "We'll call you," Mom says. "And hey—what about sleeping?"

"I'm wired right now," I say. "But I'll crash. I'm starting to get a headache."

"Headache? Buddy, once I crush you in spades, you're going to have a lot bigger headache!" Armelio toddles away to the dining room to set up the cards.

"See ya," Sarah says, hugging me.

"Bye, son." Dad shakes my hand.

"I love you," Mom says. "I'll call you with the doctors' phone numbers."

"And bring a phone card."

"And I'll bring a phone card. You hang in there, Craig."

"Yeah, I will." And as soon as they're around the bend, I head into the dining room and learn how to play spades for the rest of the afternoon, which Armelio absolutely does crush me in.

twenty-five

I'm afraid of making phone calls. The phone on Six North is a hubbub of activity, with Bobby and the blond burned-out-type, who I learn is named Johnny, fielding calls from, I assume, their respective female counterparts. Bobby starts off his calls happy and says "Baby" a lot, but then he gets angry and slams the phone down saying "bitch"; Smitty tells him not to do that; Bobby walks away leaning back with a particularly potent aura of not caring. Five minutes later, another call comes in for him, and he's back to "Baby." He doesn't ever answer the phone, though; President Armelio has that job. When he answers, he always says "Joe's Pub," and then finds whoever the call's for.

In a rare moment when Johnny and Bobby leave the phone open, I walk up to it with the phone card that Mom brought me twenty minutes after she left with Dad and Sarah. I pick up and hear the dial tone, dial the 800 number for the phone card . . .

and then stop. I can't do it. I just don't want to deal with it.

People on the outside world don't know what's happened to me—I'm in a sort of stasis right now. Things are under control. But the dam will break. Even if I'm here just through Monday, the rumors will start flying, and the homework will pile up.

Where's Craig?

He's sick.

He's not sick, he got alcohol poisoning because he can't handle real liquor.

I heard he took someone's pills and freaked out.

I heard he realized he's gay and he's coming to grips with it.

I heard his parents are sending him to a different school.

He couldn't handle it here, anyway. He was always such a loser.

He's freaking out in front of his computer. He can't move or anything. He's catatonic.

He woke up and thinks he's a horse.

Well, whatever, what's question three?

There were two messages on my phone when I came in, and now there are probably more, each one necessitating a call back, and the call back possibly necessitating another call back—Tentacles—leading me right back to where I was last night. I can't go there, so I wait. I can wait five minutes. But then Bobby's on the line. And then I wait another five minutes. And the messages are piling up. And this isn't even counting e-mail. What sort of hellish assignments have my teachers e-mailed out?

"Excuse me, are you using the phone?" the giant black woman with the cane asks as I stare at it.

"Yeah, uh." I pick up the receiver in my hands. "Yes. Yes I am."

"Okay." She smiles, rolling her gums, not showing teeth. I start dialing, enter my PIN, enter my own number.

"Please enter your password, then press the pound sign."

I obey.

"You have—three—new messages."

One more than before. Not so bad.

"First new message: message marked urgent."

Uh-oh.

"Hey, Craig, it's Nia, I just, um . . . we talked and you were sounding really bad. I just wanted to make sure you were doing all right, and since you're not answering—it's like two A.M., I mean, why would you be answering?—but I'm kinda worried that maybe you went and did something stupid because of me. Don't. I mean, it's sweet, but don't. Okay, that's it, I'm with Aaron, he's being a total dick. Bye."

"To erase this message—"

I hit 7.

"Next message."

"Craig, it's Aaron, call me back son! Let's chill—"

I hit 7-7.

"Next message."

"Hello, Mr. Gilner, this is your science teacher, Mr. Reynolds. I got your phone number from the student directory. We really need to talk about the lack of your labs; I'm missing five of them—"

7-7.

"End of messages."

I put the phone down like it's a dangerous animal. I pick back up, call home. Can't stop now.

"Sarah, can you get the phone numbers of Nia and Aaron out of my cell? And look through the recent missed calls for something from Manhattan; I have to call my science teacher."

"Sure. How are things over there?"

I look to my left. A Hasidic Jewish guy, complete with the white pants, yarmulke, tassels hanging off him, braided hair, and sandals, dashes down the hall toward me. Scraps of red food dot his dark beard, and his eyes are wild and unhinged. He says to me: "I'm Solomon."

"Um, I've heard about you. I'm Craig, but

I'm on the phone." I cup the receiver.

"I would ask you to please keep it down! I'm trying to rest!" He turns and races away, holding his pants.

"Oooh! Solomon *introduced* himself to you!" hoots the woman with the cane. "That's big."

"It's normal," I tell my sister.

"Okay, here." She gives me Nia's and Aaron's and the teacher's numbers; I write them down on a scrap of paper that Smitty has given me. I should've known these before. Nia's looks good written down—wholesome and useful. The science teacher's looks jagged and hateful. I may not be able to call him until tomorrow.

"Thanks, Sarah—bye."

I hang up and look toward the lady with the cane.

"Hey, I'm Craig," I say.

"Ebony." She nods. We shake hands.

"Ebony, it's cool if I just make one more call?"

"Of course."

I dial the 800 number, enter my PIN, dial Nia.

"Hello?"

"Hey, Nia, it's me."

"Craig, where are you?"

It's funny how people ask that as soon as they get you on the phone. I think it's a byproduct of

cell phones: people—girls and moms especially—
want to nail you down in physical space. The fact
is that you could be anywhere on a cell phone and
it shouldn't be important where you are. But it
becomes the first thing people ask.

"I'm at a friend's house. In Brooklyn."

I wonder, too, how many *lies* cell phones have
contributed to the world.

"Uh-huh, Craig. I don't think so."

"What do you mean?" I wipe sweat off my brow.
The sweat is starting again. This isn't good. I was
sweating down in the ER, but I wasn't sweating at
lunch.

"You're not at any friend's house. You're probably
at some girl's house."

I look at Ebony. She smiles and leans forward on
her cane. "Yeah, totally."

"I know you. Last night you had me on the
phone; tonight you're out hooking up with some
girl."

"Sure, Nia—"

"Seriously, how *are* you? Thanks for calling back.
I was worried."

"I know, I got your message."

"I don't want you to freak out over *me*. I think
you just need some time to decompress a little bit,
and *not* think about me, and think about someone

else. Because, like, I know we might be good for each other, but I'm with someone else, you know?"

"Right . . . um . . . I *wasn't* freaking out about you last night, actually."

"No?"

"No, I was freaking out about, like, much bigger things. I was having kind of a crisis, and I wanted to reach out to somebody who understood."

"But you asked me if we would ever have been able to be together."

"Well, I was trying to clear that up because, y'know . . . I wanted to do something stupid."

She drops her voice: "Kill yourself?"

"Yeah."

"You wanted to kill yourself over *me*?"

"No!" I scowl. "I was just in a really bad place, and you were part of it, obviously, because you're a part of my life, just like Aaron is a part of it and my family is a part of it, but I thought you could clear something up for me before I . . ."

"Craig, I'm so flattered."

"No, you have the wrong idea. Don't be flattered."

"How could I not be? I never had a boy want to kill himself for me before. It's like the most romantic thing."

"Nia, *it wasn't about you.*"

"Are you sure?"

I look down, and the answer is right there in my chest and it's resounding. "Yes. *I have bigger problems than you.*"

"Ah, okay."

"And you shouldn't assume that everything is always about you."

"Whatever. What's wrong with you?"

"Nothing. Everything's a lot better now, actually."

"You're acting like a total dick. Do you want to come out tonight?"

"I can't."

"Did Aaron call you? We're having a big party at his house."

"Right. I'm probably not going to be partying for . . . like . . . a *while*. Like *ever*, maybe."

"Is everything okay now?"

"Yeah, I'm just . . . I'm figuring some things out."

"At your friend's house."

"Correct."

"Are you like in a crack den, or something?"

"No!" I yell, and just then President Armelio walks up to me: "Hey, buddy, you want to play spades? I'll *crush you.*"

"Not now, Armelio."

"Who's that?" Nia asks.

"Leave him alone, he's talking with his *girl-friend*." Ebony taps Armelio with her cane.

"She's not my girlfriend," I whisper at her.

"Who's *that?*"

"My friend Armelio."

"No, the girl."

"My friend Ebony."

"Where *are* you, Craig?"

"I gotta go."

"All right . . ." Nia trails her voice off. "I'm glad you're doing . . . uh . . . better."

"I'm doing a lot better," I say.

She's done, I think. *She's done, and you're done with her.*

"See ya, Craig."

I hang up.

"I think that's over," I say to myself.

Then I decide to announce it to the hall: "I think that that's *over!*" Ebony stomps her cane, and Armelio claps.

Something deep in my guts, below my heart, has made a shift to the left and settled in a more comfortable place. It's not *the* Shift, but it's *a* shift. I picture Nia with her gorgeous face and little body and black hair and pouty lips and Aaron's hands all over her but also with her pot smoking and the pimples on her forehead and making fun of people all the time and the way she's always so proud of how she's dressed. And I picture her fading.

I play cards with Armelio in the dining room until Bobby pokes his head in:

"Craig? It says on your door Dr. Mahmoud is your doctor? He's making his rounds."

twenty-six

"I don't want to be here," I tell him at the entrance to my room, where I catch him before he visits Muqtada. "I don't think it's the place for me."

"Of course not." Dr. Mahmoud nods. He has on the same suit he had on earlier in the day, although that feels like last year. "If you liked it here, that would be a very bad prognosis!"

"Right." I chuckle. "Well, I mean, everybody's friendly, but I feel a lot better, and I think I'm ready to go. Maybe Monday? I don't want to miss school."

Also, doc, right now the phone messages and e-mails are bunching up and the rumors are flying. I just talked to this girl—and I did okay—but the Tentacles are coiled and the pressure is rising, getting ready to pounce on me when I leave. If I'm in here too long, I'll have that much more to do when I get out.

"We can't rush it," Dr. Mahmoud says. "The important thing is that you get better. If you try to

leave too soon—suddenly, everything is better?—
we doctors get suspicious."

"Oh. Well, you don't want the doctor who can
sign you out of the psychiatric hospital getting suspicious."

"Right. Right now, to me, you look much better,
but maybe this is a false recovery—"

"A Fake Shift."

"I'm sorry?"

"A Fake Shift. That's what I call it. When you
think you've beaten it, but you haven't."

"Exactly. We don't want one of those."

"So I'm going to be here until I have the real
Shift?"

"I don't follow."

"I'm going to be here until I'm cured?"

"Life is not cured, Mr. Gilner." Dr. Mahmoud
leans in. "Life is *managed*."

"Okay."

I'm apparently not as impressed by this as he
would like. He arches back: "We don't keep you
here until you are cured of anything; we keep
you here until you are stable—we call it 'establish-
ing the baseline.'"

"Okay, so when will my baseline be established?"

"Five days, probably."

One, two, three . . . "*Thursday?* I can't wait until

Thursday, Doctor. I have too much school. That's four days of school. If I miss four days I will be so behind. Plus, my friends . . ."

"Yes?"

"My friends will know where I am!"

"Aha. Is this a problem?"

"Yes!"

"Why?"

"Because I'm *here*!" I gesture out at the hall. Solomon shuffles by very quickly in his sandals and tells someone to be quiet, he's trying to rest.

"Mr. Gilner." Dr. Mahmoud puts a hand on my shoulder. "You have a chemical imbalance, that is all. If you were a diabetic, would you be ashamed of where you were?"

"No, but—"

"If you had to take insulin and you stopped, and you were taken to the hospital, wouldn't that make sense?"

"This is different."

"How?"

I sigh. "I don't know how much of it is really chemical. Sometimes I just think depression's one way of coping with the world. Like, some people get drunk, some people do drugs, some people get depressed. Because there's so much *stuff* out there that you have to do something to deal with it."

"Ah. This is why you need to be in here longer, to talk about these things," Dr. Mahmoud says. "You have a psychologist, correct? Have you called your psychologist?"

Shoot. I knew I was forgetting something.

"You need to call; your psychologist will come here to meet with you. What is her name? Or his?"

"Dr. Minerva."

"Oh!" Dr. Mahmoud says; his lips curl into a far-away smile. "Wonderful. Get Andrea down here."

"Andrea?" I never knew her first name. She keeps it like a big secret. It's blanked out on all her degrees. She says it's part of policy.

He waves his hand. "Make an appointment with her; then we'll be that much closer to coming up with your treatment plan and getting you out of here as soon as possible. We will try for Thursday."

"Not before Thursday."

"No."

"*Thursday*," I mumble to myself, looking across the room at Muqtada's prone lump.

"Five days, that's it! Everything will be fine, Mr. Gilner. Your life will *wait*. You just participate in the group activities and call Dr. Minerva. And when you grow up to be rich and successful, you don't forget me, okay?"

"Okay."

"Can please you close the door?" Muqtada asks from his bed.

"Mister Muqtada, you are the next: how come you are always sleeping sleeping *sleeping?*"

Dr. Mahmoud walks past me. I call Mom to report the news, and then I call Dr. Minerva. She says she's sorry I took this turn for the worse, but it's always two-steps-forward, one-step-back.

"If this is my one step back," I tell her, "what am I going to do next: win the lottery and get my own TV show?"

That'd be a good TV show, actually, I think. *A guy winning the lottery in the psych hospital.*

Dr. Minerva can't come in tomorrow, because it's Sunday, but she says she'll be in on Monday. I'm momentarily surprised by the distinction. In Six North, there probably won't be much difference.

twenty-seven

"They say there's gonna be a pizza party tonight," Humble tells me at dinner. Dinner is chicken tenders with potatoes and salad and a pear. I eat it all. "But they say that every night."

"What's a pizza party?"

"We all chip in the money and get pizza from the neighborhood. It's tough, because no one ever has any cash. It's like a big deal if we get pepperoni."

"I have eight dollars."

"*Shhh.* Don't go announcing it!" He stops chewing. "People in here don't have *any* money. I don't have two cents to rub together."

I nod. "I never heard that one before."

"No? You like it?"

"Yeah."

"What about: *I don't have a pot to piss in or a window to throw it out of.*"

"Nope."

"What about: *I got Jack and shit and Jack left town.*"

"Heh. No! Where do you get them all?"

"From the old neighborhood. *Gimme a ringy-ding. Catch ya on the flipside.* It's the best way to talk."

"A *ringy-ding*, what's that—a call?"

"Don't ask yuppie questions."

Humble scans the room for people to talk about. He enjoys talking about other people—he just enjoys talking, I've discovered, but he *especially* enjoys talking about other people—and when he does so, he puts on a peculiar sort of voice that's not quite a whisper, but is pitched at such a low monotone that no one notices it. He also seems able to throw it so it feels like he's speaking into my left ear.

"So I suppose you've become familiar with our lovely clientele here on the floor. President Armelio is the president." He nods over at Armelio, who has finished his food first and is getting up to return the tray. "You see how fast he eats? If you could harness a quarter of his energy, you could power the island of Manhattan. I'm not joking. He should really work in a place with people like us. He has such a good heart and he's never down."

"So why is he in here?"

"He's psychotic, of course. You shoulda seen him when they brought him in. He was screaming his head off about his mom. He's Greek."

"Huh."

"Now there's Ebony, She of the Ass. That is definitely the biggest ass I've ever seen. I'm not even into asses, but if you were—man, you could lose yourself in there. It's like its own municipality. I think that's why she needs the cane. She's also the only woman I've ever known who wears velvet pants; I think you have to have a butt like that to wear velvet pants. They only make them in extra extra *extra* large."

"I didn't even notice them."

"Well, give it a while. After a few days you start to notice people's clothes, seeing as how they all wear the same stuff every day."

"Things don't get dirty?"

"They do laundry on Tuesdays and Fridays. Who gave you your tour when you came in?"

"Bobby."

"He should've told you that." Humble swivels his head, then turns back. "Now Bobby and Johnny"—they're at a table together, as they were at lunch—"those two were some of the biggest methamphetamine addicts in New York City, period, in the nineties. They were called Fiend One and Fiend Two. The party didn't really start until they showed up."

That must've been such a feeling, even through

all the drugs, I think. To come into a house and have people well up and greet you: "All right, man!" "You're here!" "What's up?" That was probably as addictive as the amphetamines. People sort of do that to Aaron.

"What happened to them?" I ask.

"What happens to anybody? They got burned out, lost all their money, ended up here. Got no families, got no women—well, I think Bobby has one."

"He talks on the phone with her."

"You can't tell from that. People pretend to be on the phone all the time. Like her"—he pitches his head at the bug-eyed woman who was standing behind me when I was talking with my family— "The Professor. I've caught her on the phone talking to Dr. Dial Tone. She's a university professor. She ended up here because she thinks someone tried to spray her apartment with insecticide. She has newspaper clippings about it and everything."

Humble turns: "The black kid with the glasses: he looks pretty normal, but he has it bad. You notice he doesn't come out of his room a lot. That's because he's scared that gravity is going to reverse and he's going to fall up into the ceiling. When he goes outside, he has to be near trees so, in case the gravity stops, he'll have something to hold on to. I think he's about seventeen. Have you talked to him?"

"No."

"He doesn't really talk. I don't know how much they can do for him."

The guy looks up at the ceiling fan above the dining room, shudders, and forks food into his mouth.

"Then there's Jimmy. Jimmy's been here a lot. I've been here twenty-four days, and I've seen him come and go twice. You seem to like him."

"We came in together."

"He's a cool guy. And he has good teeth."

"Yeah, I noticed that."

"Pearly whites. Not a lot of people in here have that. I myself wonder what happened to Ebony's teeth."

"What's wrong with them?" I turn.

"*Don't look.* She has none, you didn't notice? She's on a liquid diet. Just gums. I wonder if she sold 'em, tooth by tooth. . . ."

I bite my tongue. I can't help it. I shouldn't be laughing at any of these people, and neither should Humble, but maybe it's okay, somewhere, somehow, because we're enjoying life? I'm not sure. Jimmy, two tables away, notices my stifled laughter, smiles at me, and laughs himself.

"I toldja: it *come to ya!*"

"There we go. What is going on in his *mind?*" Humble asks.

I can't help it. It's too much. I crack up. Juice and chicken tender bits spray my plate.

"Oh, I got you now," Humble continues. "And here comes the guest of honor: Solomon."

The Hasidic Jewish guy comes in holding up his pants. He still has food in his beard. He grabs his tray and opens a microwaved packet of spaghetti and starts shoveling it into his mouth, making slurping, gulping groans.

"This guy eats once a day but it's like his last day on earth," Humble says. "I think he's the most far gone of everybody. He's got like a direct audience with God."

Solomon looks up, twists his head from side to side, and resumes eating.

Humble drops to a true whisper. "He did a few hundred tabs of acid and blew his pupils out. His eyeballs are permanently dilated."

"No way."

"Absolutely. It's a certain cult of the Hasidics: the Jewish Acid-Heads. There's like a part of their holy writings that tells them it's the way to talk to God. But he took it too far."

Solomon gets up, leaves his tray disgustedly at

the table, and moves out of the room with alarming speed.

"He's like the Mole Man, back to his hole," Humble says. "The real Mole People are the anorexics; you don't even see them."

"How many people are in here?" I ask.

"They say twenty-five," Humble says. "But that's not counting the stowaways."

I look around. Charles/Jennifer isn't in the room. "Did the, uh, you know, *Charles*? Did he leave?"

"Yeah, the tranny's gone. Left this afternoon. Tranny hit on you?"

"Yeah."

"Smitty lets him do that. Gets a kick out of it."

"I can't believe he's just *gone*. They don't, like, throw a party for you when you leave?"

"No way. People here don't *want* to get out. Getting out means going back to the streets or to jail or to try and fish their things out of an impounded car, like me. Your kind of situation, with the parents and a house: that's rare. And also, with so many people coming and going, we'd be nuts to try and have a party every time. We'd end up like Fiend One and Fiend Two."

My tray is a mess from the food spraying out. "You crack me up, Humble," I tell him.

"I know. I'm a great time for everybody. Too bad

I'm in here instead of onstage getting paid for it."

"Why don't you try going onstage?"

"I'm old."

"I have to get some napkins." I rise and go out to Smitty, who hands me a stack. I return, wipe off my tray, and start in on the pear.

"You have a secret admirer," Humble says. "I should've guessed. I know how you operate."

"What?"

"She was just here. Look at your chair."

I get up and check it. There's a piece of paper lying there, face down. I flip it around, and it says HOPE YOU'RE HAVING A GOOD TIME. VISITING HOURS ARE TOMORROW FROM 7:00–7:05 P.M. I DON'T SMOKE.

"See? Your little girl with the cut-up face just left it." Humble gets up. "I had a feeling. Now you're starting to look like a rival male. I might have to keep my eye on you."

He deposits his tray and gets in line for his meds. I fold the paper up and put it in the pocket where my phone used to be.

twenty-eight

"Craig! Hey buddy! Phone!"

I'm sitting with Humble outside the smoking lounge for the 10 P.M. cigarette break, thinking about where I was at the last 10 P.M.: just getting into Mom's bed. Humble doesn't smoke, says it's disgusting, but everyone else in here does, practically, including the black guy who's afraid of gravity; and the big girl, Becca, both of whom I thought were underage. Armelio, Ebony, Bobby, Johnny, Jimmy . . . no matter how nuts they all seem, they have no problem migrating to the upper left of the H and sitting down on the couches quietly to wait for their particular brand of cigarettes, which I learn the hospital does not, in fact, provide for them—they come in with the packs themselves and the nurses keep them in a special tray. Once they pull a cigarette out of their respective packs, they walk single file through a red door, passing Nurse Monica, whose job is to light everybody up. When the door closes, the smell drifts out from under it and you hear talking—everybody talking all at once, as if they saved their words for a time when there was smoke to send them through.

"How're you doing for your first day, Craig?" Nurse Monica asked me five minutes ago, as she closed the door. "You don't smoke, I see."

"No."

"That's good. Terrible habit. And it happens so much to people your age."

"A lot of my friends smoke. I just, you know . . . never liked it."

"I see you are adjusting quite well to the floor."

"Yeah."

"Good, good, that is so important. Tomorrow we're going to talk more about your adjustment and your situation and how you're feeling."

"Okay."

"You gotta watch out for this one," Humble said. "He's crafty."

"Oh yeah?" Monica asked.

I was looking for the blond girl, Noelle—I had to remember to meet her—but she wasn't around. Neither was Solomon. Next to Humble was the woman he identified as the Professor, watching us with her bugged-out eyes. Unprompted, Humble started talking with me and Monica about this old girlfriend of his, who had, in his words, "pig-tail nipples, like curly fries, I kid you not." Monica laughed and laughed. The Professor said Humble was disgusting. Monica said it was okay to laugh once in a while, and did she have a story to share?

"Yeah, we all know you had some indiscretions in your youth, Professor," Humble prodded.

The Professor got a dreamy look in her eyes. I almost thought she was going to have a seizure. And she said, in a light little voice, with a nasal twinge: "I had a lot of guys, but I only had one *man*."

I was wondering where I'd heard that before, when Armelio interrupted.

"C'mon buddy! Phone is for you!"

"Right." I get up.

"You're lucky, buddy. It's after ten. They usually shut the phone off at ten."

Shut the phone off. I picture a big lever in my mind, a man heaving it down.

"What happens if someone calls and the phone's off?"

"It just rings and rings," Humble yells out, "and people know they're not in Kansas anymore."

I walk down the hall. The pay-phone receiver is hanging and swaying. I pick it up.

"Hello?"

"Hey, is this the loony bin?" It's Aaron. It's Aaron, high.

"How'd you get this number?" I ask. The man with the beard, who I saw rocking in the dining room when I first came in, is pacing the central hall, staring at me.

"My girl gave it to me, what do you think? What's it like in there, dude?" Aaron asks.

"How do you know where I am?"

"I looked it up, man! You think I'm an idiot? I go to the same school as you! I did a reverse number search and found exactly where you are: Argenon Hospital, Adult Psychiatric! Dude, how'd you get in *adult*? Do they serve beer up there?"

"Aaron, c'mon."

"I'm serious. How about girls? Are there any hot girls around—*ow!*"

I hear laughing in the background, above rap. "Gimme the phone!" Ronny's high-pitched bleat comes through the line. "Lemme talk!"

Ronny comes into focus: "Dude, can you get me any Vicodin?"

Howls. Howls of laughter. And in the background, Nia protesting: "Guys, don't bother him."

"*Gimme*—Craig, no, seriously." Aaron is back on. "I'm really sorry dude. I . . . just, how *are* you, man?"

"I'm . . . okay." I'm starting to sweat.

"What happened?"

"I didn't have a good night, and I checked myself into the hospital."

"What's that mean, 'didn't have a good night'?"

The man in my stomach is back, tugging at me. I want to vomit *through* the phone.

"I'm depressed, okay, Aaron?"

"Yeah, I know, about what?"

"No, man, I'm depressed *in general*. I have like, clinical depression."

"No way! You're like the happiest guy I know!"

"What are you *talking* about?"

"That's a joke, Craig. You're like the craziest person I know. Remember on the bridge? But, you know, the problem is you don't *chill* enough. Like even when you're here, you're always worried about school or something; you never just kick back and let things *slide*, you know what I mean? We're having a party tonight—where are you gonna be?"

"Aaron, who's in the room?"

"Nia, Ronny, Scruggs, uh . . . my friend Delilah."

I don't even know Delilah.

"So all these people know where I am now."

"Dude, we think it's awesome where you are! We want to visit!"

"I can't believe you."

"What?"

"I can't believe you're doing this."

"Don't be a girl. You know if I was in the mental ward, you'd call me up and rag on me a little. It's because we're friends, man!"

"It's not a mental ward."

"What?"

"It's a psychiatric hospital. It's for short-stay patients. A mental ward is longer."

"Well, clearly you've been there long enough to be an expert. How long are you staying?"

"Until I have a baseline established."

"What does that mean? Wait, I still don't get it: what was wrong with you in the first place?"

"I told you, I'm depressed. I take pills for it like your girlfriend."

"Like my girlfriend?"

"Craig, shut up!" Nia yells in the background.

"My girlfriend doesn't take any pills," Aaron says.

Ronny yells, "The only thing she takes is—" The rest is cut off by laughter and I hear him getting hit with something.

"Maybe you should talk to her a little more and figure out what she's actually like," I say. "You might learn something."

"You're telling me how to treat Nia now?" Aaron

asks. I hear him lick his lips. "What, like I don't know what this is really about?"

"What, Aaron. What is it really about?"

"You want my girl, dude. You've wanted her for like two years. You're mad that you didn't get her, and now you've decided to turn being mad into being depressed, and now you're off somewhere, probably getting turned into somebody's bitch, trying to play the pity card to get her to end up with you . . . And I call you *as a friend* to try and lighten your mood and you hit me with all of this crap? Who do you think you *are?*"

"Yo, Aaron."

"What."

I'm going to do a trick Ronny showed me. He used to do it a long time ago, and I think Aaron's forgotten it.

"Yo."

"What?"

"Yo."

"What?!"

"Yo, yo, yo, yo, yo—"

I pause. Hold it, hold it . . .

"Fuck you."

And I slam the phone down.

It hits my finger and I go howling into my room, next to Muqtada.

"What happened?" he asks.

"I don't have any friends," I say, jumping and holding my finger.

"This is tough thing to learn."

I look out the window, through the blinds, into the night. Now I'm really screwed. I run my finger under cold water in our bathroom. I didn't think I could get more screwed than last night, but here I am. I'm in a hospital. I've sunk to the lowest place I can be. I'm in a place where I'm not allowed to shave by myself—even if I needed to shave biologically—because they're worried that I'll use the razors on myself. *And everyone knows.* I'm in a place where people have no teeth and eat liquid food. *And everyone knows.* I'm in a place where the guy I eat with lives in his car. *And everyone knows.*

I can't function here anymore. I mean in life: I can't function in this life. I'm no better off than when I was in bed last night, with one difference: when I was in my own bed—or my mom's—I could do something about it; now that I'm here I can't do anything. I can't ride my bike to the Brooklyn Bridge; I can't take a whole bunch of pills and go for the good sleep; the only thing I can do is crush my head in the toilet seat, and I still don't even know if that would work. They take away your options and all you can do is *live*, and it's just like Humble said: *I'm not afraid of dying; I'm afraid of living.* I was afraid before, but I'm afraid even more now that I'm a public joke. The teachers are going to hear from the students. They'll think I'm trying to make an excuse for bad work.

I get in bed and put the single topsheet over me. "This sucks."

"You are depressed?" Muqtada says.

"Yeah."

"I, too, suffer from depression."

I feel the Cycling starting again—I'm going to get out of here at some point and have to go back into my real life. This place isn't real. This is a facsimile of life, for broken people. I can handle the facsimile, but I can't handle the real thing. I'm going to have to go back to Executive Pre-Professional and deal with teachers and Aaron and Nia because what the hell else do I know? I staked everything on that stupid test. What else am I good at?

Nothing. I'm good at nothing.

I get up and go to the nurses' station.

"I'm not going to be able to sleep."

"You're not able to sleep?" The nurse is a white-haired little old lady with glasses.

"No, I *know* I'm not going to be *able* to sleep," I

respond. "I'm taking preemptive action."

"We have a sedative, called Atavan. It's injectable. It'll relax you and make you sleep."

"Let's do it," I say, and with Smitty's supervision, over by the phones, I sit down and have a small needle attached to what looks like a butterfly clip stuck in my arm. I stare forward as something yellow is pumped into me and then I stumble off into my room—stumble because I can feel it hitting me even as I get up from the chair. It's some kind of powerful muscle relaxant, and loving hands pull me down as I crash into bed past Muqtada, but the last thought I have before I go to sleep is:

Great, soldier, now you're depressed and in the hospital and a drug addict. And everyone knows.

twenty-nine

I'm awakened by a guy in light blue scrubs taking my blood. That's an interesting way to wake up. The guy comes into the room with a cart—carts are very popular here—as light creeps through the blinds.

"I need your bloods. For downstairs."

"Uh, okay."

I present my arm. I'm too beat to ask any questions. He takes a little bit of blood expertly through the back of my hand under my middle-finger knuckle—doesn't leave any kind of mark—and rolls along, leaving Muqtada asleep, or awake and paralyzed by life; it's tough to tell. I want to get more sleep, but once you've been stuck you're inclined to get up, so I move out of bed and take a shower with the hospital-provided towels and my parent-provided shampoo and the generic soap that I pump out of the wall. The shower is searing and wonderful, but I don't want to stay too long—I have to break my habit of languishing in the bathroom—so I dry off and drop my stuff back at the nurses' station. Smitty isn't there; instead there's a big guy who introduces himself as Harold and tells me to dump the towels in a hamper that looks just like a garbage can by the dining room, something that I know I've seen Humble and Bobby dump apple cores and banana peels into.

"Hey, buddy, you're up!" Armelio calls out, bounding down the hall at me. "How'd you sleep?"

"Not good. I needed a shot."

"That's okay, buddy, we all need shots once in a while."

"Heh." I crack the day's first smile. Armelio uncorks one of his own.

"It's time to wake everyone up for vitals," he says, treading down the hall. "*All right, everybody! Vitals! Time to take your vitals!*"

A caravan of my fellow bleary mental patients— or wait, I think we're called in-patient psychiatric treatment recipients, technically—emerge from their compartments, rubbing their eyes and staggering as if they have a job to get to and they just need that first cup of coffee. Surprised by my good fortune, I put myself at the front of the line and become the first to get my blood pressure and pulse taken. 120/80. I continue to be the picture of health.

"Craig?" Harold, the big guy, asks when everyone is done.

"Yeah?"

"You haven't been filling out your menus."

"What are those?"

"Every day, you're supposed to put down what sort of meals you want. On one of these."

He holds up what looks like a placemat, with columns of food: *Breakfast, Lunch, Dinner.*

"You should have gotten this in your welcome packet the nurse gave you."

Ah, the one I completely ignored. I nod.

"I just . . . didn't . . ."

"It's okay, but if you don't mark up your menus, you're going to get a meal we pick for you every time. So fill one out for lunch and dinner today. For breakfast you're going to have to have one of the omelets."

I put my elbows down on the desk and eye the menu choices: hamburger, fish nuggets, French-cut beans, turkey with stuffing, fresh fruit, pudding, oatmeal, orange juice, milk 4oz, milk 8oz, 2% milk, skim milk, tea, coffee, hot chocolate, split pea soup, minestrone soup, fruit salad, cottage cheese, bagel, cream cheese, butter, jelly . . . highly processed food. I'm not going to have a problem eating this. My eyes swim over the choices.

"Circle what you want," Harold explains. I start circling.

"If you want two of anything, put two-x by it." I start putting 2xs.

I wish the world were like this, if I just woke up and marked the food I'd be eating and it came to me later in the day. I suppose it *is* like that, except you have to pay for whatever you want to eat, so maybe what I'm asking for is communism, but I think it's actually deeper than communism—I'm asking for simplicity, for purity and ease of choice and no pressure. I'm asking for something that no politics is going to provide, something that probably you only get in preschool. I'm asking for preschool.

"After breakfast, fill one out for tomorrow," Harold says as I hand in my menu.

Breakfast comes to the dining room and the omelet is like a science experiment: is the lack of cheese explained by the mysterious holes that dot the alleged egg?

"Your first omelet," Bobby says. Today, for a change, I sit with him instead of Humble. Johnny rounds out the table.

"It's really gross." I pick at it.

"It's like a rite of passage," Johnny says. He speaks slowly and without any accents in his words. "'Everyone must eat the omelet.'"

"Yeah, you're *in* now," Bobby says.

"Huh." Johnny exhales.

"How did everybody sleep?" I try.

"I'm anxious, real anxious," Bobby says.

"Why?"

"I've got that interview tomorrow, with the adult home."

"What's that?"

"Huh." Johnny exhales. "It's where people like us live."

"It's a place like this, basically, except you have to hold a job," Bobby explains. "You don't need a pass to leave; you can leave whenever you want, but you have to prove you're employed and be back by seven o'clock."

"Wait, you can leave here with a pass?"

"Yeah, once you have five days inside, they have to give you a pass if you ask for it."

"I'm gonna try and be *out* in five days."

"Huh," Johnny exhales. "Good luck."

I start in on my orange, which is about two hundred times more edible than the omelet. "Why are you nervous about the interview?" I ask Bobby.

"Anxious, not nervous. It's different. It's medical."

"Why are you anxious, then? I'm sure you'll get in."

"You can't be sure of a thing like that. And if I mess it up, I've got problems: I've been here too long; my coverage isn't going to last. Once you're giving the tours, it's really time to leave." He takes a slow bite of oatmeal. "The last place wouldn't let me in because I'm too much of a picky eater. It's not like this place. You can't pick your food."

"So now you know what not to say!" I point out.

"Yeah, that's true."

"See, when you mess something up," I muse, "you learn for the next time. It's when people *compliment* you that you're in trouble. That means they expect you to keep it up."

Bobby nods. "Very, very true."

"Huh, yeah," Johnny says. "My mom was always complimenting me, and look how I turned out."

"This kid has some promise." Bobby laughs. "He's on the level."

"Huh, yeah, on the level. You play guitar, kid?"

"No."

"Johnny here's a great guitarist," Bobby says. "*Really* great. He had a deal in the eighties."

"Oh yeah?"

"*Shhh,*" Johnny says. "It ain't nothin'."

Bobby continues: "He can play better than the guy they bring in here to play for us. But he's a cool guy, that guy."

"Yeah, he's on the level."

"He's on the level. Is he coming in today for group?"

"That's tomorrow. Today is art."

"With Joanie."

"Right."

Bobby sips his coffee. "If there wasn't coffee on this earth, I'd be dead."

I scan the room: everyone's here but Solomon, the Anorexics (who I've now seen peeking out of their rooms like, literally, skeletons in closets), and Noelle. I wonder where she is. She didn't show up for vitals. Maybe she's out on a pass. I hope she'll be around tonight for our date. Technically, it'll be my first date.

"You know, I'll tell you why I'm *really* anxious," Bobby pipes up, leaning in over his coffee. "It's this stupid shirt." He pushes forward his Marvin the Martian WORLD DOMINATOR sweatshirt. "How'm I gonna do an interview in this?"

"Huh." Johnny exhales. "Never underestimate the power of Marvin."

"*Shhh*, man. I'm serious."

"I have shirts," I say.

"What?" Bobby looks up.

"I have shirts. I'll lend you a shirt."

"What? You would do that?"

"Sure. What size are you?"

"Medium. What are you?"

"Uh, child's large."

"What is that in normal?" Bobby turns to Johnny.

"I didn't even know children had sizes," Johnny says.

"I think it would fit," I stand up. Bobby gets up next to me and, although his posture is way different—backward, really—he looks like a decent match.

"I have a blue-collared shirt that my mom makes me wear to church every week. I can have her bring it."

"Today? The interview's tomorrow."

"Yeah. No problem. She's two blocks away."

"You would do that for me?"

"Sure!"

"All right," Bobby says. We shake hands. "You're *really* on the level. You're a good person." We look into each other's eyes as we shake. His are still full of death and horror, but in them I see my face reflected, and inside my tiny eyes inside his, I think I see some hope.

"Good person," Johnny echoes. Bobby sits down. I put my tray back in the cart and Humble comes up behind me.

"You didn't sit with me, I'm very hurt," he says. "I might have to jump you for your lunch money later."

thirty

Nurse Monica brings me into the same office that I was interviewed in the day before, to ask me how I'm adjusting. I look at the white walls and the table where she showed me the pain chart and think that I've actually come kind of far since yesterday; I've eaten and slept; you can't deny that. Eating and sleeping will do a body good. I needed the shot, though.

"How are we feeling today?" she asks.

"Fine. Well, I couldn't sleep last night. I had to take a shot."

"I saw on your chart. Why do you think you couldn't sleep?"

"My friends called. They were kind of . . . making fun of my whole situation."

"And why would they do that?"

"I don't know."

"Maybe they are not your friends."

"Well, I told them . . . 'Screw you,' basically.

The main one, Aaron. I told him 'Screw you.'"

"Did that make you feel good?"

I sigh. "Yeah. There was a girl too."

"Who would that be?"

"Nia. One of the friends."

"And her?"

"I'm done with her, too."

"So you made a lot of big decisions on your first day here."

"Yes."

"This happens to many people: they come and make big decisions. Sometimes they are good decisions, sometimes bad."

"Well, I hope good, obviously."

"Me too. How do you *feel* about the decisions?"

I picture Nia and Aaron dissolving, replaced by Johnny and Bobby.

"It was the right thing to do."

"Wonderful. Now, you've made some new friends here as well, isn't that true?"

"Sure."

"I noticed you talking with Humboldt Koper outside the smoking lounge last night."

"Is that his real name?" I laugh. "Yeah, well, right, you were talking, too. We all were."

"Yes. Now, you might not want to become so friendly with your fellow patients on the floor."

"Why not?"

"That can distract people from the healing process."

"How?"

"This is a hospital. It's not a place to make friends. Friends are wonderful, but this place is about *you* and making you feel better."

"But . . ." I fidget. "I *respect* Humble. I *respect* Bobby. I have more respect for them after a day and a half than I do for most people . . . in the *world*, really."

"Just be careful of forming close relationships, Craig. Focus on *yourself*."

"Okay."

"Only then does healing take place."

"All right."

Nurse Monica leans back with her moon face.

"As you know, we have certain activities on the floor."

"Right."

"On your first day you are excused from activities, but after that you are expected to attend on a daily basis."

"Okay."

"That means you start today. This is an opportunity for you to explore your interests. So I ask you: what are your hobbies?"

Bad question, Monica.

"I don't have any."

"*Aha*. None at all?"

"No."

I work, Monica, and I think about work, and I freak out about work, and I think about how much I think about work, and I freak out about how much I think about how much I think about work, and I think about how freaked out I get about how much I think about how much I think about work. Does that count as a hobby?

"I see." She takes some notes. "So we can put you in any activity group."

"I guess."

"And you'll go?"

"Can I play cards with Armelio in the groups?"

"No."

"Will participating in them get me out of here on Thursday?"

"I cannot say for sure. But not participating will be viewed as a step back in the healing process."

"Okay. Sign me up."

Nurse Monica marks a sheet in her lap. "Your first activity will be arts and crafts this evening, before dinner, with Joanie in the activity lounge, which is through the doors behind the nurses' station."

"I thought those doors didn't open."

"We can open them, Craig."

"When does it start?"

"Seven."

"Oh. I won't be there exactly at seven."

"Why's that?"

"I have to meet with someone at seven."

"A visitor?"

"Sure," I lie.

"A friend?"

"Well, yeah. So far. I hope so."

thirty-one

At 6:55 P.M. I position myself at the end of the hall where I met with my parents yesterday and again today—around three, without Sarah this time; she was at a friend's house. Dad didn't crack any jokes and Mom brought the shirt for Bobby, who shook her hand and told her *Your son is great* and she told him she knew that. Dad asked whether we got to watch movies, and I told him that we did, but that since so many people were older, it was really boring movies with Cary Grant and Greta Garbo and stuff, and he asked if I wouldn't enjoy him bringing over *Blade II* on DVD. And I checked with Howard and it turned out the hospital had a DVD player like everyone else in the world and so Dad and I made a date for Wednesday night, in three days, when he didn't have to work late. He'd come by with *Blade II* and we'd all watch it.

The place I'm sitting in is the part of the H that mirrors the part next to the smoking lounge;

Noelle said she didn't smoke, so I think she wants to meet here. I didn't tell my parents about her. I did tell them that I talked to my friends, that it didn't go well, but that they were probably part of the problem anyway and it was good to stay away from them for a while. Mom said she knew my friends smoked pot and they were probably a bad influence anyway. Dad said *Now you yourself haven't smoked pot, right, Craig?* and I told him no, no I hadn't, not before the SATs like he told me. And we all laughed.

They asked how I was eating and I told them I was eating fine, which was true.

They asked how I was sleeping and I told them I was sleeping fine, which I hoped would be true tonight.

Now I sit with my legs crossed, only I think that looks weird, so I uncross them, only now I'm cold and nervous, so I cross them again. Right at 7:00 P.M. Noelle, in the same clothes I saw her in yesterday—dark Capri pants and a white wife-beater—comes down the hall.

She sits in the chair next to me and moves the hair away from her face with small fingers with no nail polish on them.

"You came," she says.

"Well, yeah, you passed me a note. That's like

the first time a girl passed me a *note*." I smile. I try to sit up and look good in my chair.

"We're going to make this quick," she says. "And it's going to be a game."

"Five minutes, right?"

"Right. Here's the game: it's just questions. I ask you a question, and you ask me a question."

"Okay. Do you have to answer?"

"If you want, you can answer. But no matter what, you have to end with another question."

"So we're trading questions. Like twenty questions. Why do we have to talk like this?"

"It's the best way to get to know a person. And in five minutes we can do way more than twenty questions. If we don't dilly-dally. I'm starting. Ready?"

I concentrate. "Yeah."

"No, answer with a question. Don't tell me you're stupid. Are you stupid?"

"No!" I shake my head. "Uh . . . are *you* ready?"

"There you go. We're on. First question: Do you think I'm gross-looking?"

Gosh, she cuts right to the chase. I look her over. I'm a little ashamed of how I do it, because I look at her from the bottom up, like I would if she were on the Internet. I look at her feet ending in simple black sneakers and her small ankles and her pale lower legs and the indentation in the Capri pants where the pants start, under her knee, and up her body to her small waist and then the sharp bulge of her breasts and then her neck, coming through the uneven, distended neckline of her wife-beater, and her small chin and lips. The cuts on her face line her cheeks and forehead: little parallel slashes, three together in each place, with clumps of white skin on the ends where they're healing. They don't look like very deep cuts, and they're thin—I have a feeling that when they heal up she'll look just fine. And she's beautiful. No question. Her eyes are green and knowing.

"No, you look awesome," I say.

"What's your question?"

"Uh, why did you pass me the note?"

"I thought you were interesting. Why did you do what it said?"

"I . . ." I can't think up a fake answer quickly enough. "I'm a straight guy, you know. So if a girl talks to me or whatever, I'll do exactly what she says." Wait, now: *make it a compliment.* "Especially if it's a *pretty* girl." I smile.

"You're not very good at this game. What's your *question?*"

"Oh. Right. Ah . . . are you straight?"

She sighs. "*Yes.* Don't get too excited. You don't have a boner, do you?"

"*No!*" I cross my legs. "No. So . . . how'd you get here?"

"Oh, that's a big one. Crossing the line. What do you think?"

"Someone came in on you while you were cutting your face?"

"*Ding ding ding!* Afterward, actually. I was bleeding all over the sink. How'd you get here?"

"I checked myself in. *When* did you get here?"

"*Why* did you check yourself in? Twenty-one days ago. Whoops. Reverse those. Pretend I ended with the question." She rubs her arms.

"I wasn't doing well. I called, you know, the Suicide Hotline, and they told me to come here. Why have you been here so long?"

"They're not sure I won't hurt myself again. What medication are you on?"

"Zoloft. What about you?"

"Paxil. Where do you live?"

"Around here. Where do you live?"

"Manhattan. What do your parents do?"

"My mom designs greeting cards and my dad works in health insurance. What about yours?"

"My mom's a lawyer and my dad's dead. Do you want to know how he died?"

"I'm sorry. How? *Do* I want to know?"

"That's two questions. Yes, you do. He died fish-ing. He fell off a boat. Isn't that the stupidest thing you ever heard?"

"No. Not by a *long shot*," I say. "You want to know what I think is the stupidest way to die?"

"What?"

"Auto-erotic asphyxiation. You know what that is?"

"When people put ropes around themselves while they're jerking off, right?"

"Right. I read about it in the *DSM*. Have you ever read the *DSM*?"

"The big book of psych disorders?"

"Yeah!"

"Of course. Have you ever heard of Ondine's Curse?"

"Oh my God! I thought I was the only one who knew about that. Where you forget how to breathe. Uh . . . where did you first see the *DSM*?"

"On my shrink's bookshelf. You?"

"Same. You call them 'shrinks' too?"

"That's what they are, right?"

"What does that even mean?"

"I think 'headshrinks,' because they shrink people's heads. You think I have all the answers?"

I stop. I need a break. I put my hands on my knees and rock forward. This game is hard. "Is your name really Noelle?"

"Why wouldn't it be?"

"After the whole thing at lunch yesterday, I don't know what to believe. Do you know what my name is?"

"Of course. Craig Gilner. You think I'm an idiot?"

"How'd you know my last name?"

"I read your bracelet. You want to read mine?"

"'Noelle Hinton.' Hey . . ." I think, "So here's one: Did you know what was going to *happen* at lunch yesterday?"

"With 'Jennifer'? Of course. He does that to everybody. What I'm curious about is this: why'd you come over?"

"I thought she—uh, he—was, y'know, a *girl*. And I got asked—"

"Why did you come *here*?"

"Wait, I forgot to ask you a question."

"That's okay. You have one point. Why'd you come here?"

"Um, I thought I said: because you're a girl. And you asked me. And you seem cool?" *You already said she's beautiful; now show you're not shallow and say she's cool.*

"Watching you try and answer these questions right is hilarious. You're a silly boy. You know you're silly, right?"

Noelle leans back and stretches. Her hair falls away from her face and her cuts scream up into the light. The lines of her wife-beater echo her hair.

"You know those cuts on your face really aren't that bad?"

"How long have I been here, Craig?"

"You told me twenty-one days. Is that true?"

"Yeah. Can you imagine what they looked like when I came in?"

"Are they going to scar?"

"I have to have surgery to clear them up. You think I should?"

"No. Why hide what you've been through?"

"I don't know if that's really a question. It's too obvious. Wouldn't I be happier without scars?"

"I don't know. It's tough to tell what would make you happy. I thought I'd be happier in a really tough high school, and I ended up here. Wait, where do you go to school?"

"Delfin." That's a private school in Manhattan; I think it's the last one where they have to wear uniforms. "You?"

"Executive Pre-Professional. Do you have to wear uniforms?"

"Are you like a school-uniform pervert?"

"No. Well . . . *no.*"

"Two points. You didn't ask a question. Do you like this game?"

"I like talking to you. It's like a math problem. Do you like talking to me?"

"It's all right. Do you like math?"

"I thought I was good at it, but it turns out I'm a year behind everybody else. You?"

"I'm bad in school. I spend most of my time in ballet. But I'm not tall enough for that. Have you ever been not tall enough for anything?"

"Maybe some rides, when I was a little kid. Why?"

"I'm still too short for those rides. It sucks to be short. Remember that." She stops.

"One point for you."

"That's three for you. Game over."

"Okay, cool." I sit back in my seat. "*Phew.* What now?"

"*That's* a good question. I have no idea. I've got to go to arts and crafts."

"Me too."

"You want to go together?"

"Sure." I stop. That's a come-on, isn't it? "Can we . . . uh . . . can I like kiss you or whatever?"

Noelle leans back and laughs and laughs. "No you can't *kiss* me! What, you think we play the game once and you get to *kiss* me?"

"Well, I thought we had a thing going."

"Craig." She leans in and looks me right in the eyes. "No." She smiles. The cuts crinkle.

"Do you know when you're leaving?" I ask.

"Thursday."

My heart jumps. "Me too." I start to lean forward—

"No. *No*, Craig. Arts and crafts."

"Okay." I get up. I hold out my hand for Noelle. She ignores it.

"Race you!" she says, and sprints down the hall into the activity lounge, with me following, trying to keep up—how can I not, when my legs are so much longer? Does ballet teach you to run? Howard yells at us as we pass the nurses' station—"Kids! Kids! No running on the floor!"—but I really don't care.

thirty-two

"*So who here likes to draw-awww?*" Joanie asks. Joanie is a big smiling lady with lots of makeup and bracelets. She rules the activity lounge, which is *exactly* like the art room I had when I was in kindergarten. There are patient-contributed paintings of hamburgers and dogs and kites on the walls and then there are posters—OBSTACLES ARE THOSE FRIGHTENING THINGS THAT APPEAR WHEN WE TAKE OUR MIND OFF OUR GOALS; DREAMS ARE ONLY DREAMS UNTIL YOU WAKE UP AND MAKE THEM REAL; THINGS I HAVE TO DO TODAY: 1) BREATHE IN 2) BREATHE OUT. The alphabet, thankfully, is nowhere to be seen; if I saw *Aa Bb* I'd probably start the Cycling again. There is one interesting poster: PEOPLE WITH MENTAL ILLNESS CONTRIBUTE TO OUR WORLD. It lists Abraham Lincoln, Ernest Hemingway, Winston Churchill, Isaac Newton, Sylvia Plath, and a bunch of other smart people who were kind of nuts.

It's depressing, though. I mean, this room is what I *expect* a mental hospital to look like. Adults reduced to children, sitting with finger paints; a jolly supervisor telling them that everything they do is *great*. But isn't this what I was asking for when I was filling out my menus?

You wanted preschool, soldier, you got preschool.

I wanted the comfort of preschool, not the ambience.

You gotta take the good with the bad. Like your little chicky here. I bet you didn't think you'd come in here and find a fine filly like that.

Well, she's not a filly.

I have a feeling *filly* means *girlfriend*. I look at Noelle. We're trying to decide where to sit.

I only talked with her once.

She likes you, boy, and if you can't tell that, you aren't going to be able to tell a rifle from a cap gun in this war.

What war is that, again?

The one you're fighting with your own head.

Right, how are we doing?

You're making gains, soldier, can't you see that?

Noelle and I sit with Humble and the Professor.

"I see you two have made each other's acquaintance," Humble says.

"Leave them alone," the Professor says.

"Where were you?" Humble continues. "Were you in a tree, *K-I-S-S-I-N-G?*"

"No."

"Nothing's happening," Noelle says.

"We're just sitting together," I say.

"'Craig and No-elle, sitting in a tree—'" He gets up and puts his hands on his hips, sashaying.

"Hold on, now, what's going on here?" Joanie comes over. "Is there a problem, Mr. Koper?"

"No. What? What are you talking about?" He holds up his hands, sits down. "You mean *me*?"

Joanie scoffs and announces: "This is free-period arts recreational therapy, for all you latecomers!" Humble points at me and Noelle, making a little *shame on you* gesture. "That means you can draw whatever you feel like. It's a great chance to explore your creativity and find out what you like to do for leisure! Leisure is *very important!*"

Joanie comes up behind me when she's done announcing: "You're new. Hi, my name is Joanie. I'm the recreation director."

"Craig," I shake her hand.

"You want pencil and paper, Craig?"

"No. I don't have anything to do. I can't draw."

"Sure you can. It doesn't have to be representative. You can do abstract. Do you want *crayons*?"

"No." God, it's so embarrassing. Being asked if you want *crayons*.

"How about paints?"

"I told you, I can't draw."

"Paints are for painting, not drawing."

"Well, I can't do that either."

"What about markers?"

"No."

"Everyone?" Joanie turns to the room. "Our new guest, Craig, has what we call an *artistic block*. He doesn't have anything to draw!"

"That's too bad, buddy!" Armelio yells from his table. "You want to play cards?"

"Armelio, no cards in here. Now, can anyone give Craig something he can draw?"

"Fish!" Bobby yells out. "Fish are easy."

"Pills," Johnny says.

"Johnny," Joanie admonishes. "We do *not* draw pills."

"Salad," says Ebony.

"She wants you to draw it, but she sure as hell can't eat it," Humble guffaws.

"*Mister* Koper! That's it. Please leave the room."

"*Ohh-hhhhhh,*" everybody says.

"That's *right!*" Ebony calls. She makes the umpire gesture. "You're *outta here!*"

"Fine," Humble stands up. "Whatever. Blame me. Blame the guy who has total respect for everybody else." He gathers his things, which is nothing, and steps out of the activity lounge. "You're all a bunch of yuppies!"

I watch him go.

"You can draw a cat!" the guy who's afraid of gravity says. "I used to have one. It died."

"Rolling pin," the bearded man says. It's the first words I've heard him say since I saw him in the dining room on my way in. He still rocks and he still paces the halls whenever he isn't shuttled into a room.

"What was that, Robert?" Joanie asks. "That's *very* good. *What* did you say?"

But he clams up. He won't say it again. *Rolling pin*. I wonder what that means to him. If I had one thing to say, I don't think it would be rolling pin. It would probably be *sex*. Or *Shift*.

"He can draw something from his childhood," Noelle says next to me.

"Oh, there's a good one. Noelle, you want to speak up?"

She sighs, then announces to the room: "Craig can draw something from his *childhood*."

"That's right," Joanie nods. "Craig, do you like any of these suggestions?"

But I'm already gone. I've got the river started at the top of the page, looping down to meet with a second river. No, wait, you have to put in the roads first, because the bridges go over the water, remember? Highways first, then rivers, then streets. It's all coming back to me. How long has it been since I did this? Since I was *nine*? How could I forget? I slash a highway across the center of the page and make it meet with another in a beautiful spaghetti interchange. One ramp goes off the junction through a park and ends in a circle, a nice hubbub of residential activity. The blocks start out from there. The map is forming. My own city.

"Oh, somebody got Craig's mind unblocked!" Joanie announces from the other end of the room. I glance back. Ebony, who's been sitting over there, goes through the arduous process of getting up with her cane and walks toward me. "I want to see."

"Huh, thanks Ebony," I say, turning back to the map.

She looks over my shoulder. "*Oooh* that's pretty," she says.

"What is it?" Armelio yells.

"Let's not yell across the room," Joanie says.

"That is extraordinary," the Professor says next to me.

"I deserve half-credit," says Noelle, sketching out a flower to my right. She glances at me through the sides of her eyes. "You know I do."

"You do," I tell her, taking a break to look at her.

I go back to the map. It's flowing out of me.

"Is that somebody's *brain*?" Ebony asks.

I look up at her, rolling her mouth and smiling down. I look at the map. It's not a brain, clearly; it's a *map*; can't she see the rivers and highways and interchanges? But I see how it *could* look like a brain, like if all roads were twisted neurons, pulling your emotions from one place to another, bringing the city to life. A working brain is probably a lot like a map, where anybody can get from one place to another on the freeways. It's the nonworking brains that get blocked, that have dead ends, that are under construction like mine.

"Yeah," I say, nodding up at her. "Yeah. That's exactly what it is. It's a brain." And I stop my map in the middle—this was always a problem for me, *finishing* the damn things; I always ran out of energy before I got to the edge of the page—and draw a head around it. I put a nose and two paired indentations for lips and a neck running down. I draw the head so that right where the brain would be is this blob of city street map. I make a traffic circle the eye and bring down boulevards to lead to the mouth, and Ebony giggles above me, taps her cane.

"It's so pretty!"

"It's all right," I say, looking down. I decide it's done. I can do better. I put my initials in the bottom—CG, like "computer-generated"—and put the picture aside. I ask for more paper and start the next one.

It's easy. It's easy and pretty and I can do it. I can make these things forever. For the rest of arts and crafts, I make five.

I get so concentrated that I don't even notice when Noelle leaves. I only find her note, sitting next to me, decorated with a flower, as I gather up my things from the room.

I'M TAKING A BREAK FROM YOU. CAN'T GET TOO ATTACHED. THE NEXT MEETING WILL BE TUESDAY, SAME TIME AND PLACE. DON'T BE WORRIED THAT IT'S SUCH A LONG WAIT. I THINK YOU'RE LOVELY.

I fold the note and put it in my pocket next to the other one. After arts and crafts is dinner, where Humble tells me he forgives me for getting him in trouble, and I thank him, and after dinner is cards with Armelio, who tells me that now that I've gotten a little experience under my belt, I might be ready for the big card tournament they're having tomorrow night.

"Do you play with real money?" I ask.

"Nope, buddy! We play with buttons!"

I hang outside the lounge during cigarette break—I basically just follow the group; wherever they go, I go—and talk with Bobby about my day.

Then I go into my room with my map/brain art. My bed hasn't been made during the day—they don't pamper you in Six North—but the pillow has returned to its normal shape, no longer dented in by my sweaty head, and when I lie down it lets out air in the most slow, soothing hiss I've ever heard.

"You are feeling better?" Muqtada asks.

"Quite a bit," I say. "You've really got to get out of the room more, Muqtada. There's a whole world out there."

"I pray every day that someday I will get better like you."

"I'm not that much better, man."

But I'm good enough to sleep. No shot necessary.

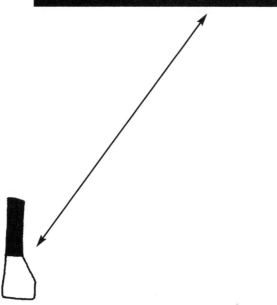

PART 7: SIX NORTH, MONDAY

thirty-three

The next day is Monday and I should be at school.

I shouldn't be eating with Humble and hearing about what his girlfriend used to do to him every time they passed a Burger King. I should be at school.

I shouldn't be explaining to Ebony's friend on the phone that what I drew was a map of a human brain and having her echo "He's so *good*, Marlene, he's so *good*." I should be at school.

I shouldn't be taking my Zoloft in line behind Bobby, who is dressed in my shirt for his interview. I should be at school.

I work up the courage to get to the phones at 11 A.M. and check the messages.

"Hey, Craig, it's Aaron, listen, I'm really sorry, man. The truth is, I probably—well, I got in a big fight with Nia after you told me she was on pills and . . . I think I might have some of that depression stuff, too. Lately, I've been like, unable to get out of bed sometimes and I'm just . . . y'know, really sleepy and I lose my train of thought. So like, I probably called you the other night like that because I was *projecting*, that's what Nia says, and I'm seriously interested in visiting you. Me and Nia are having problems."

I call him back and leave a message for him. I tell him that if he feels depressed, he should go to his general physician first and get a referral to a psychopharmacologist and go through the process like I did. I tell him that it's nothing to be ashamed of. I tell him I'm glad he called but I don't know whether he should visit because I'm really sorting my stuff out here and I think I'd like to keep in here and the outside world as separate as possible. And I ask him what's going on between him and Nia, whether they made up yet.

"Hello, Craig, this is Mr. Reynolds again—"

I call him back and leave a message that I'm in the hospital for personal reasons and that he'll have his labs when I'm good and ready to do them. I tell him that I'll provide any documentation from doctors—including psychopharmacologists, psychiatrists, psychologists, nurses, recreation directors, and President Armelio—that I am being cared for right now in a facility where the stresses of doing labs are not allowed. And I tell him that if he wants to talk to me again, he can call the number here, and don't be alarmed if someone answers "Joe's Pub."

"Hey, Craig, this is Jenna, I'm one of Nia's friends, and like . . . okay, this is really embarrassing, but do you want to hang out anytime soon? I heard about all this stuff you went through, like you're in the hospital or whatever, and my last boyfriend was really insensitive about that stuff, because I kind of go through that stuff too? And so I thought you'd probably understand me, and I always thought you were cute—we met each other a couple times—but I always thought that you were so shy that you wouldn't be fun to hang out with; I didn't realize you were like, *depressed*. And I think that's really brave of you to admit it and I just think we should hang out."

Well. I call Jenna back and leave her a message that I can hang out with her next week maybe.

That's it. The other messages are from Ronny and Scruggs and they're about pot and I ignore them. I put the phone down without slamming it on my finger. Muqtada is right in front of me.

"I follow your advice. Come out of room."

"Hey, good morning! How are you?"

He shrugs. "Okay. What is to do?"

"There's lots of stuff to do. Do you like to draw?"

"*Eh.*"

"Do you like to play cards?"

"*Eh.*"

"Do you like to . . . listen to music?"

"Yes."

"Great! Okay—"

"Only Egypt music."

"Huh." I try to think of where I can get Egyptian music, or even what it's called, when suddenly Solomon flops past in his sandals.

"Excuse me if you please I am trying to rest!" he yells at us. Muqtada takes one look at him and curls his face into a laugh, his glasses rising above his nose.

"What is the problem?" Solomon asks.

"Seventeen days!" Muqtada says. "Seventeen days the Jew will not talk to me! And now he does. I am honored."

"I wasn't talking to you, I was talking to him," Solomon points at me.

"Have you guys met?" I ask.

Muqtada and Solomon shake hands—Solomon's pants fall down a little but he bows his legs to hold them up. Then he takes his hand back and stalks off. Muqtada turns to me: "This I think is enough for one day." And he goes back into our room.

I shake my head.

The phone rings next to me. I call for Armelio. He scoots up, grabs the receiver, says "Joe's Pub," and hands the phone to me.

"Me?"

"Yeah, buddy."

I take the phone. "I'm looking for Craig Gilner," an authoritative voice says through the line.

"Ah, speaking. Who is this?"

"This is Mr. Alfred Janowitz, Craig. I'm your principal at Executive Pre-Professional High?"

"Holy crap!" I say, and I hang up.

The phone starts ringing again. I stand by it and ignore it, explaining to Armelio and everyone else who passes that it's for me but that I can't answer. They understand completely. *It's the principal.* I was right. I've seen this guy before; he's the one who greeted us on that first day when I was high with Aaron, and told us that only the best had been accepted and only the best would be rewarded. He's the one who drops by classes and looks us over as we take tests and gives out chocolates as if that makes up for it. He's the one who says "your school day shouldn't end until five o'clock" and is always in the newspapers as the most no-nonsense principal around and now he's on my ass because he knows I'm crazy and knows I haven't been doing my homework. I never should have left that message for

Mr. Reynolds. This is it. I'm being expelled. I'm out of school. I'm never going to go to high school again. I'm never going to go to college.

When the phone finally dies, I start pacing.

I was right all along. What was I thinking? You add up your little victories in here and think they count for something. You get lulled into thinking Six North is the real world. You make friends and have a pithy little conversation with a girl, and you think you've succeeded, Craig? You haven't succeeded in the slightest. You haven't won anything. You haven't proven anything. You haven't gotten better. You haven't gotten a job. You aren't making any money. You're in here costing the state money, taking the same pills you took before. You're wasting your parents' money and the taxpayers' money. You don't have anything really wrong with you.

This was all an excuse, I think. I was doing fine. I had a 93 average and I was holding my head above water. I had good friends and a loving family. And because I needed to be the center of attention, because I needed something more, I ended up here, wallowing in myself, trying to convince everybody around me that I have some kind of . . . disease.

I don't have any disease. I keep pacing. Depression isn't a disease. It's a pretext for being a prima donna. Everybody knows that. My friends know it; my principal knows it. The sweating has started again. I can feel the Cycling roaring up in my brain. I haven't done anything right. What have I done, made a bunch of little pictures? That doesn't count as anything. I'm finished. My principal just called me and I hung up on him and didn't call back. I'm finished. I'm expelled. I'm finished.

The man is back in my stomach and I rush to my bathroom, but something about me won't let it go. I hunch over the toilet moaning and hacking, but it won't come so I wash my mouth out and get into bed.

"What happened?" Muqtada asks. "You never sleep during the day."

"I'm in big trouble," I say, and I lie there, getting up only to munch through lunch, until Dr. Minerva comes by at three o'clock and pokes her head into my room.

"Craig? I'm here to talk."

thirty-four

"I'm really glad to see you." We're back in the room that Nurse Monica checks me out in. Dr. Minerva seems very familiar with it.

"I'm glad to see you, too. I'm glad to see you well," she says.

"Yeah, it's really been a roller coaster, I have to say."

"An emotional roller coaster."

"Yes."

"Where is that roller coaster right now, Craig?"

"Down. Way down."

"What's got you down?"

"I got a phone call from my school principal."

"And what did he want?"

"I don't know. I hung up."

"What do you think he wanted, Craig?"

"To expel me."

"And why would he want to do that?"

"Hello? Because I'm here? Because I'm not *in* school?"

"Craig, your principal can't expel you for being in a psychiatric hospital."

"Well, you know all my other problems."

"What are those?"

"Hanging out with my friends all the time, getting depressed, not doing homework . . ."

"Uh-huh. Let's hold off on that for a moment, Craig. I haven't seen you since Friday. Can you talk a little bit about how you came to be here?"

I give her the rap. There's much more to add to it now, about being on Six North. About Noelle and the eating and the not throwing up and the sleeping, where I'm one for two.

"What's it like compared to Friday, Craig?"

"Better. Much, much better. But the question is, am I really better, or am I just lulled into a false sense of security by this fake environment? I mean, it's *not* normal here."

"Nowhere is normal, Craig."

"I guess not. What's been the news since I've been in here?"

"Someone tried to gas the Four Seasons in Manhattan."

"Jeez!"

"I know." Dr. Minerva smirks. Then she leans in. "Craig, there's one thing you didn't mention that your recreation director did. She said you've been doing art while you've been here."

"Oh, yeah, that's nothing, really. Just yesterday."

"What is it like?"

"Well, remember how I told you last time that I liked to draw maps when I was a little kid? It sort of came from that."

"How so?"

"When they gave me a pencil and paper in arts and crafts, I remembered—well, I didn't remember, I was actually prompted by Noelle—"

"That's the girl you met?"

"Right."

"From the way you describe her I can see a real friendship developing."

"Oh, forget a friendship. We are totally going to be going out when I leave, I think."

"You think you're ready for that, Craig?"

"Absolutely."

"All right." She takes a note. "So how did Noelle help you?"

"She suggested that I draw something from my childhood, and that made me remember the maps."

"I see."

"And I started drawing one, but then Ebony came over—"

"You're on a first-name basis with all these people."

"Of course."

"Have you ever considered yourself good at making friends, Craig?"

"No."

"But you can make friends here."

"Right. Well, here is different."

"*How* is it different?"

"It's, I dunno . . . there's no pressure."

"No pressure to make friends?"

"No, no pressure to *work* hard."

"As there is in the outside world."

"Right."

"Tremendous pressure out there. Your Tentacles."

"Yeah."

"Are there Tentacles in here, Craig?"

I stop and think. The way they run things on Six North has become clear to me: it's all about keeping people occupied and passing the time. You wake up and you've immediately got a blood pressure gauge around your arm and somebody taking your pulse. Then it's breakfast. Then you get your meds and then there's a smoking break, and then *maybe* you have fifteen minutes to yourself before there's some kind of activity. That leads to lunch which leads to more meds and more smoking and more activities, and then all of a sudden the day is over; it's time for dinner, and everyone's trading salt and desserts, and then it's the 10 P.M. cigarette break and bedtime.

"No, there aren't any Tentacles in here," I say. "The opposite of a Tentacle is a simple task, something that's placed before you and that you do without question. That's what they have in here."

"Right. Your only Tentacles in here are your phone calls, which are what got you so down just now."

"Correct."

Dr. Minerva takes notes. "Now, here's an important question, Craig. Are there any *Anchors* in here?"

"Huh."

"Anything you can hold on to."

I think about it. If an Anchor is a constant, there are lots of those. There's the constant lite FM, which occasionally borders on dangerously funky, coming out of the nurses' station whether Smitty or Howard is behind it. There's the constant schedule: the food coming and going, the meds being dished out, the announcements of Armelio. There's the constant of Armelio himself, always ready to play cards. And Jimmy is always around going, "It'll come *to ya!*"

"The people are Anchors," I say.

"People don't make good Anchors, though, Craig. They change. The people here are going to change. The patients are going to leave. You can't rely on them."

"When will they leave?"

"I can't know that."

"What about the staff?"

"They change too, just on a different time scale. People always come and go."

"Noelle. She's beautiful and smart and I really like her. She could be an Anchor."

"You don't want any of your Anchors being members of the opposite sex you're attracted to," Dr. Minerva says. "Relationships change even more than people. It's like two people changing. It's exponentially more volatile. Especially two teenagers."

"But Romeo and Juliet were teenagers," I point out.

"And what happened to Romeo and Juliet?"

"Oh," I mumble. "Right."

"And have we gone beyond that, Craig? Have we gone beyond thinking those thoughts?"

"Yes," I nod.

"Because if you have those thoughts again you know you have to come back here."

"I know. I won't."

"Why not?"

"It's just . . . It would suck to kill myself. I'd hurt a lot of people and . . . it would suck."

"That's right," Dr. Minerva leans across the table. "It *would* suck. And not just for other people. For you."

"It's not noble or anything," I say. "Like this guy Muqtada who's my roommate, he's practically dead. He doesn't do anything. He just lies in bed all day."

"Right."

"And I don't want to ever be like him. I don't want to live that way. And if I were dead, I'd basically be living that way."

"Excellent, Craig."

She stops. Like I say, the good shrinks know when to throw in a dramatic pause.

I tap my feet. The fluorescent lights hum.

"I want to pick back up on your Anchors," Dr. Minerva says. "Can you think of anything else you've found in here that could occupy your time when you leave?"

I think. I know there's something. It's at the tip of my brain-tongue. But it won't come.

"No."

"Okay, not a problem. You've made a lot of progress today. There's only one more thing we have to do: call your principal."

"No!" I tell her, but she's already at it, pulling out her cell phone, which is apparently allowed up here. "Yes, I'd like the number for Executive

Pre-Professional High School in Manhattan."

"You can't you can't you *can't*," I say, leaning across the table, grabbing at the phone. Luckily the blinds are drawn so no one can see in here; if they did they'd probably have me sedated. She gets up and walks to the door, points outside. *Do I want security in here?* I sit back down.

"Yes," she says. "I need to speak with the principal. I'm returning a call of his to one of your students regarding a health and legal matter. I'm the mother."

A pause.

"Great." She cups the phone. "I'm being connected."

"I can't believe you're doing this," I say.

"I can't believe you'd be worried about me doing this . . . yes, hello? Is this Mr. . . . ." she looks at me.

"Janowitz," I mouth.

"Janowitz?"

I hear an affirmative *mumph* through the line.

"I'm Dr. Minerva, calling for your student Craig Gilner. You called him before at Argenon Hospital psychiatric facility in Brooklyn. I'm Craig's licensed therapist and I'm right here with him; would you like to speak with him?"

She nods. "Here you go, Craig."

I take the cell phone—it's smaller than mine, more buzzy. "Um, hello?"

"Craig, why'd you hang up on me?" His booming voice is light and gentle, almost laughing.

"Ah . . . I thought I was in trouble. I thought I was being expelled. You called me, you know, in the *hospital*."

"Craig, I called you because I got a message from one of our teachers. I just wanted to tell you that you have the school's full support in everything you're going through and that we're more than willing to have your semester repeated, or given over the summer, or for work to be provided for you where you are now, if you should miss enough days to warrant that."

"Oh."

"We don't pass judgment on our students for being in the *hospital*, my goodness, Craig."

"No? But it's, like, a psychiatric—"

"I know what kind of hospital it is. You think we don't have other kids in these situations? It's a *very* common problem among young people."

"Oh. Uh, thanks."

"Are you doing okay?"

"I'm doing better."

"Do you know when you'll be leaving?"

I don't want to tell him Thursday and then have it be Friday. Or next Thursday. Or next year.

"Soon," I say.

"Okay. You just hang in there, and whenever you come back, we'll be waiting for you at Executive Pre-Professional."

"Thanks, Mr. Janowitz." And I picture it in my mind: me going back to school. My little group of friends—only they're not even my friends any-more—buffered by this new collection of girls who like me because I'm depressed and teachers who are sympathizing and the suddenly nice principal. It's something I want to get excited about. But I can't.

"See, was that so bad?" Dr. Minerva asks. And I have to admit that it wasn't. But it was kind of like getting told that the prison is happy that you've been granted a temporary reprieve but we'll be *right here* with open arms to take you in when you come back.

"The plan right now is to discharge you Thursday, Craig, and I'll be here to talk to you on Wednesday, all right?" Dr. Minerva asks. I shake her hand and thank her. I tell her what I tell her when I feel really good about talking to her, which is that she knows how to do her job. Then I go back to my room and draw some brain maps. I'm excited for tonight, for Armelio's big card tournament.

thirty-five

"O-kay!" says Armelio. "Everybody here?"

We're back in the activities lounge. Johnny, Humble, Ebony, and the Professor are here. Everyone shaved today—it turns out that the shaving rule is only enforced on weekdays—and they look ten times better. Even Rolling Pin Robert, pacing the halls outside, looks serviceable. I'll have to remember that: shaving can make even a psych patient look good.

"Huh." Johnny exhales. "Bobby's still at his interview."

"Yeah," Ebony says. "Craig lent him a shirt. You're so *nice*, Craig."

"Thanks."

"When are you going to do more of your art?"

"Maybe tonight, after cards."

"That's right, buddy, cards is what we need to focus on," Armelio announces. He stands at the head of the table, which is covered with paint drops, crayon marks, and ink smears over uneven wood. In the middle is a plastic container with the buttons, separated into four even partitions. It looks like at some point the buttons were ordered by size or color, but now they're all mixed up—every conceivable hue, shape, and ornamentation. They look like jewels.

"I don't want any of my buttons missing at the end!" Joanie says from the back. She's at the other table, reading a romance novel and supervising.

"That's right, we're still looking for the Blue Button Bandit," Humble says. "Anybody who can suddenly keep their pants up, we're going to be very suspicious. Watch out for Solomon, that means. And Ebony."

"I told you once, stupid, to stop talking about my pants."

"Okay, everybody ready?" Armelio asks. "Take your buttons!"

Our hands dive into the middle of the table, grabbing fistfuls. We pour the buttons in front of us and use our fingertips to spread them into a one-button-thick layer. Armelio gets to judge whether we have an equal amount.

"Humble, put back six buttons. Ebony, put back ten. Johnny, what's going on, buddy? You have like two hundred buttons too many!"

"I got a button bonus," Johnny says, and just then Bobby comes into the activity room.

He moves with his normal loping gait, leaning back with my shirt on. He stops at the end of our table, makes sure he has our attention, raises his right hand, shakes it in the air like he's doing a magic trick, and then slams both his fists down on the table so his arms make a 'V' shape, as if he were Chairman of the Board. He grins:

"I got it."

Silence holds the room.

Joanie starts the clapping from the back, slowly, but with reverence and purpose. Then Armelio joins in and the tempo starts to spiral.

"All right!"

"Congratulations!"

"Hooray for Brooklyn scumbags!"

"Bob-by! Bob-by!"

In a small room, eight people clapping can be a lot. The posters seem to shake with the applause. As it gets louder there's howling and hooting and cheering. Tommy gets up and gives Bobby a bear hug, the kind that you can see between two men who've known one another for twenty years, who've been Fiend One and Fiend Two, for whom one's victory counts just as much for the other.

"Bobby, buddy, you the man!" Armelio walks

over to the hugging pair and smacks Bobby's back, nearly toppling Bobby *and* Johnny.

"Wait a minute," Bobby says. He extracts himself from the hug and holds up his right hand. "Before we get too crazy, 'cause I see the buttons are out, I gotta thank this young man over here." He walks toward me. "This kid literally gave me the shirt off his back—this blue one right here—and he didn't know me from Adam, and there ain't no question, without him, I wouldn't have gotten this home. This new home."

I stand up and Bobby hugs me, his big bony hands wrapping around my back, and I feel the smooth old skin of his cheek and the well-knit fabric of my shirt doing a better job on him than it ever did on me. I think about how much this means to this guy, about how much more important it is than going to any high school or getting with any girl or being friends with anybody. This guy just got a place to *live*. Me? I have one. I'll always have one. I don't have any reason to worry about it. My stupid fantasies about ending up homeless are just that— the fact is that my parents will take me in anytime, anywhere. But some people have to get lucky just to live. And I never knew I could make anybody lucky.

If Bobby can get a place to live, I think, *then I can get a life worth living.*

"Thank you, kid," Bobby says.

"It's nothing," I mumble. "Thanks for the tour."

"All right, guys, we gonna play cards or what?" Armelio asks, but Bobby stops him.

"One more thing: I'm really sorry, Craig, but I accidentally fell in something on my way back from the interview." He turns around. There's a . . . wait a minute . . .

There's a giant piece of dog shit ground into the back of my shirt, right above his belt.

"Ah . . ." I can't believe I didn't *smell* it. Did I touch it when I hugged him? "Ah, Bobby . . . it's okay . . . my mom can wash it out—"

"It ain't real!" Bobby reaches back and pulls it off, throws it at me. It bounces off my shirt (a tie-dye T-shirt that everyone on Six North likes) and lands on the table in the buttons.

"It's plastic! I've had it since the eighties! Ha! I love it!"

Armelio cracks up. "Holy crap! Look at that! It looks like something my mom would leave in my bedroom!"

Everyone stops, turns.

"President Armelio, we did not need to know that," says Humble.

"Your mother would defecate in your bedroom?" the Professor asks.

"Who said that?" Armelio asks. "I was talking about plastic—what'sthematter with you?"

"Everybody just cool it a little," says Joanie, standing up with her book at her side. "Let's have fun, but keep calm."

"All right, who gets the doodie button?" Humble holds up the poop. "I think it counts for two."

Bobby sits down and we ante up. The game is poker, seven-card stud. I'm no good at it. The hands start and people begin betting crazy, throwing in three or four buttons right at the beginning. I can't match them. I have a limited number. And I don't seem to be getting any good hands. So I fold. I fold three times in a row. The third time, Johnny says, "You might as well bet. It's just buttons."

"Yeah," Humble says. "Let me show you a secret." He reaches into the button container and takes out a handful. "*See?*"

"*I see,*" Armelio says, looking over his cards. "Don't think that's not cheating, Humble. Any more and you're out."

I laugh and bet six buttons.

"What am I out of, exactly?" Humble asks Armelio. "The button jackpot?"

"Be nice," the Professor says.

"Oh, listen to her," Humble jerks his thumb. "Trying to be the mediator." He leans in to me.

"Don't let her grandma look fool you. She's a real hustler."

"Excuse me?" The Professor puts down her cards. "What do you mean, 'grandma?'"

"Nothing, you just have that little old granny look about you, to lull people into your trap of playing good cards!" Humble gestures at himself disbelievingly.

"You're saying I'm old."

"I'm not! I'm saying you're a grandma!"

"Humble, apologize," Joanie says from the back.

"Why? Grandmas are wonderful things."

"For your information I'll have you know," the Professor says, "that unlike certain people around here I *act* my age."

"Oh, so now I'm a liar?" Humble asks, standing up.

"We all *know* that's what you are," says the Professor.

"Peo-*ple* . . ." Joanie warns.

"If I'm a liar, you know what you are?"

"What? You better not call me old because I'll take this cane and whack you in the head right in front of everybody."

"You ain't taking nothing of mine!" Ebony holds her cane close. Quietly, she has far and away the most buttons.

"You're a yuppie!" Humble yells, and he picks up the dog doo and throws it at her head. "A stupid yuppie with no respect for anybody!"

"*Aaaagh!*" The Professor holds her face. "He broke it! He broke my nose!" The dog doo has bounced all the way across the room and Joanie jumps over it lightly as she beats a hasty retreat.

"Uh-oh," Armelio says. "Now you guys did it. We were having such a good card game."

Harold comes into the room with two big guys in light blue jumpsuits, Joanie behind them. Humble raises his hands. "What? I didn't do it!"

"C'mon, Mr. Koper," Harold says.

"I can't believe it!" Humble says. "She insulted me! It wasn't even my dog poop! I didn't have the weapon!" He starts pointing at Bobby. "He's an accomplice. If I'm going, he's going."

"Humble, you have three seconds to get over here."

"All right, all right." Humble throws down his cards. "You guys have fun with your buttons." He's escorted out by Harold and the security guards, getting a resounding slap on the butt from the Professor. She still has one hand on her face, claiming that she's bleeding, but when she removes her hand there isn't any kind of mark. Joanie sits back down at her table.

"You all saw what happened. He attacked me," the Professor says.

"Yeah yeah, we saw, Doomba," says Armelio.

"Excuse me?"

"You're the Doomba; we all know you are."

"What's a Doomba?" I ask.

"If you asking, maybe you're a Doomba, too!" Armelio looks mad. This is the first time I've seen it.

"Huh," Johnny breathes.

"Craig ain't no Doomba," Bobby says. "He's on the level."

"Aren't I the winner yet?" asks Ebony.

"How can you have so many buttons?" asks Armelio. "You're not winning any hands!"

"It's cuz I don't over-bet," Ebony says, leaning over, and a stream of buttons comes roaring out of her top.

"Whoops!"

They keep coming—a mountain spilling over the ante pile. She starts laughing and laughing, showing us her very neat and clean gums while she howls: "Ooooooh, I *got you!* I got *alla you!*"

"That's it," Armelio says, throwing down his cards. "Every Monday the card tournament always gets messed up! I quit!"

"Do you resign your position as President?" Bobby asks him.

"Forget you, buddy!"

My tongue hurts from so much biting. It might not have been a regulation game, but it definitely had as many emotional ups-and-downs as the poker on TV. I clean up with Bobby and Joanie. Tonight, when I get in bed, I'm too busy wondering about what a Doomba is, and when Ebony stuck the buttons in her breasts, and what that even feels like, and Noelle and the fact that I get to see her tomorrow, to do anything but sleep.

PART 8: SIX NORTH, TUESDAY

thirty-six

The next day Humble isn't around for breakfast. I sit with Bobby and Johnny, collect my shirt, perfectly folded, and put it on the back of my chair. I drink the day's first "Swee-Touch-Nee" tea and ask what they did with Humble.

"Oh, he's happy. They went and gave him some serious drugs, probably."

"Like what?"

"You know about drugs? Pills?"

"Sure. I'm a teenager."

"Well, Humble is psychotic and depressed," Bobby explains. "So he gets SSRIs, lithium, Xanax—"

"Vicodin," Johnny says.

"Vicodin, Valium . . . he's like the most heavily medicated guy in here."

"So when they took him away they gave him all that stuff?"

"No, that's what he gets *normally*. When they

take him away they give him shots, I bet. Atavan."

"I had that."

"You did? That'll knock you right out. Was it fun?"

"It was okay. I don't want to be taking stuff like that all the time."

"Huh. That's the right attitude," says Johnny. "We got a little sidetracked by drugs, me and Bobby."

"Yeah, no kiddin'," Bobby says. He shakes his head, looks up, chews, and folds his hands. "Sidetracked isn't even the word. We were off the face of *this planet*. We were holed up twenty-four hours a day. I missed so many concerts."

"I'm sorry—"

"—Santana, Zeppelin, what's that later one with the junkie, Nirvana . . . I coulda seen Rush, Van Halen, Mötley Crüe, everybody. All this back when it cost ten bucks to get in. And I was too much of a garbage-head to care."

"What's a garbage-head?"

"Somebody who does anything, whatever," Bobby explains. "You give it to me, I'd do it. Just to see what it was like."

Jeez. I'll admit that it sounds a little sexy. I see the appeal. But maybe that's why I'm in here, to meet guys who take the appeal away.

"Do you think Humble stages scenes so he can get drugs?" I'm spreading cream cheese on a bagel now. I started ordering bagels x2 for breakfast; they're far and away the best option.

"That's the kinda thing you just can't speculate about," Bobby says. "Oh, here comes your girl."

She rushes in with a tray and sits down in a corner, drinks her juice, dips at her oatmeal. She glances over at me. I wave as lightly as I can, so people think maybe I have a spasmodic twitch. I haven't seen her since Sunday; I don't know what she did all of yesterday. I don't know how she eats if she doesn't leave her room. Same with Muqtada. Maybe they deliver food to her? There's still so much I don't know about this place.

"Huh, she *is* a cutie," Johnny says.

"C'mon, man, don't be saying that. She's like thirteen," Bobby says.

"So? *He's* like thirteen."

"I'm fifteen."

"Well, let *him* say it, then," Bobby says to Johnny. "Leave the thirteen-year-olds to the thirteen-year-olds."

"I'm fifteen," I interject.

"Craig, you should probably wait a few years, because sex at thirteen can mess you up."

"I'm fifteen!"

"Huh, I was doing stuff when I was fifteen," says Johnny.

"Yeah," says Bobby. "With *guys*."

Pause. If Ronny were here, he would say it out loud: "Pause."

"Huh. This food sucks." Johnny pushes his waffles aside. "Kid," he says. "Just do this for me. If you get with her, freak her a little bit. You know what I mean?"

"Stop it," Bobby looks at Johnny. "You got a daughter that age."

"I'd set him up with my daughter, too. Probably do her good."

"Wait, how do you guys even *know* about this? I only talked with her once, and it was really short. Nothing happened."

"Yeah, but you came into the activity center with her."

"We notice everything."

I shake my head. "What's going on today?"

"At eleven the guitar guy is coming. Johnny here'll play."

"Oh, yeah?"

"Huh, if the inclination hits."

I finish up my bagel. I know what I'm going to do until the guitar guy comes: I'm going to make brain maps. I kind of have an audience now. Joanie lent me some high-quality pencils and glossy paper since I helped her out with clean-up after the card tournament debacle, so I can draw whenever I want. When I do, people line up to watch me work. Ebony is my biggest fan; she seems to like nothing better than to sit behind me and see the maps fill out in the people's heads; I think she likes them more than I do. The Professor is big into them too; she says my art is "extraordinary" and I could sell it on the street if I wanted. I'm branching out into variations: maps in people's bodies, maps in animals, maps connecting two people together. It comes naturally and it passes the time and it feels a little more accomplished than playing cards.

"I'm gonna work on my art," I tell the guys.

"If I had half your initiative, things woulda turned out different," says Bobby.

"Huh, yeah; I want to be you when I grow up," says Johnny.

I walk out with my tray.

thirty-seven

The guitar guy's name is Neil; he has a black goatee and a black shirt and suede pants and he looks totally stoned. He comes in with a vintage-looking electric guitar—I don't know brands, but it looks like something the Beatles would have had—and plugs it into his amp on a chair before we file in. There's something I didn't expect in the room—instruments on all the seats around the circle—and people run for the ones they want. We have visitors today, nursing students who are learning what it's like to work in a psych hospital, and they wade in with us and take seats and mediate disputes over who gets the bongo drums, the conga drums, the two sticks you bang together, the washboard, and the coveted seat by the electric keyboard.

"Hey, everybody!" Neil sways. "Welcome to musical exploration!"

He's playing simple chords in a studded beat that I think is supposed to be reggae, and after a while

I realize it's "I Shot the Sheriff." He starts singing and he's just got a terrible voice, like an albino Jamaican frog, but we chime in as best we can with our voices and whatever instruments we ended up with.

Armelio bangs on his chair with some sticks and gets bored, leaves the room.

Becca, the big girl, asks if she can trade her bongos (the little ones) for my congas (the big ones), and I switch. I try to play the fills that come after the choruses in "I Shot the Sheriff" and Neil recognizes that I'm trying, gives me a chance to shine each time, but I can't pull them off.

Noelle, directly across from me, shakes maracas and her hair, smiling. I occasionally fire off a bongo fill just for her but I'm not sure if she notices.

The star of the show is Jimmy.

I didn't have any idea that the high-pitched noises he made were *singing*. Once the music starts he goes right into the Jimmy-verse, banging against his washboard and letting it all hang out in a piercing falsetto that's surprisingly on key. The thing is, he doesn't sing "I Shot the Sheriff." He sings only one phrase:

"How sweet it is!"

Doesn't matter where the song is or what it is; Jimmy will hum along to the tune as necessary, and then, as soon as there's a break that he can be heard over, remind us: *"How sweet it is!"* He sounds a little like Mr. Hankey from *South Park*. The nursing students, who are all West Indian like Nurse Monica, and young, unlike her, absolutely adore him and give him big smiles, which increases his activity. Jimmy may have only a few sentences in his repertoire, but he knows to keep going when pretty girls pay attention to him.

I send out a fill for him. He sings back. I'm convinced that some part of him knows we came in together.

When "I Shot the Sheriff" finishes in a crescendo of percussion that seems destined never to end (everybody wants to hit that last note, including me), Neil starts in on the Beatles: "I Wanna Hold Your Hand," "I Feel Fine." The Beatles are apparently the cue for people to get up and dance. It begins with Becca, at Neil's left. A nursing student pulls her up, she leaves her conga aside and starts wiggling her big butt in the middle of the circle—we yell out encouragement. She turns red and grins, and when she sits down, it's Bobby's turn—he moves like John Travolta in *Pulp Fiction*, shaking his hips with a laconic tilt, turning his feet more than his body.

Johnny refuses to dance but bobs his head. The

nursing students dance with one another and with Neil. Then it comes around to me. I hate dancing. I've never been good at it and I don't mean that in the traditional scared teenager way: I'm really *not* good.

But a nursing student has both her hands out to me, and Noelle is across the room.

I put my bongos aside and try to think about what I'm doing as I do it. I know that you're not supposed to think about dancing—what is that stupid expression, *Sing like no one's listening, dance like no one's watching?*—whatever. I want to dance like Bobby did, and I know the way to do that is to move my hips, so I focus there and think a *lot*. I don't think about my arms. I don't think about my legs. I don't think about my head. I think about shaking my hips back and forth and then in and out and then in circles, and all of a sudden the nursing student is behind me—I had my eyes closed—and there's another one in front of me, making a Craig Gilner sandwich, and I'm dancing as if I were one of those cool club guys with two chicks—heck, I *have* two chicks.

I hold out my hand to Noelle in a fit of confidence. She gets up and we go to the middle of the floor and shake our hips at each other, never touching, never talking, just smiling and keeping our eyes locked. I think she's actually looking to *me* for tips, so I mouth to her: "Shake your hips!"

She does, her arms as out of place as my own, hanging at her sides with nowhere sexy to go. Where are you supposed to put your arms when you dance? It's like the Universal Question. I guess you're supposed to put them around someone.

When it's Jimmy's turn to dance, he gets up, throws down his washboard, and puts his finger over his lips at Neil. Neil stops playing. Jimmy does a pirouette over the unaccompanied wild percussion that we've built up and lands on his knee: "*How sweet it is!*"

thirty-eight

When Neil's guitar is packed up he comes over.

"Good job with those drum fills."

"Yeah?"

"Yeah. I haven't seen you before. What's your name?"

"Craig."

"You had good rhythm; you got people moving. Ah, I hope you don't mind me asking this but . . . why are you here? You seem pretty, you know, *good*."

"I have depression," I say. "I had it really bad. I'm getting out in two days."

"Great, wonderful, that's great to hear. I have a lot of friends with that." He nods at me. "Once you're out, do you ever think you might consider . . . volunteering in a place like this?"

"Volunteering with what?"

"Well, do you play instruments?"

"No."

"You probably could. You have a good musical sense."

"Thanks. I do art."

"What kind of art?"

I lead him out of the activity center past the nurses' station and the phone, to my room, where Muqtada is in bed.

"Craig, I hear you all in music room," he says.

"You should have come."

Neil smiles at him: "Hello."

"Hm."

I pull my stack of my brain maps out for Neil. "I do these." I give him a whole armful, maybe fifteen of the best of them by now. The one on top is a duo, a guy and girl with a bridge connecting the cities in their minds.

"These are *cool*," Neil says. He flips through them. "Have you done these for a long time?"

"That depends," I say. "Ten years or a couple days, depending on how you count it."

"Can I have one?"

"I don't know if I can give them away for free."

"Ha! Listen, for real, here's my card." Neil pulls out a simple black-and-white business card that identifies him as a *Guitar Therapist*. "Whenever you're out of here, and I'm sure it'll be soon, give me a call and we can talk about volunteering, and—I'm serious—I might like to buy some of these. How old are you? You should be on the teen floor, right, but they're renovating?"

"I'm young," I say.

"I'm glad you came here and got the help you needed," Neil says, and he shakes my hand in that way that people do in here to remind themselves that you're the patient and they're the doctor/volunteer/employee. They like you, and they genuinely want you to do better, but when they shake your hand you feel that distance, that slight disconnect because they know that you're still broken somewhere, that you might snap at any moment.

Neil leaves the room and I spend the rest of the day drawing and playing cards with Armelio. Around one-thirty I call Mom, tell her about the sing-along and the card tournament and how I danced, and she affirms that I'm sounding better and that she heard from Dr. Mahmoud that Thursday is a solid day and she and Dad will be ready when it's time to pick me up. Even though it's only a few blocks back to my house, they have to pick me up in person.

In the late afternoon, while I'm playing spit with Armelio and getting crushed, Smitty pops in and tells me I have a visitor.

I know it's not Mom or Dad or Sarah; they're

coming tomorrow for one last time, when Dad brings *Blade II*. I hope to God it isn't Aaron or one of his friends.

It's Nia.

I see her through the big window in the dining room, looking like she's been crying or she's about to cry, or both. She comes slinking timidly down the hall and I walk away from Armelio without a word to go up to her.

thirty-nine

"What are you doing here?" I ask, then pause. That's really a question other people should be asking *me*.

"What do you think?" She has on light makeup that makes her lips sparkle and her cheeks a slight Asian red; her hair is drawn back to accent the curved proportions of her face. "I'm here to see you."

"Why?"

She turns away. "I'm having a really hard time right now, okay Craig?"

"All right," I get in step with her. "Come on, the best place to talk is over here."

I lead her through the hall with a familiarity and confidence that she seems surprised by. I guess I'm a veteran here now. Sort of an alpha male. Which reminds me: still no Humble.

"Here." I sit her in the chairs where I sat with my parents and Noelle. "What's going on?"

She puts her hands on her knees. She has on a little beige combat outfit with black boots; she looks like a Soviet soldier recruit. The light comes in behind her and makes her skin sparkle. I've seen her in this get-up before; it's one of her particularly hottest ones: when you bind up little breasts in guy-type clothing they're just that much more intriguing.

"Aaron and I broke up," she says.

"No." I open my eyes wide.

"Yes, Craig." She wipes her face. "After that night when he called here? And you told him I was on Prozac?"

"What? Are you saying that it's my fault?"

"I'm not saying it's anybody's fault!" She chops her arms against her thighs and takes a deep breath.

The Professor peers out of her room.

"Who are you?" Nia turns.

"I'm Amanda," she says. "I'm Craig's friend."

"Well, we're trying to have a conversation; I'm really sorry." Nia wipes her hair.

"It's okay. But you shouldn't yell. Solomon will come out."

"Who's Solomon?" Nia turns to me. "Is he dangerous?"

"Nobody here is dangerous," I say, and as I say it I put my hand over Nia's, on her thigh. I'm not sure why I do it—to reassure her? I guess it's just an instinct, a reaction. Subconsciously I suppose I'm thinking that it's a really hot thigh and that I would love to have my hand there without her hand serving as a buffer. I haven't really gotten the chance to touch any girl's thigh, and Nia's beige ones seem just about as alluring as thighs get. I even think it's a sexy word: *thigh*.

"Craig, hello?"

"Sorry, I was spacing out."

She looks down at my hand and gives a little smirk. She doesn't move it away. "You're funny. I was asking you if you *like* it here."

"It's not bad. It's better than school."

"I believe that." Now her hand—her other hand—is on top of my hand on top of her thigh. I think of the dancing sandwich I was in before in the activity lounge. I feel how warm she is and remember how I noticed that at the party, eons ago. "I've been thinking about going to a place like this."

"What?" I pull my body away but keep my hand under hers. "What do you mean?"

"I've been thinking of, you know, checking myself in, spending some time here, or somewhere like it, re-centering, like you."

"Nia." I shake my head. "You can't just come in here because you want to."

"Isn't that what you did?"

"No!"

"What did you do, then?" She tilts her head.

"I . . . I had like a *medical emergency*," I explain. "I called up the Suicide Hotline and they sent me here."

Nia leans back. "You called the *Suicide* Hotline?" She holds my hand up, clutches it. "Oh, Craig!"

I look at my crotch. I'm springing up. I can't help it. She's so close. This face is so close to mine and it's the same face I've jerked off to so many times. I've conditioned myself to want this face. I want her. I feel her on me and I want her right now in her little Russian army outfit. I want to see what she looks like with it off. I want to see what she looks like with it *half* off.

"I didn't realize . . ." she continues. "I knew you wanted to kill yourself; I never knew you wanted to *kill yourself*. I never would have told Aaron that you called me from that weird number if I'd known it was so *serious*."

"Well, what do you think people come here for?" My hand twitches around hers.

"To get better?" she asks.

"Yeah, exactly. But you have to be really bad before they make you get better *here*."

Nia swishes her head and her hair slides around

her dark eyes. "I thought that you got bad because of me. And I thought *I* could make you better."

She's so cute. The way she holds her face, it's like she always knows the best angles. We hold each other's eyes. I see myself in hers. I look expectant, ready, eager, stupid, willing to do anything.

I don't like how I look. Humble wouldn't like it either; it doesn't have any strength or will. But *I* don't have any strength or will when I'm with her. I don't have any choice. We're going to do whatever she wants.

"What about Aaron?" I ask.

"I told you." She drops almost to a whisper. "I broke up with him."

"*You* broke up with *him*?" I want it clarified.

"It was mutual. Is that important?"

"Permanently broke up?"

"Looks like it."

"Don't you think it's a little soon for you to be coming in here and, like, touching me?"

She shakes her head and purses her lower lip.

"I've been thinking about you since we talked on the phone Friday night. And now I know you so much *better*. You've told me all this stuff about you and you're really . . . I don't know . . . you're mature. You're not like all these other people with their stupid little problems. You're like, really *screwed up*."

She giggles. "In the good way. The way that gives experience."

"Huh." I'm not sure what to say. No, wait, I know what to say: Go *away, leave, I don't need you; I finished with you on the phone before; I met a girl here who's cooler and smarter*; but when you've got a really gorgeous girl in front of you and she's biting her lip and talking low and smiling—and you're hard—what are you going to do?

"Huh . . . uh . . . well . . ." I'm back to stuttering. Maybe it was Nia that made me stutter. I'm sweating too.

"Do you want to show me your room?" she asks.

That's a bad idea. It's a bad idea just as much as it's a bad idea to skip meals or stay awake in bed in the morning or stop taking your Zoloft, but there's no hope for me now. I cede control to my lower half, which is actually *pointing* toward my room, and lead Nia to it.

forty

Muqtada isn't in the room. I can't believe it—it's like the first time since I've been here. I look at his rumpled sheets and try to make out a human form, but there isn't enough bulk to account for him. I peek in the bathroom—nothing.

"You have a roommate?" Nia asks.

"Yeah, uh, he's usually here . . ."

"*Ewwww* . . ." She waves in front of her nose. "Something *smells*."

"The roommate's Egyptian; I don't think he wears deodorant."

"Me *either*."

I make like I'm cleaning up my stuff near my bed, but really I'm just taking my brain maps and flipping them over.

"You don't get a TV?"

"No."

"Do you read in here?"

"I like to read out in the hall with other people.

My sister gave me a *Star* magazine, but the nurses took it away to read themselves."

She walks toward me, looking up idly glib and innocent. "Do you get lonely here?"

"Actually, no," I tell her. I move hair that is stuck to my forehead. I'm really sweating now. "It's very social here. I made friends."

"Who?"

"That lady you were talking to outside."

"Her? She's so rude. She totally horned in on our conversation."

"She thinks someone sprayed insecticide in her apartment, Nia. She gets paranoid."

"Really? That's crazy. That's really crazy."

"I dunno. She might be right." Nia is a few feet away from me now. Her shoulders are tilted up at me. I could pick her up and throw her on my unmade bed just like Aaron has done for the past two years. These words we're saying are just a front. "She's a college professor. There might be something to it."

"Craig . . ." She's right in front of me now. "Do you remember when you called me"—she touches my forehead—"oh, you're sweating!"

"Yeah, I do that. When I get nervous."

"Are you okay? You're *really* sweating."

"I'm all right." I wipe it away.

"Seriously, Craig, that is gross." She scowls, then

gets back to where she was. "When you called me, you remember how you asked what I would do if you came over and grabbed me and kissed me?"

"Yeah." My stomach is tight. The man is down there pulling on the rope. I thought I had him beat. I'd been eating so well.

"I'd *let* you," she says. "You know I would."

Now she's got her glossy, sparkly lips turned up at me, and I feel this amazing dichotomy going on. It's almost like before I came in here, when I was in my mom's bed, when my brain wanted to die but my heart wanted to live. Now, quite literally, everything from my stomach up wants to run to the bathroom, to throw up, to talk to Armelio or Bobby or Smitty, to kick Nia out, to get ready for my second date with Noelle. But the bottom half has been denied too long. It's been ready for this for two years, and it knows what it wants. It says that the real cause of all my problems is that I haven't been satisfying it.

And these aren't any lips, either, that I'm presented with to rectify my lack of play. These are lips that I've had access to for years in my mind. I've done terrible, horrible things to these lips in the privacy of my bathroom. So screw it. You've gotta try sometime.

I lean down and grab Nia and push her back on Muqtada's bed.

I didn't mean to; I meant to turn her around and put her on *my* bed, but she happened to be in front of me and I couldn't switch directions in mid-grab. I cover her with my thin body and kiss her upper lip first, encase it in my lips, then do the lower one, then try to do them both at once, only that doesn't really work, it's like trying to pull the lips off her head, and she laughs, which gives me her beautiful smile to kiss, the hard white teeth—I don't mind—and then I use my tongue the way I've seen in movies and put my hands on her soldier outfit and feel what I don't have and have wanted for years pressing back at me, taut and yielding at the same time. *Two* of them.

"*Mmmmmm*," Nia mmmmmmms, putting her small hands on the back of my head. She feels my hair; I shake against her. I can't believe how good it feels. This is how good it feels? Why the hell did I ever get depressed?

I remember what Aaron said about the inside of a girl's cheek feeling like another place and I lick the insides of hers. She shivers; she likes it; it's like Aaron said: *she likes sex*; her tongue becomes a jittery dart flicking in and out of my mouth. I feel the ring—a little metal bubble, something to add texture, foreign and dirty. Forget it. Let's do it. I reach up to the buttons on her outfit. My eyes are closed, because if I open them I think I might get a little too excited and ruin my pants, and Mom didn't bring me any pants.

Darn, the button I'm grabbing is in the middle. Up one. No. That's not it. One more.

"God." she pulls away. "I always wanted to hook up in a hospital."

"What?" I look up at her chin. I'm still on top of her on Muqtada's bed, my legs sticking way off, almost hitting my bed.

"This was totally on my checklist." She looks down. "Me and Aaron never did anything like this."

That's a body blow to my whole body: the lower half that wanted this and the upper half that warned me about it. I can't think what to say: *Please don't compare me to Aaron? Please don't mention Aaron? What checklist?* So I say: "Uh . . . um . . ."

"*Sex!*" I hear from the doorway.

It's Muqtada.

"Sex! Sex in my bed! *Children* make sex in my bed!" He runs over to us; I jump off Nia and hold my hands up, thinking he's going to *hit* me, but he grabs me and holds me close to his square smelly body and carries me like a girder to the corner of the room.

"Um, Muqtada—"

"Craig, who is *that?*" Nia yells.

"I live here! You terrible girl corrupt my friend!"

Muqtada puts me down, turns and stands with his arms crossed at Nia, guarding me. "You leave!" He points at the open door.

"There's no *door*?!" Nia peers at it. On some kind of incredible girl-time, she's gotten up, smoothed out her outfit, and collected her purse from near Muqtada's pillow. She already has her cell phone out; it's blinking at her side. She's gesturing at me with it.

"There's a door, yeah," I say, standing on tiptoes to talk over Muqtada's shoulder. "We just didn't close it—"

"Don't talk to her!" Muqtada turns and shakes his finger at me. "She try and make sex in my bed!"

"It wasn't just *me*, okay?" Nia bends her face in at him. He turns back. "In case you didn't notice, Craig was on top of *me*. And we weren't going to have *sex*."

"Woman is temptress. My wife leave me. I know."

"Craig, I'm outta here."

"Uh, okay!" I answer into Muqtada's back. "Ah—" I try and think how to sum it up. "I like making out with you . . . but I don't really like you as a person. . . ."

"Yeah, same here," says Nia.

"What is going on in here?" It's Smitty. He shadows the door. "Muqtada, what are you doing? And excuse me, young lady?"

"I was just leaving," Nia says.

"You're the visitor for Craig, right?"

"Not anymore."

"What happened in here?"

"Nothing," says Muqtada. "Everything fine." He steps aside, turns, and gives me what I guess he thinks is a wink through his glasses.

"Yeah, absolutely." I catch on. "Muqtada just came in and was surprised to see two people in the room."

"Well, he should be," says Smitty, "because you're not supposed to have visitors in your room. Don't let it happen again, okay?"

"No problem."

"Yeah, because you won't be *seeing* me again," says Nia, and Smitty gives her a disbelieving look as she walks away from him, stomping down the hall, slamming her shoes with each step. He shrugs at us.

"All right," he says to her back. "Sign out on your way out, miss."

"Craig, what kind of girl is going to put up with this . . . crap?" Nia turns around, spreads her arms, and gestures to the hall as if she owns it while she backs away.

"Be quiet, Doomba!" yells President Armelio from somewhere. She turns back around and doesn't give any more looks back.

"Huh," Smitty says. "Lovely girl. Everything cool, guys?"

We nod like kindergartners. "Yes."

"Don't let anything like that happen again, Craig."

"I won't."

"Otherwise you'll be here a long time." Smitty walks away from the door; Muqtada waits a few moments and then turns to me.

"Craig, I am sorry I only have very important beliefs about sex."

"No, I understand. You did a good thing."

"You are not in trouble, yes?"

"No, I'm fine. You handled it perfectly, man." I put out my hand to get a slap from him, but he misinterprets that as a handshake attempt, so I take the initiative and turn it into a hug, a big smelly one. His glasses smack against me.

"I am out trying to get Egyptian music in hospital," he says. "You give me idea. But they have none. Now I rest." And he climbs back in bed, rearranges his sheet, curls into a fetal position, and stares through me.

I glance at the door. Right there, with her bright green eyes wide open, is Noelle.

I rush out to talk to her, but she flies down to her room and closes her door. I run up to it and knock, but there's no answer, and when Smitty passes me, shooting a look, I have to stop knocking.

I check the clock in the hall and sigh. It's five. Two hours until our second date.

forty-one

"I only have a couple of questions for you," Noelle says, walking up fast at seven o'clock as I sit in the chair that I've come to call my conference chair, since I meet with so many people in it. I wonder what else has happened in this chair—people have probably peed on it, licked it, drummed their heads against it, and writhed around in it spouting gibberish. That gives me comfort. It feels like a chair with some history.

I didn't think Noelle was going to show up, so I almost didn't come—but then I decided I didn't want any regrets. I'm done with those; regrets are an excuse for people who have failed. When I get out in the world, from now on, if I start to regret something, I'm going to remind myself that whatever I could have done, it won't change the fact that I was in a psychiatric hospital. This, right here, is the biggest regret I could ever have. And it's not so bad.

Noelle seems to be looking at me for comment.

But I'm amazed at how she looks. New clothes: a pair of tight blue jeans cut down dangerously low and a sliver of white underwear sticking out above them. The underwear looks like it has pink stars on it—do girls' underwear really have pink stars?—and I almost stare, before my eyes are drawn by the soft curve of her stomach to her T-shirt, which is wrapped against her with some kind of mystical female force, reading I HATE BOYS.

How come girls are coming to me dressed all hot all of a sudden?

Above the shirt is her face, bordered by blond hair pulled back, and highlighted by her cuts.

"Uh . . . Why'd you wear that T-shirt?" I ask. "Is that a message to me?"

"No. I hate *boys*, not you. And this is one reason why: they're so arrogant. Why is that?" She stands with her hands on her hips.

"Well . . ." I think. "Do you want like, a real, honest answer?" My brain is working better than it did before. It has bagels and soup and sugar and chicken in it. It's firing almost like it used to.

"No, Craig, I want a big, dumb, fake answer." Noelle rolls her eyes. I think her breasts roll in synch with them. Girls' breasts are so amazing.

"Wait, you didn't ask a question!" I smirk. "One point for you."

"We're not playing the game, Craig. We were going to, but I'm too mad."

"Okay, well, darn . . ." I start. "What were we talking about?"

"Why guys are so arrogant."

"Right. Well, you know, we're born into the world seeing that we're just a little bit . . . We tend to have things a little bit easier than girls. And we tend to assume therefore that the world was built for us, and that we're, you know, the culmination of everything that came before us. And then we get told that having a little bit of this attitude is called *balls*, and that *balls* are good, and we kind of take it from there."

"Wow, you are honest," she says, sitting down. "An honest asshole." *Yes! She sat down!* "Who the hell was that girl?"

"A girl I know."

"She's pretty." (It's amazing how girls can say this and make it the most withering insult.) "Is she your girlfriend?"

"No. I don't have a girlfriend. Never had a girlfriend."

"So she was just a girl you were hooking up with in your room?"

"You saw, huh."

"I saw everything: from out here to your room-mate's bed."

"What, you were *following* me?"

"I'm not allowed?"

"Well, no—"

"You don't *like* it?" She leans in. "You don't like some poor little girl"—she throws on a Little Bo-Peep voice, fluffs her hair—"following big, manly Craig around the ward?"

"It's not a ward, it's a psych hospital." *But yes, yes I do like you following me around; yes, that's awesome.* "I can't believe I didn't notice you. . . ." I think of the flashes of time with Nia, if I ever glanced down the hall or checked behind me.

"You were in a state of excitement; that's why."

"Well. You want to know who she was?"

"No. I lost interest."

"You did?"

"*No!* Tell me!"

"Okay, okay, she was this girl I've known for a long time, and she came in here—"

"Just overcome with lust for you?"

"Yeah, sure, exactly; she came in overcome with lust and I took advantage of her." I flick my hand. "No, what really happened is she came in here lonely and confused, I think, and thinking that she belonged in a place like this . . ."

"That was pretty funny when your roommate caught you. That kinda made the whole thing worthwhile."

"I'm glad you think so."

"You're never going to be a good cheater. You're going to be one of those guys who gets caught on the first try."

"Is that good?"

"You *didn't even* close the door. How'd you know the girl?"

"She was my best friend's girlfriend since we were like thirteen."

"How old are you now?"

"Fifteen."

"Me too."

I look at her anew. There's something about people who are the same age. It's like you got piped out in the same shipment. You've got to stick together. Because deep down I believe my year was a special year: it produced me.

"So you macked your best friend's girlfriend?"

"No, they broke up."

"When?"

"Uh, a few days ago."

"She moves *fast!*"

"I think," I think out loud, "she's just one of these girls who's never really *not* had a boyfriend."

"Sometimes we call those girls sluts. Do you think she had a boyfriend when she was eight?"

"*Ew.*"

"Maybe she was letting—"

"*Stop!* Stop! I don't want to hear it."

"It happens." Noelle looks at me.

I nod, and pause, and let that sink it. It does happen.

"Um . . . how are *you?*" I ask.

"You think you're really smart, don't you?"

I laugh. "*No.* That's one of the reasons I came in here, actually. Thinking I was dumb."

"Why would you think that? You're in a smart school."

"I wasn't doing well there."

"What were you getting?"

"Ninety-threes."

"Oh." Noelle nods.

"Yeah." I fold my arms. "I think *you're* really smart. *You* probably get good grades."

"Not really." She puts her chin in her palms like someone in a painting. "You're not very good at giving compliments."

"What?"

"I'm *smart?* C'mon."

"You're attractive, too!" I say. "Does that work?

You're attractive! Did I say that already? I said it the other day, right?"

"Attractive? Craig, real estate is attractive. Houses."

"Sorry, you're beautiful. What about that?" I can't believe I'm saying it. We'll both be out of here in two days; that's why I'm saying it. No regrets.

"Beautiful's all *right*. There are better ones."

"Okay, okay, cool." I crack my neck—

"*Ewwww*."

"What?"

"Don't do that. Especially when you're about to compliment me."

"Fine, okay. What are better words than beautiful?"

She puts on a Southern accent: "'*Go*-geous.'"

"Okay, okay, you're gorgeous."

"That sounds terrible. Do it my way: go-geous."

I do it.

"You can't even do a Southern accent? Oh my gosh, are you even from America?"

"Gimme a break! I'm from *here*!"

"Brooklyn?

"Yeah."

"This neighborhood?"

"Yeah."

"I have friends here."

"We should meet up sometime."

"You're so terrible. Try some more compliments."

"Okay." I dig down deep. I got nothing. "Um . . ."

"You don't know any more?"

"I'm not good at words."

"See, this is why the math nerds don't get girls."

"Who said I was a math nerd? I told you my grades suck."

"You might be one of those nerds who's not *smart*. Those are the worst kind."

"Listen," I stop her. "I'm really glad you're here talking with me, and I've met a lot of people in here."

"Uh-oh," she says. "Is this the part where it gets all serious?"

"Yes," I say. And when I say it, the way that I say it, I see that she understands that I'm serious about being serious. I can be serious now. I've been through some serious shit and I can be serious like somebody older.

"I like you a lot," I start. No regrets. "Because you're funny and smart and because you seem to like me. I know that's not a good reason, but I can't help it; if a girl likes me I tend to like her back."

She doesn't say anything. I dip my head at her. "Um, do you want to say anything?"

"No. No! This is fine. Keep going."

"Well, okay, I've been thinking about how to put this. I like you for all this stuff but I also kind of like you for the cuts on your face—"

"Oh no, are you a fetishist?"

"What?"

"Are you like a blood fetishist? There was one of them in here before. He wanted to make me like his Queen of the Night or something."

"No! It's nothing like that. It's like this: when people have problems, you know . . . I come in here and I see that people from all over have problems. I mean, the people that I've made friends with are pretty much a bunch of lowlifes, old drug addicts, people who can't hold jobs; but then every few days, someone new comes in who looks like he just got out of a business meeting."

Noelle nods. She's seen them too: the scruffy youngish guy who came in today with a pile of books as if it were a reading retreat. The guy who came in yesterday in a suit and told me in the most practical way that he heard voices and they were a real pain in the ass; they didn't say anything scary but they were always saying the stupidest stuff while he was in trial.

"And not only in here: all over. My friends are all calling me up now: this one's depressed, that one's depressed. I look at what the doctors hand out, and there are studies that show like, one fifth of Americans suffer from a mental illness, and suicide is the number-two killer among teenagers and all this crap . . . I mean *everybody's* messed up."

"What's your point?"

"We *wear* our problems differently. Like I didn't talk and stopped eating and threw up all the time—"

"You threw up?"

"Yeah. Bad. And I stopped sleeping. And when I started doing that, my parents noticed and my friends noticed, sort of—they kinda made fun of me—but I could go through the world without really letting on what was wrong. Until I came here. Now it's like: something is wrong. Or was wrong, because it feels like it's getting better."

"What does this have to do with me?"

"You're out there about your problems," I say. "You put them on your face."

She stops, puts her hand in her hair.

"I cut my face because too many—too many people *wanted* something from me," she tries to explain. "There was so much pressure, it was—"

"Something to live up to?"

"Exactly."

"People told you you were hot and then all of a sudden they treated you different?"

"Right."

"How?"

She sighs. "You have to be the prude or the slut, and if you pick one, other people hate you for it, and you can't *trust* anyone anymore, because they're all after the same thing, and you see that you can never go back to how it was before . . ."

She pulls her face into one of those faces that could be laughing or crying—they use so many of the same muscles—and leans forward.

"And I didn't want to be part of it," she says. "I didn't want to be part of that world."

I grab her leaning into me, feel for the first time the soft dimple of her body. "Me neither."

She puts her arms around me and we hold each other like that from our two chairs, like a house constructed over them, and I don't move my hands at all and neither does she.

"I didn't want to play the smart game," I tell her. "And you didn't want to play the pretty game."

"The pretty game's worse," she whispers. "Nobody wants to *use* you for being smart."

"People wanted to use you?"

"Someone did. Someone who shouldn't."

I stop.

"I'm sorry."

"It wasn't you."

"Should I not touch you?"

"No, no, you didn't do anything. It's okay. But . . . yeah. It happened. And I lied before."

"About what?"

"It doesn't matter what kind of surgery I have. I did it with half a scissor, Craig. It's going to leave scars. I'll have scars for the rest of my life. I didn't know what I was doing. I just wanted to get off the world a little after this . . . this *thing* . . . and now I'm never going to be able to have a job or anything. What are they going to say when I go into a job interview looking like . . ." She sniffles, chuckles, and snot comes out. ". . . like a Klingon?"

"There are places in California where they speak Klingon. You can get a job there."

"Stop it."

We're still holding each other. I don't want to look up. I keep my eyes closed. "There are anti-discrimination laws too. They can't not hire you if you're qualified."

"But I look like a *freak* now."

"I told you, Noelle," I say into her ear. "*Everybody* has problems. Some people just hide their crap better than others. But people aren't going to look at you and run away. They're going to look at you and think that they can talk to you, and that you'll understand, and that you're brave, and that you're strong. And you are. You're brave and strong."

"You're getting better at the compliments."

"Nah. I'm nothing. I can barely hold food down."

"Yeah, you're skinny." She laughs. "We need to fatten you up."

"I know."

"I'm glad I met you."

"You're bare and honest, Noelle; that's what you are." Words come into my head like they've always been there. "And in Africa your scarring would be highly prized."

She sniffles again. "I didn't like seeing you with that other girl."

"I know."

"You like me more, right?"

"Right."

"Why?"

I pull away from her—maybe the first time in my life I've ended a hug—because a level of eye contact is required.

"I owe you a lot more than I do her. You really opened my eyes to something." My actual eyes have been closed for so long on Noelle's shoulder that the hall is blinding. But when they readjust I see the Professor, watching us from her door, holding the doorknob with one hand and her shoulder with the other.

"I wanted to show you this." I reach under my chair to pick up something for our meeting—I had it down there as a trump card. I didn't think the date would go like this; I thought it would all be Noelle yelling at me and I'd have to do something drastic. But now I can do something drastic and it'll be like a cherry on top.

I pull out my couple's brain map and show it to her.

"It's beautiful!"

"It's a guy and a girl, see? I didn't do any hair, but you can see how one has a feminine profile and the other is masculine." They're lying down, not on top of each other, just side by side, floating in space. They have sketched-out legs and arms at their sides, but that's the whole point of my brain maps—you don't need to spend a lot of time on the legs or the arms. What they really have are *brains*—full and complete with whirling bridges and intersections and plazas and parks. They're the most elaborate ones I've done yet: divided thoroughfares, alleys, *cul de sacs*, tunnels, toll plazas, and traffic circles. The paper is 14" x 17" and I had room to make the maps *huge*; the bodies are small and unimportant; the key thing that your eye is drawn to (because I understand now, somehow, that that's how art works) is a soaring bridge between the two heads, longer than the Verrazano, even, with coils of ramps like ribbons mashed up at each end.

"It might be my best yet," I say.

She looks it over; I see the red in her eyes, fading. There aren't any tear streaks—I still haven't seen actual tear streaks on anyone. Her tears went right into my shirt; they cool and chafe now on my shoulder.

"You were the one who suggested I do stuff from childhood," I continue. "I used to do these when I was a kid, and I forgot how fun they were."

"I bet you never did them like this."

"No, well, this is easier, because I don't have to finish the maps."

"It's beautiful."

"Thanks for getting me started. I owe you big."

"Thank you. Do I get to keep it?" She looks up.

"Not yet. I have to fix it up." I stand, stretch my back, and shrug down at her.

Do it, soldier.

Yes, sir!

"But, um, I kind of wondered if I could have your phone number, so I can call you when we're out of here."

She smiles and her cuts outline her face like a cat's whiskers. "Crafty."

"I am a guy," I say.

"And I hate boys," she says.

"But a guy's different," I say.

"Maybe a little," she says.

forty-two

Humble is back at dinner. He has entirely new clothes, a sparkly clean-shaven face, and eyes that won't quite open all the way; he stations himself at his usual table under the TV in the dining room, which everyone left empty while he was gone. Noelle's there too, at the next table, her back to him; I walk in, say hi to both of them, grab the tables, put them together, and sit between them, smiling.

"Noelle, I don't know if you've had the chance to meet Humble."

"Not really," she says. She's still grinning. From our date, I hope.

"Humble, Noelle. Noelle, Humble."

"*Uhhhhhh . . .*" he says, squinting his eyes. "Those cuts on your face are *trippy*."

"Thanks?" They shake hands.

"You have a good handshake for a girl," says Humble.

"You have a good one for a guy."

My dinner is beans and hot dogs and salad,

with cookies and a pear at the end. I tackle it.

"So where'd they take you?" I ask between bites.

"Across the hall to geriatric," says Humble.

"With the old people?" Noelle asks.

"Yeah. That's where they take you when they have to get you *whacked outta your mind.*"

"Where'd you hear the term 'wack'?" Noelle asks.

"'Whacked?'" Humble picks a piece of salad out of his teeth with his thumb.

"No, she thinks you're saying 'wack,' like 'that's wack,'" I explain.

"Wack, wacky, whacked, it's all the same word. This is an old word. I used to have an uncle named Wacky—what are you laughing at? Man, don't start with me. This kid is a lot of trouble."

"Yeah, I know," says Noelle. And she bangs her knee against my thigh. Awesome. A girl hasn't done that to me since like fourth grade. "He's a mess."

"I know," says Humble. "It's because he's too smart for his own good. He comes in here; he's burned out. I've seen it before. I see it all the time, but in people in their *twenties, thirties.* This guy is so smart that he got burnt out in half the time. He's having like a midlife crisis as a teenager."

"Forget the midlife crisis," I say. "It's all about the *sixth-life crisis.*"

"What the hell is that?"

"Well . . ." I look at Noelle. She's not going to hit me with her leg again? I'm not sure if I want to talk. I don't want to bore her. But I know I won't bore Humble, and if I don't bore her *either*, that would make it like a major victory.

"Well, first there's the quarter-life crisis," I say. "That's like the characters on *Friends*—people freaking out that they won't get married. Twenty-year-olds. That's probably true that people get quarter-life crises; I wouldn't know. But I know that now things work faster. Before you had to wait until you were twenty to have enough choices of things to do with your life to start getting freaked out. But now there's so much stuff for you to buy, and so many ways you can spend your time, and so many specialties that you need to get started on very early in life—like ballet, right, Noelle, when did you start ballet?"

"Four."

"Okay. I started Tae Bo at six. So there are like— so many *people* angling for success and so many colleges you're supposed to get into, and so many women you're supposed to have sex with—"

"You gotta freak them," says Johnny from across the room.

"Were we talking to you?" Humble asks.

"Huh, eat your salt."

"What, tough guy? How about I knock your head off, how would you like that—"

"Boys." Noelle stands up and pulls her hair away from her cheeks, which are red in addition to being cut up. Everybody shuts up.

"So now," I continue, "instead of a quarter-life crisis they've got a fifth-life crisis—that's when you're eighteen—and a sixth-life crisis—that's when you're fourteen. I think that's what a lot of people have."

"What you have."

"Not just me. It's the . . . um . . . should I keep going?"

"Yes," Noelle says.

"Well, there are lot of people who make a lot of money off the fifth- and sixth-life crises. All of a sudden they have a ton of consumers scared out of their minds and willing to buy facial cream, designer jeans, SAT test prep courses, condoms, cars, scooters, self-help books, watches, wallets, stocks, whatever . . . all the crap that the twenty-somethings used to buy, they now have the ten-somethings buying. They doubled their market!"

Bobby has pulled up a chair next to me. "This kid is a freakin' lunatic," he says.

"I hope they keep him in here," says Humble.

"So pretty soon." I keep thinking. "There'll be seventh- and eighth-life crises. Then eventually a baby will be born and the doctors will look at it and wonder right away if it's unequipped to deal with the world; if they decide it doesn't look happy, they'll put it on antidepressants, get it started on that particular consumer track."

"*Hmmmmmmmmmmmmm,*" Humble says. I think he's going to follow it up with something, but instead he says: "*Hmmmmmmmmmmmm.*"

Then:

"Your problem is you have a worldview totally informed by depression." He leans in. "What about *rage?*"

"I was never big on rage."

"Why?"

"It's so much more angry in my head than it could ever be outside."

"Extra cookies!"

It's one of the nurses. We all get in line; it's oatmeal and peanut butter. As I shuffle forward, Noelle nudges me from behind; when I turn to her, she turns her face away as if I were trying to kiss her but she wouldn't let me.

"You're trouble," I say.

"You're silly," she answers.

I did it. I talked and she liked me; she thought I

was smart. I start to develop a plan. Once I get my cookies, I go to the phone to call Dad, who's already bringing *Blade II* tomorrow night. I want him to bring something else too.

PART 9: SIX NORTH, WEDNESDAY

forty-three

This is your last full day at the hospital, is what I think when I get up—no one's taking my blood today (it's only happened once since Sunday) so I don't get up super-early, but I'm still the first one in the halls. I take my shower and think about how much life would suck if hot water didn't come out of the showerhead when you wanted. I've tried to take cold showers and they're wonderful when they're over, but during the process they feel like some form of animal torture. But then again, that's the point—when you take a cold shower you're supposed to get in and out as fast as possible; that's why they do it in the army.

That's right! Want to take a shot, soldier?

I don't think so. Sir.

C'mon, what's the matter with you? You got a lot going for you; you don't want to keep it going?

I need a cold shower to keep things going?

That's right. Less time in the shower, more in the battlefield.

Fine.

I can do this. I reach out and twist the temperature knob slowly to the left, then decide that I'm never going to get it done gradually so I'll have to do it like a Band-Aid—I jerk it over. The water goes from toasty warm to frigid so quickly that it feels like it burns me. I bend my groin out of its path but I know that's cheating, so I stick it back in as I furiously lather myself. Leg: up! Down! Other leg: up! Down! Crotch: uh, scrub scrub scrub. Chest: wipe. Arm: down! Back! Other arm: down! Back! Neck, face, turn around, wash your butt, and I'm out! Straight to the towel. I wrap it around myself and shiver.

I'm so desperate to put my clothes on that my socks stick to my wet feet. I go out to talk with Smitty.

"You okay?"

"First cold shower."

"Of the day?"

"Of my *life.*"

"Yeah, that'll knock ya."

"What's the news?"

Smitty holds up his paper. It seems that a new candidate is running for Mayor of New York promising to give everyone who votes for him a lap dance. He's a multibillionaire, and at $100 per

lap dance, he thinks he can lock up the vote. A lot
of women are supporting him.

"That's crazy." I shiver. "It's like . . . Who's out
there and who's in here, you know?"

"Absolutely. Better music in here, though."
Smitty turns up the radio.

"By the way, that's a question I have—can I play
some music on the hall tonight? At the other end?"

"What kind?"

"There's no words, don't worry, nothing offen-
sive. It's something one of the people on the hall
will like. Like a gift."

"I'll have to see it first."

"Okay. And you know I'm bringing that *Blade II*
movie tonight to watch with the group."

"You think about that a minute. You're bringing
a vampire movie onto a floor full of psych patients."

"They can handle it."

"I'm not gonna get any nightmares?"

"Promise."

"Nightmares are a big problem in my job, Craig."

"Understood."

Smitty sighs, puts his paper down, and gets up.
"You want me to do your vitals?"

He straps me in on the chair, pumps me up, and
puts his soft fingertips on my wrist. Today I'm
120/70. First day I haven't been perfect.

forty-four

"How're you doing?" Dr. Minerva is like.

It's 11 A.M. I sigh. After vitals was breakfast, where the guy who was afraid of gravity and Rolling Pin Robert were gone—Humble told me and Noelle that they got discharged. Toward the end of the meal, Noelle touched her leg against mine for as long as it took me to drink the first sip of my after-breakfast Swee-Touch-Nee tea, which was a big sip. Then Monica announced that we'd be screening *Blade II* tonight opposite the smoking lounge and everybody got excited, especially Johnny: "Huh, that movie is cool; a lotta vampires die." No announcements about my music, but then again it hadn't arrived yet.

I took my Zoloft in my little plastic cup and drew some brain maps by the window in the corner of the hall next to Jimmy. I handled my phone messages, started thinking seriously about what I'd do the moment I got out—would I buy a cup of coffee?

Walk to the park? Go home and start in on the e-mail?—and *that* got me started thinking about e-mail, and all of a sudden I was really glad to have Dr. Minerva to go to.

"I'm doing okay, I think."

She looks at me calm and steady. Maybe *she's* my Anchor.

"What's got you in doubt, Craig?"

"Excuse me?"

"You said you were okay 'you think.' Why do you just *think* it?"

"That's an expression," I say.

"This isn't the place to be leaving if you're not feeling better, Craig."

"Right, well, I've been thinking about my e-mail."

"Yes?"

"I'm really worried about getting out there and having to check it. The phones I'm caught up with, but the e-mail might be pretty deadly."

"Deadly . . . How can e-mail be deadly, Craig?"

"Well." I lean back, take a deep breath. Then I remember something. "You know how I had a lot of problems with starting and stopping my sentences before?"

"Yes."

"Not lately."

"Really?"

"Yeah, it's like the opposite, like words can just pour out of me, the way they used to, when I used to get in trouble in class."

"Which was . . ." She focuses on her pad to write this down.

"A year ago . . . Before I went to Executive Pre-Professional."

"Right—now tell me about the e-mail."

"The e-mail." I put my hands on the table. "I hate it. Like, right now, I haven't been checking it for five days, okay?"

"Since Saturday." She nods.

"That's right. Now, what are people thinking while they're trying to reach me? These are people who probably already have some idea where I am because Nia told Aaron the number and he figured it out."

"Right: a big source of shame for you."

"Yes. But even if someone has no idea where I am, what are they thinking? *Five days.* They're like: *He's crazy. He must have OD'ed or something.* Everyone is expecting me to answer them instantly and I'm not able to."

"Who e-mails you, Craig?"

"People who want homework assignments, teachers, school clubs, announcements about charities I should volunteer in, invitations to Executive Pre-

Professional football, basketball, squash games . . ."

"So they're mostly school-related."

"They're *all* school-related. My friends don't e-mail me. They call."

"So why don't you just ignore the e-mails?"

"I can't!"

"Why not?"

"Because then people will be offended!"

"And what happens then?"

"Well, I won't get to join clubs, get credits, participate in stuff, get extra-credit . . . I'll *fail*."

"At school."

"Right." I pause. No, it's not exactly school. It's what comes after school. "At life."

"Ah." She pauses. "Life."

"Right."

"Failing at school is failing at life."

"Well . . . I'm *in* school! That's the one thing I'm supposed to do. I know a lot of famous people didn't do well at school, like James Brown; he dropped out in fifth grade to be an entertainer, I respect that . . . but that's not going to be me. I'm not going to be able to do anything but work as hard as possible all the time and compete with everyone I know all the time to make it. And right now school's the *one thing* I need to do. And I'm away from the e-mail and I can't do it."

"But your definition of school isn't really one thing, it's many different things, Craig: extracurricular activities plus sports plus volunteering. That's not to mention homework."

"Right."

"How anxious would you say you are about all of this, Craig?"

I think back to what Bobby said, about anxiety being a *medical* thing. The e-mail has been in the back of my mind since I got here, the nagging knowledge that when I get out I'll have to sit on the computer for five or six hours going through everything I've missed, answering it in reverse order because that's the way it comes in and therefore taking the longest time to respond to the people who e-mailed me in the most distant past. And then as I'm answering them more will *come in*, and they'll sit on top of my stack and mock me, dare me to answer them before digging down, telling me that I need them, as opposed to the one or two e-mails that are actually about something I care about. Those will get saved to the end, and by the time I have the time to deal with them, they'll be so out of date that I'll just have to apologize: *Sorry, man. I haven't been able to answer my e-mail. No, I'm not important, just incapable.*

"Craig?"

"Very anxious," I answer.

"The e-mail anxiety, and the failure talk . . . These are subjects you've brought up before. They're very distressing to you."

"I know. I'm sweating."

"You are?"

"Yeah. And I haven't been sweating for a while."

"You've been away from your Tentacles."

"Right. Not anymore. Now I get to go back and they're all right there for me."

"Do you remember what I asked you last time, about whether or not you'd found any Anchors in here?"

"Yes."

She pauses. In order to ask a question, it is often possible for Dr. Minerva only to intimate that she might ask a question.

"I think I've found one," I sigh.

"What's that?"

"Can I get up and get it?"

"Absolutely."

I leave the office and walk down the hall, where Bobby is leading a new recruit on his welcoming tour—a black guy with wild teeth and a stained blue sweatsuit.

"This is Craig," Bobby says. "He's real young, but he's on the level. He does drawings."

I shake the man's hand. That's right. I do drawings.

"Human Being," the man says.

"That's his name," Bobby explains, rolling his eyes.

"Your name isn't Craig; it's Human Being too," the man says.

I nod, break the handshake, and keep walking to my room. It's literally like breaking away from a monster—the further I get from thinking about e-mail and Dr. Minerva and the fact that I'm going to have to leave here and go back to Executive Pre-Professional, the calmer I get. And the closer I get to the brain maps, to this little stupid thing I can do, the calmer I get.

I walk past Muqtada—he's staring and trying to sleep—and take my art off the radiator cover. I cradle it in a stack past Bobby and Human Being—who's now explaining how his real last name is Green and that's what he needs, some green—back into the office.

"I kinda like it in here," I say to Dr. Minerva.

"This room?"

"No, the hospital."

"When you're finished, you can volunteer."

"I talked to the guitar guy Neil about that. I think I'll try. I can get school credit!"

"Is that the reason you should volunteer, Craig—"

"No, no . . ." I shake my head. "I'm just *joking*."

"Ah." Dr. Minerva cuts her face into a wide smile. "So what do we have here?"

I plop them down on the table. There are two dozen now. No kind of crazy breakthroughs, just variations on a theme: pigs with brain maps that resemble St. Louis, my couple for Noelle joined by the sweeping bridge, a family of metropolises.

"Your artwork," she says.

She leafs through them, going "Oh, my" at the particularly good ones. I constructed this stack last night—not just for Dr. Minerva, for anybody. The brain maps have a certain order. Ever since I've been doing them, they've been making it clear that they should be stacked for presentation.

"Craig, these are wonderful."

"Thanks." I sit down. We were both standing. I didn't even notice.

"You started these because you used to do them when you were four?"

"Right. Well. Something like them."

"And how do they make you feel?"

I look at the pile. "Awesome."

She leans in. "Why?"

I have to think about that one, and when Dr. Minerva makes me think, I don't get embarrassed and try to skip it. I look to the left and stroke my chin.

"Because I do them," I say. "I do them and they're done. It's almost like, you know, peeing?"

"Yes . . ." Dr. Minerva nods. "Something you enjoy."

"Right. I do it; it's successful; it feels good; and I know it's good. When I finish one of these up I feel like I've actually done something and like the rest of my day can be spent doing whatever, stupid crap, e-mail, phone calls, all the rest of it."

"Craig, have you ever considered the fact that you might be an artist?"

"I have other stuff too," I keep going. *What'd she say?* "First of all I was thinking about this perpetual candle, like a candle on the ground with another candle hanging upside-down over it, and as the first candle melts the wax is kept molten by some kind of hot containment unit and gets pumped up to the second candle and drips down like a stalactite-stalagmite thing, and then I was also thinking: what if you filled a shoe with whipped cream? Just a man's shoe, filled with whipped cream? That's pretty easy to do. And then you could keep going: a T-shirt filled with Jell-O, a hat full of applesauce . . . that's art, right? That kind of stuff. What'd you say about artists?"

She chuckles. "You seem to enjoy what you're doing here."

"Yeah, well, duh, it's not the most difficult thing in the world."

"You're not sweating now."

"This is a good Anchor for me," I say. I admit. I admit it. It's a stupid thing to admit. It means that I'm not practical. But then again, I'm already in the loony bin; how practical am I going to get? I might have to give up on practical.

"That's right, Craig. This *can* be your Anchor." Dr. Minerva stares at me and doesn't blink. I look at her face, the wall behind her, the door, the shades, the table, my hands on the table, the Brain Maps between us. I could do the one on the top a little better. I could try putting some wood grain in there with the streets. Knots of wood in people's heads. That could work. "This can be my Anchor." I nod. "But . . ."

"What, Craig?"

"What am I going to do about school? I can't go to Executive Pre-Professional for *art*."

"I'm going to throw a wild notion at you." Dr. Minerva leans back, then forward. "Have you ever thought about going to a *different school?*"

I stare ahead.

I hadn't. I honestly hadn't.

Not once, not in my whole life, not since I started there. That's my *school*. I worked harder to get in than I did for anything else, ever. I went there because, coming out of it, I'd be able to be President. Or a lawyer. Rich, that's the point. Rich and successful.

And look where it got me. One stupid year—not even one, like three quarters of one—and here I am with not one, but *two* bracelets on my wrist, next to a shrink in a room adjacent to a hall where there's a guy named Human Being walking around. If I keep doing this for three more years, where will I be? I'll be a complete loser. And what if I *keep* on? What if I do okay, live with the depression, get into College, do College, go to Grad School, get the Job, get the Money, get Kids and a Wife and a Nice Car? What kind of crap will I be in then? I'll be *completely crazy*.

I don't want to be *completely* crazy. I don't like being here *that* much. I like being a little crazy: enough to volunteer here, not enough to ever, ever, ever come back.

"Yes," I say. "Yes. I have thought about it."

"When? Just now?"

I smile. "Absolutely."

"And what do you think?"

I clap my hands together and stand up. "I think I should call my parents and tell them that I want to transfer schools."

forty-five

"Visitor, Craig," Smitty pokes his head into the dining room. I slide my chair back from the table, where I'm playing after-lunch poker with Jimmy and Noelle and Armelio. Jimmy doesn't really have any idea how to play, but we deal him cards and he plays them face down and smiles and we give him more chips (we're using scraps of paper; the buttons are locked up due to our recklessness) whenever he pockets his or chews them up.

"I'll be back," I say.

"This guy, so busy," says Armelio.

"He thinks he's all important," Noelle says.

"I woke up, and the bed was on *fire!*" says Jimmy.

We all look at him. "You okay, Jimmy?" I ask.

"My mom hit me in the head. She hit me in the head with a *hammer.*"

"Oh, wow." I turn to Armelio. "I heard him say stuff like this down in the ER. Has he talked about this before?"

"No, *nuh-uh*, buddy."

"Hey, Jimmy, it's okay." I put my hand on his shoulder. At the same time, I bite my tongue. You can think someone's hilarious and want to help them at the same time.

"She hit me in the *head*," he says. "With a *hammer!*"

"Yeah, but you're here now," Noelle says. "You're safe. Nobody's going to hit you in the head with anything."

Jimmy nods. I keep my hand on his shoulder. I keep my tongue bit down, but I make little chuffing noises as I try to keep from laughing, and he looks up and notices. He smiles at me, then laughs himself, then picks his cards up and claps my back.

"It'll *come* to ya," he says.

"That's right. I know it will."

I excuse myself from the room and head down the hall. Right at the end is Aaron, holding the record I want. Dad didn't have it.

"Hey, man," he says sheepishly, and as I approach, he leans it against the wall. He's a dick, but I'm not perfect either so I come up and hug him.

"Hey."

"Well, you were right. My dad had it—*Egyptian Masters Volume Three*."

"I so appreciate this." I take the record. It's got a

picture on the cover of what looks like the Nile at dusk, with a palm tree lilting left, echoing the brightening moon, and the purple sky rolling up from the horizon.

"Yeah, I'm sorry about everything," Aaron says. "I . . . uh . . . I've had a weird couple of days."

"You know what?" I look him in the eyes. "Me too."

"I bet." He smiles.

"Yeah, from now on, whenever crap goes down, you can be like 'Oh, Craig, I had a bad few days,' because I *will* get what you're talking about."

"What's it like in here?" he asks.

"There's people whose lives have been screwed up for a long time, and then there are people like me, whose lives have been screwed up for . . . you know . . . shorter."

"Did they put you on new drugs?"

"No, same ones I was on before."

"So are you feeling better?"

"Yeah."

"What changed?"

"I'm going to leave school."

"You're *what*?"

"I'm done. I'm going somewhere else."

"Where?"

"I don't know yet. I'm going to talk it over with my parents. Somewhere for art."

"You want to do art?"

"Yeah. I've been doing some in here. I'm good at it."

"You're pretty good at school too, man."

I shrug. I don't really need to explain this to Aaron. He's been demoted from most important friend to friend, and he's going to have to earn that, even. And you know what else? I don't owe people anything, and I don't have to talk to them any more than I feel I need to.

"What's up with Nia?" I ask. Have to tread carefully here. "I got your message, about how things were bad."

"They got worked out. It was my fault. I got all freaked out about her being on pills and we broke up for like, a few days."

"Why did that freak you out?"

"I don't need any more of that in my life, you know? I mean, it's bad enough with my dad."

"He's on medication?"

"Every form of medication in the *book*. Mom, too. And then me, with the pot . . . when you come right down to it, there isn't anybody in the household who isn't seriously drugged except the fish."

"And you didn't want your girlfriend to be, too."

"Her smoking is one thing; I just . . . I can't really explain it. I guess you'll have to go out with someone for a long time to understand. If you're with somebody and then you learn that they need to . . . *take* something on a daily basis, you wonder—how good can you be for them?"

"That's pretty stupid," I say. "I met this girl in here—"

"Oh yeah?"

"Yeah, and she's really screwed up, as screwed up as me, but I don't look at that as an insult. I look at that as a chance to connect."

"Yeah, well."

"People are screwed up in this world. I'd rather be with someone screwed up and open about it than somebody perfect and . . . you know . . . ready to explode."

"I'm sorry, Craig." Aaron looks at me deep and holds out a hand for me to slap. "I'm sorry I was a bitch to you."

"You *were* a bitch." I slap his hand. "This album partly makes up for it. Just, don't do it again."

"All right." He nods.

We stand still a minute. We haven't moved from the crux of the hallways near the entrance of Six North. The double doors that I came in through are eight feet behind him.

"Well, listen," he says. "Enjoy the record. And—hey, they have a record player in here?"

"They still *smoke* in here, Aaron. They're kind of back in time."

"Enjoy it and be in touch, and I'm sorry once again. I guess you won't be chilling for a while."

"I don't know. I may never be chilling again."

"Did you almost kill yourself to get in here?" Aaron asks. "That's what Nia told me."

"Yeah."

"Why?"

"Because I wasn't capable of dealing with the real world."

"Craig, don't kill yourself, okay?"

"Thanks."

"Just . . . don't."

"I won't."

"I'll see you soon, man."

Aaron turns and the nurses open the door for him. He's not a bad guy. He's just someone who hasn't had his stay on Six North yet. I take the record to Smitty to store behind the nurses' station.

forty-six

Six North doesn't need a PA system, because of President Armelio, but it does have one, used regularly for the simple and rhythmic messages of "Lunch is served," "Medication," and "All smokers to the smoking lounge; smokers, get your smokes." This afternoon it pipes up with a longer message, courtesy of Monica.

"Ladies and gentlemen, this afternoon our patient Craig Gilner, who is leaving tomorrow, is going to be drawing his artwork for everyone on the floor. If you'd like your own personal piece of Craig's art, come to the end of the hallway by the dining room. End of the dining-room hallway, five minutes. Have fun!"

I sit down in the backmost chair, by the window that peers out over the avenue that crosses the street I live on, so close to my real life. I look over at my conference chair where I meet with my parents and Noelle. I have a second chair set up in front of me as an art desk, with stacks of board games on it and a chessboard on top. It's a little flimsy, but it'll do.

President Armelio is first to approach. He strides up, barrel-chested and sure of himself, like a torpedo.

"Hey, buddy, this is great! You gonna make me one of your heads with the maps inside?"

"That's right."

"Well let's go, buddy. I ain't got all day!"

Right. Armelio is going to have to be done fast because he *is* fast. I sketch the outline of his head and shoulders without a second thought and start in on his brain map. Highways, that's what Armelio has in his head—six-lane highways running parallel, streaking through a city, with purpose and minimal on-ramps. He doesn't have any quiet little streets or parks; it's highways and a grid, and no rivers either. The highways hardly even connect because Armelio doesn't mix up his thoughts; he has one and does it and then he moves on to the next. It's a great way to live. Especially when the biggest thought is wanting to play cards. Cards have to be represented in Armelio's brain somewhere. So I sketch some streets into an ace of spades right in the middle—it's not a *great* ace of spades, but Armelio gets it.

"Spades! Buddy, I *crush* you in spades."

I put my initials on it, big and bold, "CG" like "computer-generated."

"I'm gonna keep this, for real," Armelio says. "You a good guy, Craig." He shakes my hand. "You want my number for when you go?"

"Sure." I take out a piece of paper.

"It's an adult home," Armelio says. "You're gonna have to ask for Spyros, which is my other name." He gives me the number and moves aside, and there's Ebony, with her cane and her velvet pants, smacking her lips.

"I *heard* . . . that you were making your brains for people," she says.

"That's right! And you know who the first person who said they were brains was?"

"Me!"

"Absolutely. Now, look" —I gesture at my stack of work on the floor—"now I've got all this."

"So I get paid, right?" Ebony laughs.

"Not quite; I haven't really made it yet. As an artist."

"I know. It's tough."

"So you just get a brain map for yourself, okay?"

"Good!"

I trace her head freehand, looking at her, not the paper. I look down and it's pretty good. Ebony's brain . . . what's in there? A lot of circles, for all the buttons she stole. She was a nut with those buttons. Didn't mess around. Quite a schemer. And with all of her gambling skill, she needs to have a Strip, like Vegas. So I get a big boulevard in the middle and lots of traffic circles around it, with circular parks, circular malls, little circle lakes. It comes out looking less like a city and more like a necklace with a central band and tons of bunched-up jewels hanging off.

"It's *pretty!*" she says.

"And you're done." I hand it to her.

"You like doing these, huh?"

"Yeah. It helps, you know . . . with my depression. I came in here with depression."

"Imagine having depression when you were *eleven years old*," Ebony says. "If all my children were in this hall, this hall would be full up, I tell you."

"You have kids?" I ask, keeping my voice down.

"I had thirteen miscarriages," she says. "Imagine that." And she looks at me without any of the humor or attitude that she usually puts on, just with big wide eyes and empty questions.

"I'm so sorry," I say.

"I know. I know you are. That's the thing."

Ebony shuffles away showing off her portrait ("That's me! See? *Me!*"); she doesn't leave a phone number. Humble is next.

"All right, man, what kinda scam you got going on here?"

"It's nothing." I start in on Humble's bald head. Bald heads are easy. You know, if I had to right now, I think I could handle the lower tip of Manhattan. I look at Humble. He raises his eyebrows at me.

"Make me look good, all right?"

I laugh. Inside Humble's head is industrial chaos. I don't make any small blocks, just big ones—the kind of blocks where you'd find lumber shops and factories and bars where Humble would hang out at and work. I put the ocean in there, to represent his hometown, Bensonhurst, which borders the ocean, where he hooked up with all those girls way back when. Then I splash it with highways, erasing the streets and putting them over the top, throwing in crazy interchanges for no reason, making the whole thing look violent and random, but also powerful and true—the kind of mind that could come up with some great stuff if you harnessed it right. When I'm done, I look up.

"I guess it's okay." He shrugs.

I chuckle. "Thanks, Humble."

"I want you to remember me," he says. "No joke. When you're a big-time artist or whatever, you gotta invite me to one of the parties."

"It's a deal," I say. "But how am I going to be in touch?"

"Oh, right—I got a number!" Humble says. "I'm gonna be staying in Seaside Paradise; it's the same home that Armelio is going to, but I'm going to be on a different floor." He gives me the number; I put it on the same sheet as Armelio's.

"You're not gonna be in touch," Humble says.

"I will," I say.

"No you won't; I can tell. But it's okay. You have a lot going for you. Just don't burn out again."

We shake hands. Up next is Noelle.

"Hey, girl!"

"Don't you dare start calling me that. This is very nice of you to do."

"Least I could do. They're all such cool people."

"You're like a celebrity now. Everyone wants to know if I'm your girlfriend."

"And what do you tell them?"

"'No!' And then I walk away."

"Good call."

"So what are you trying to pull? You already made one of these for me. You just said it wasn't finished."

I pull out the one I made for her, with the guy and girl connected by the bridge, and write my phone number on the back of it.

"Oh my *gosh*."

"*Now* it's done." I smile, standing up. I lean in

and whisper: "It took me like twice as long as any of the others. And I'll make you an ever better one when I get out—"

She pushes me away. "Yeah, like I want your stupid art."

"You *do*." I lean back. "I saw how you looked at it before."

"I'll keep it to make you feel good," she says. "That's *it*."

"Fine."

She leans in and kisses my cheek. "Thank you, for real."

"You're welcome. Hey, what are you doing tonight?"

"Well . . . I thought I'd be hanging out in the psych hospital. What about you?"

"I've got big plans," I say. "We've got a movie coming in—"

"Right, I'm not seeing that stupid movie."

"I know." I drop to a whisper. "But when it's halfway done, do you want to meet in my room?"

"You're kidding."

"No. Seriously."

"Your roommate will be there! He's always there!"

"Trust me. Come to the room."

"Are you going to try and make out with me?"

"If you must know? Yes."

"I appreciate your honesty. We'll see."

I give her a hug; she holds the brain map with her hands wrapped around me. "And I already have your number," I say.

"You don't get any second chances if you lose it," she says. "I don't give that number out twice."

I take a quick wanting look at her as we pull away from each other and she moves off to the side.

Bobby is next.

"Who's that behind you?"

"Huh, who do you think?" Johnny answers.

"Come on up together, guys. I'll do you both at once."

"Cool," Bobby says, standing off to the side. Johnny stands next to him and I start drawing them, their shaggy hair and baggy clothing making for great outlines.

"So he's *drawin'* us?" Johnny asks Bobby.

"Be quiet, all right?"

"Where did you guys hang out?" I ask Bobby, not looking up from the paper. "Back when you were garbage-heads?"

"What? You're gonna draw that?"

"No." I look up. "I'm just curious. What neighborhood?"

"It was the Lower East Side, but don't draw the Lower East Side," says Bobby. "I don't want to go back there."

"All right, fair enough. Where do you want to live?"

"On the Upper East Side, with all the rich people," Bobby answers.

"Huh, me too," says Johnny.

"Wait, no, you're getting a guitar," I say.

"Oh, cool."

I start on Bobby's and Johnny's brains. With Johnny, it's fun to do a guitar in a street grid—some diagonal streets meeting for the body and then a big wide boulevard for the neck, a park for the head. Then I turn to Bobby. I know the Upper East Side pretty well; it's in Manhattan and the big thing that it has is Central Park, so I draw that on the inside left of his head. Then I put in the stately grid of rich streets. I know the Guggenheim Museum is somewhere up there; I mark that with an arrow. And then I put an "X" right next to it, on a corner where an apartment probably costs $20 million, and write *Bobby's pad*.

"Bobby's pad! That's right! That's where I'm headed." He raises his arms. "Movin' on up."

"Enjoy." I hand them the piece.

"Who gets what?" Johnny asks. "You want us to rip it apart?"

"No, man, we're supposed to keep it together

because we're *friends*," says Bobby. "I'll make a photocopy."

"Where's the photocopy machine in here?"

"There isn't one! I'll do it when I get out."

"Where's that gonna leave me?"

"With a copy!"

"I don't want a copy!"

"Would you listen to this guy? Nothing's good enough for him—"

"Hey, Bobby," I interrupt. "Any way I can get yours and Johnny's phone numbers to talk to you after you leave?"

Johnny starts to say something, but Bobby leans in and stops him: "It's not a good idea, Craig."

"What? Why?"

He sighs. "I've been in and out of this place a lot, right?"

"Yeah."

"There are good things about this place; I mean, the food is the best around; there are good people here . . . but it's still not a place to meet people."

"Why not? I met you guys and you're really cool!"

"Yeah, well, all the worse, then, when you try to call me or Johnny up and find out that we've OD'ed, or been shot, or come back here even worse, or just disappeared."

"That's a pretty negative view."

"I've seen it before. You just remember us, okay? We meet in the outside world, it just ruins it. You'll be embarrassed of me and I . . ." He smiles. ". . . I might be embarrassed of me, too. And I might be embarrassed of *you*, if you don't keep your stuff together."

"Thanks. You sure no numbers?"

Bobby shakes my hand. "If we need to, we'll meet."

Johnny shakes my hand. "What he said."

The last guy in line is Jimmy.

"I tell you, what'd I say? You play those numbers—"

"It'll come to ya!" I answer.

"*It the truth!*" He grins.

Ah, Jimmy. What's in Jimmy's brain? Chaos. I do up his nearly bald head and shoulders and then start putting the most complicated, unnecessary, wild highways through him from ear to ear. I connect them in intricate spaghetti ramps. In one nexus, five highways meet; I have to erase and redraw the ramps a few times. Then I put in the grid—a grid laid out by a hyperactive designer, with blocks going in all different directions. When Jimmy's brain map is done it might look the best—a catalog of a schizophrenic mind, but one that works somehow.

"Here you go," I tell him. He's sitting in a seat that he took next to me to watch me work.

"It'll come to ya!" he says, and takes the map. I want him to finally open up, to call me Craig, to tell me that we came in together, but he's still Jimmy—his vocabulary is still limited.

We sit back in our respective chairs; I doze off a bit. Making art on demand is tiring. But the last thing I see before I go to sleep is Jimmy unfolding his brain map next to me and comparing with Ebony, who says *of course hers is a lot prettier*. That's not a bad thing to go to sleep to.

forty-seven

"Craig, are you okay?" Mom asks. I jolt up and I have a momentary seizure that it was all a dream, all of it—the whole Sixth North bit—but then I wonder, where would the dream start? If it were a nightmare, it would have to have started somewhere before I got bad; it would be like a yearlong dream. You don't have those. And if it were a good dream, that would mean I was still back where it started, leaning over my parents' toilet or lying in bed listening to my heart. I didn't need that.

"Yeah! I'm—whoa." I sit up. They're all there—Dad, Mom, Sarah.

"Are you forcing yourself to sleep?" Mom asks. "Are you depressed?"

"Are you on drugs?" Sarah asks. "Can you hear me?"

"I was taking a nap! Jeez!"

"Oh, okay. It's six o'clock."

"Wow, I was asleep for a while. I was drawing my brain maps for people."

"Oh, boy," says Dad. "This doesn't sound good."

"What are brain maps?" Sarah asks.

"That's his art," says Mom. "This is why he wants to change schools. Making this art makes you happy, right Craig?"

"Yeah, wanna see?"

"Absolutely."

I take the stack from beside me and pass it around. This is really what I was creating the stack for, I think; to show my parents.

"Some of the best were the ones I just did, for the patients."

"Very original," Dad says.

"I like this one," says Sarah, pointing at the pig with quasi–St. Louis inside him.

"You put a lot of time into these, I see," Mom says.

"Right, that's the thing: they don't actually take me much time," I explain. "I'm starting to get a little bored of them, actually; I want to move to something else."

"So how are you feeling, Craig?" Dad puts the stack back on the floor.

"You *look* a lot better," Mom says.

"I do?"

"Yeah," Sarah says. "You don't look all freaky as much."

"I used to look *freaky?*"

"She doesn't mean *freaky*," Mom tells us both. "She just means that when you were down, you looked a little under the weather. Isn't that right, Sarah?"

"No, he looked freaky."

"A flat affect, that's what the doctors call it." I smile.

"Right, well you don't have that as much anymore," Sarah says.

"So you want to quit school?" Dad brings us back to the real-deal stuff.

"I don't want to *quit.*" I turn to him. "I want to *transfer.*"

"But that means quitting the school you're currently at—"

"He can't handle the other school!" Sarah says. "Look at—"

"Hold on a second. I can talk," I say. "Guys." I look at all three of them in turn. "One thing that they do in here is give you a lot of time to think. I can't explain it; once you come in, time just slows down—"

"Well, you don't have any interruptions, that's probably it—"

"Also I think the clocks are a little off—"

I wave my hand. "Point is, you have time to

think about how you got here. Because obviously, nobody wants to come back. *I* don't want come back—"

"Good. Me neither," says Dad. "What I said last time, about actually wanting to be here; that was a joke."

"Right. Hey, did you bring the movie?"

"Of course. I can watch some of it with you, right?"

"Absolutely. So anyway, I've been thinking about when things started getting bad for me. I realized: it started after I got into high school."

"Uh-huh," Mom says.

"That was the happiest moment of my life. The happiest day. And from there on it was all downhill."

"Right, this happens to a lot of adults," Dad says.

"Will you stop interrupting him?" Sarah interrupts. Dad folds his hands behind him and straightens his back.

"It's okay, Sarah. I just . . . I think I was concentrated on getting into Executive Pre-Professional because it was like, a challenge. I wanted to have that feeling of triumph. I never really thought about the fact that I'd have to, you know, *go* to the school."

"So you want to do art," Mom says.

"Well, let's consider. I never really liked math. I

was good at it, but only because I liked having basic information in front of me to get through, to reach that feeling of accomplishment. I never really liked English. This"—I point at the brain maps—"this is something different. This is something I *love*. So I'd better do it."

"You'd better love it," Dad says. "Because it's a hard life. It's mostly the artists who end up in places like this."

"Well, then he has to be an artist; that's where he is!" Sarah says.

"Heh. It's pretty simple." I stand up. "Take a look around. I tried to go to the best high school in the city. And this is where I ended up."

"True." Mom looks behind her. Solomon rushes across our field of view.

"If I don't make some kind of big change, I'm going to come out of here wondering how anything is different from before, and I'm going to end up right back here."

"Right," says Mom. "I'm with you, Craig."

"What art school are you going to go to?" Dad asks.

"Manhattan Arts Academy? It's easy to transfer to with my grades—"

"Oh, but Craig, that's the school for kids who are all screwed up," Dad says.

I look at him. "Yeah? Dad?" I raise my wrist, show him the bracelets. I have pride in them now. They're true, and people can't screw with them. And when you say the truth you get stronger.

Dad stands still for a minute, looks down at his feet, and then looks up.

"Okay," he says. "We'll do whatever we have to do. You have to stay in school until you transfer, though. That's going to be . . . until the end of the year at least, I think."

"I'll handle it," I say.

"I know you will. We'll help."

"Dinner, get ready for dinner!" President Armelio walks toward us. "Craig and his family, dinner is almost here!"

"How've you been eating?" Mom asks as I stretch my legs.

"I have been. That's good."

"It's wonderful, Craig."

"Okay, so I'm leaving the DVD here with you." Dad hands it to me. "And I'm going to be back to watch it when you're done with dinner. When will that be?"

"Seven is good. But visiting hours end at eight. You won't get to watch the whole thing."

"We'll see how long I can stay. You might be surprised."

I swallow. I actually don't want him sticking around that long. I'll make sure Smitty gets him out.

"I'll see you tomorrow," Mom says. "The staff tells us we're picking you up early in the morning, before I go to work."

"I'll be ready."

"We've got lots of good food at home."

"I'll see you when I come home from school." Sarah hugs my waist. "I'm so happy you're back."

I pat her head. "Are you embarrassed by this place?"

"Yeah, but whatever."

"I am too," I say. "It's just a good type of embarrassment."

forty-eight

Blade II . . . well, you have to like action movies to like it. I myself am a big fan of action movies. They're like the blues; there's a certain formula. You have the hero and the villain and the girl. The hero is going to almost die but not quite, and if there's a dog it'll be the same story with him. There's going to be one sub-villain with a distinguishing facial characteristic, and he's going to get killed in a printing press or a pool.

The plot of *Blade II* is that Blade is a guy who runs around killing vampires. He wears a leather coat with a *sword stuck in the back of it*; he regularly just walks around with this thing. I guess it's possible that you could walk around a city with a sword and not have people notice, but the chances of your not cutting your butt open seem close to nil, especially if you're running or doing jump flips.

Now, the real kicker is the way the vampires die. They digitally dissolve into multicolored ash—*in slow motion.* I could watch these vampires die all day. It's so *clean* the way they go; they don't leave a body or anything.

I explain all this to Humble as we help Monica roll out the TV from the activity center and plug it in. Monica has no idea how to use a DVD—the whole metal shiny disc concept scares her. We pop it in and have to hit the TV a few times to get it going, but then it's blasting into our eyes: Blade killing his first swath of vampires in Prague by skidding down fire escapes, jumping over motorcycles, and stabbing dudes with his sword.

The audience is a good cross-section of Six North—Humble, Bobby, and Johnny; the Professor; Ebony; the new guy Human Being; Becca; and Dad. He came in right at seven and sat down in the corner, staying very quiet, blending in. Jimmy came by as soon as he heard the noise of the film and took a seat beside him.

"Hello," Dad said.

"Your son?" Jimmy asked, pointing at me.

"Yes."

"How sweet it is!"

Dad nodded and said, "Yes, yes it is."

On the screen, Blade slices a vampire right through from his groin up to his skull.

"Whoa, this is *wild*," says Humble. "Did you

see that? That's worse than gonorrhea, man."

"Did you ever have gonorrhea?"

"Please. I've had everything. You know what they say: the Jews cut 'em off, the Irish wear 'em off."

"*Ewwww,*" I say. "You're Irish?"

"Half," says Humble.

"Could you be quiet? I'm trying to watch the film," the Professor says.

"Oh, don't start. You don't care about this movie; Cary Grant's not in it," says Humble.

"Cary Grant was a *real man.* Don't you say anything about him."

"I can say whatever—"

"What's that guy doing?" Bobby asks.

"He's sucking that girl's blood, can't you see?"

"I thought she was a vampire, though."

"So? Vampires have blood."

"Vampires ain't got no blood," says Human Being. "Vampires ain't got nothing but *green* running in their veins, and green means money."

"You don't know what you're talking about," Humble says. "If you drink blood, how are you not going to have blood?"

"I met a lotta vampires in my time, and their blood was always green. Been sucking me dry in their little temples."

"What temples?" Becca asks. "I go to temple. You better not be talking about the Jewish people."

"I'm Jewish too," says the Professor. "That's why they tried to insecticide my house."

Noelle walks toward the TV from down the hall, wearing a long black skirt and a white top with little frills around the shoulders, locking eyes with me. I look around; no seat for her.

Dad notices as soon as she becomes visible. He leans over and gives me a look:

So is this why you've been feeling better, son?

I shrug.

She comes up to me. "There's nowhere to sit."

"Here!" I stand up and point at my armrest.

She sits down right in the middle of the chair. "*Ooh*, you warmed it! Thank you."

"No, I meant—where am *I* going to sit?"

She pats the armrest.

"Darn, girl."

I sit down and we watch Blade slice up some more vampires. Topics discussed among the audience include surgery, the moon, chicken, prostitution, and jobs in the Sanitation Department. Dad leans back and lets his eyes fall; I had a feeling that would happen. As soon as I see him breathing heavy and steady I get up, go to Smitty, and I tell him that it's after eight o'clock.

"You want me to kick out your own Dad?" he asks.

"I need to be independent," I say.

"All right." Smitty walks down the hall with me. "Mr. Gilner—I'm sorry; visiting hours are over."

"Oh, hm!" He gets up. "Right. So, Craig, you'll bring this back tomorrow?"

"Yeah," I tell him. "Thanks."

"Thank you for getting here and getting help." He hugs me. Smitty backs away. It's a big hug, and long, and right in front of the television, but no one says anything.

"I love you," I mumble. "Even though I'm a teenager and I'm not supposed to."

"I love you too," Dad says. "Even though . . . eh . . . No. I don't have any jokes about it. I just do."

We separate and shake hands and he makes his way down the hall, waving without looking back.

"Good-bye Mister Gilner!" a chorus of those paying attention calls out.

I dip down next to Noelle, whisper in her ear. "That's one; I gotta settle one more thing, and then I'll see you in my room."

"Okay."

I walk down the hall and pop into my room, where Muqtada is putting his distinctive shape in the bed, turned toward the window, in his continuous dead reverie.

"Muqtada?"

"Yes."

"You remember how you wanted Egyptian music?"

"Yes, Craig."

"I got some for you."

"You did?" He pulls his top sheet aside. "Where?"

"I got a record over," I say. "You know we're watching a movie, right?"

"Yes, I hear. This sounds very violent, no good for me."

"Right, well, in the other hall, by where the smoking area is, I asked Smitty to put the Egyptian music."

"And he did this thing?"

"It's ready to go on right now. You want to hear?"

"Yes." Muqtada pushes the sheets aside in a gesture of hope and strength and determination. It's tough to get out of bed; I know that myself. You can lie there for an hour and a half without thinking anything, just worrying about what the day holds and knowing that you won't be able to deal with it. And Muqtada did that for years. He did that until he needed to be hospitalized. And now he's getting up. Not for good, but for real.

I walk with him out of the room, passing Smitty at the nurses' station and nodding at him. He opens a door behind his desk and goes in to turn on the turntables, changing the PA music from the normal funky lite FM to the sounds of deep plucked strings, and rolling over it, a voice of dangerous clarity and yearning, hitting three ascending notes and then bending one beyond where I thought you couldn't bend a human voice, sounding like a man drawn out and smacked to vibrate around a little.

"*Umm Kulthum!*" Muqtada says.

"Yeah! Uh . . . Who's that?"

"This is Egypt's greatest singer!" he yells. "How you find this?"

"I have a friend whose dad has some records."

"This I have not heard in so long!" He's grinning so much I think his glasses are going to fall off.

Armelio is playing solitaire in the back of the hall, by the smoking lounge. "You're out of your room, buddy? What's going on? Is there a fire?"

"This music!" Muqtada points up to it. "This is Egyptian!"

"You Egyptian, buddy?"

"Yes."

"I'm from Greece."

"The Greeks, they took all our music."

"This?" Armelio looks up. "This ain't nothing like Greek music, buddy."

"You want to sit, Muqtada?" I ask him.

He looks around, then up at the music.

"The best seat'll be over here, right by the speaker."

"Yes," he says, and sits down.

"I don't like this," Armelio looks up.

"What kind of music do you like, Armelio?" I ask.

"Techno."

"Just . . . techno?"

"Yeah. *Utz-utz-utz-utz.* Like that."

"Heh heh." Muqtada laughs. "The Greek man is funny."

"Of course I'm funny, buddy! I'm always funny! You just don't leave your room. You want to play cards?"

Muqtada starts to leave; I stand over him and hold my hands out. "Wait one second, man. I know you can't play cards for money, but Armelio doesn't play for money."

"This I know; I do not want to play."

"Are you sure? He's got no one else to play with."

"That's right. My friends are all watching this stupid movie. You want to play spades? I'll *crush* you in spades."

"Muqtada," I say. He's still looking up at me, hands on his armrests, ready to spring. "Remember when you saved me from that girl?"

"Yes."

"I'm trying to do the same thing for you now, to get you out of your room and save you. Please. Play with Armelio."

He looks at me, then at the speakers.

"This I do for you, Craig. But only for you. And only because of music."

"Great." I pat his back. "Go easy on him, Armelio."

"You know that's not going to happen, buddy!"

I smile and walk down the hall, waving at them. As soon as I get to the corner, I run—I don't have much time—but skid to a leisurely pace by Smitty and then, moving as slowly and calmly as I can, enter my room. Noelle picked up on what was happening: she's already there, sitting on my bed, looking out the window.

"You're very crafty," she whispers. I shrug. "Come and sit. It's a pretty view through your blinds."

forty-nine

I sit down next to Noelle and it starts off right away, like it was destined to—though I don't believe in destiny; I just believe in biology, and hotness, and wanting girls. There's been so much hesitation in so many parts of my life that it's shocking to not have any here, to just lean in and have this girl's mouth open to mine, to be easing her down and touching her face and feeling the cuts there but understanding, not getting freaked out, just moving my hands down to her neck, which is clean and smooth, and her hitting my pillow and me next to her with my legs off the bed, still on the floor like I was sitting in class, like my lower half had no part in this. K-I-S-S-I-N-G.

"You're beautiful," I stop and tell her.

"*Shh*, they'll hear."

She has her hand in my hair and that reminds me that my hands should be doing something—right now they're just sort of touching her neck while I try and figure out what it is about her that's so much more sexy than Nia. It's her tongue, I think—it's a whole different creature than Nia's. Nia's was small and flighty; Noelle's is *overwhelming*—she slides it in and it almost fills me up. It's like some deep dark part of her that I've gotten out, that no one else has access to. She presses it through my teeth and I keep my eyes open, although there's nothing in the room but scattered moonlight to see her by. We press against each other as if we both had prizes at the back of our mouths and we could only get them out with the tips of our tongues.

It frickin' *rocks*.

I put my hands on her white top and she doesn't stop me, not at all, and there they are, right through the soft fabric—one on each side, that is *so cool*— my palms envelop them and then rise from them and then envelop again. I'm not really sure what to do with them. They're bigger than Nia's; they fill up my hands. Should I squeeze them? I try that. I look up. She's nodding. I squeeze them again, the whole things, both at once, and move my mouth down her chin to her neck, kissing the underside of it where an Adam's apple would be, only this is a *real girl*.

She moves her hips against me. Not her hips, her crotch—I mean, that is a crotch, right? Girls have crotches? Or do they have like a prettier name for them? Wow, how far is this going to go? She presses it—whatever it is—against my thigh. My feet have levitated somehow and now I'm horizontal on the bed next to her, with my hands squeezing her and my shoes—my Rockport shoes—clanking against each other.

She says nothing. Everything is touching.

"Do you want me to?" I ask.

She nods. Or maybe shakes her head. I don't know. But I take two fingers of my right hand and put them through the soft seam in her top. Underneath is a bra, I'm pretty sure—something made of mesh that wraps around her. I twiddle my finger against it, not sure if she can feel it. Can you feel things through a bra?

She makes noises like someone about to sneeze. When I squeeze her breasts, she makes more; when I twiddle the side of the bra, she doesn't make any. So I put my fingers in all the way through her shirt and feel up the dome of the bra—the highest point on her. An inch and a half above sea level.

"Hold on." Noelle lifts her butt off the bed and inserts her hands, flat, palms-down, below herself. Now she's got no hands. She wasn't doing anything with them anyway, but it's weird.

"Keep going," she says.

"Okay," I slide my fingers, still outside her bra, around her nipple. I decide to try something. I get the nipple right between the knuckles on my index and middle finger, and I squeeze.

You can't get much of a squeeze on through a bra, but the noises are immediate.

"*Unhh.*"

"Um?" I look up.

"*Mmmmmmn.*"

Oh, *this* is awesome.

"*Shh,*" I whisper. "Smitty will come."

"How much time do we have?" she asks.

"I don't know. A little while."

"You're going to call me, right? When you're out? And we're going to hang out?"

"I want to go out with you," I say. "I really do."

"That's what I mean. We will." She smiles. "Where will I tell people I met you?"

"In the psych hospital. Then they won't ask any questions."

She giggles—yup, a real giggle. Now we've sort of lost the sexual nature of things. Can I get it back just by squeezing? It's worth a shot.

"*Mmmmmm.*"

All right, cool, only now there's one more voice that wants me to do *one more thing*. It's the same voice that got me hooking up with Nia; it's the voice of the lower half of me, but it feels truer now, and it knows it can't get away with everything it wants to do, but it insists that we try something.

We need to test out that claim of Aaron's.

My hand moves down Noelle's body, down the seam of the frilly white shirt to the skirt, which has a slightly different grain to the fabric. I move down to its end, by her knees, shocked that I don't get any resistance or hesitancy or punches in the face. I roll the skirt up—I'm really in danger of putting a hole through this bed at this point—and there I find underwear. Not underwear. Panties. Real panties!

Holy crap, I'm actually going to figure this out!

"Wow!"

Noelle gasps.

"It *is* like the inside of a cheek!"

"What?"

Noelle pushes me off her. The distended seam of the shirt is repositioned; the panties are jerked back in place; the skirt is down and the girl is up at the head of the bed, staring at me.

"What did you say about my cheeks?!"

"No, no, *shhhhh*," I tell her. "Not your cheeks, um . . . your . . . your other cheeks."

"My *butt* cheeks?" She pulls her hair over her real cheeks, holding it there, eyes wide and angry in the moonlight.

"No," I whisper. Then sigh. "Let me explain. Do you want me to explain?"

"Yes!"

"All right, but this is like privileged boy information. I'm only telling you because we're going to be hanging out when we get out of here."

"Maybe we're not even. What did you say about my cheeks?"

"No, listen, it doesn't have anything to do with your cheeks and your cuts, all right?"

"What does it have to do with?"

I tell her.

When I'm done, there's a terrible pregnant pause, a pause that could hold all the hatred and yelling and screaming in the world as well as the possibility of me getting discovered as having another girl in my room (how did I get two? Am I a "player"?) and having to stay here for another week, never talking to Noelle again, going back to the Cycling, to being unable to eat, to move, to wake up, ending up like Muqtada. Single moments contain the potential for complete failure, always. But they also contain potential for a pretty girl to say—

"That is the stupidest thing I've ever heard."

—and to put her own finger in her mouth to test it out.

I hug her.

"What?" she asks, mouth clogged. "I don't get it. It doesn't feel the same at all."

I pull back. "You're so cool." I look at her. "How did you get so cool?"

"Please," she says. "We should go. The movie's almost over."

I hug her one more time and pull her down to the bed. And in my mind, I rise up from the bed and look down on us, and look down at everybody else in this hospital who might have the good fortune of holding a pretty girl right now, and then at the entire Brooklyn block, and then the neighborhood, and then Brooklyn, and then New York City, and then the whole Tri-State Area, and then this little corner of America—with laser eyes I can see into every house—and then the whole country and the hemisphere and now the whole stupid world, everyone in every bed, couch, futon, chair, hammock, love seat, and tent, everyone kissing or touching each other . . . and I know that I'm the happiest of all of them.

PART 10: SIX NORTH, THURSDAY

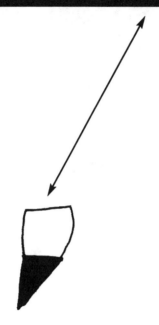

fifty

Mom and Dad are dressed up to bring me out; I'm wearing what I wore all the time in here—some khaki pants and my tie-dyed T-shirt and my dressy shoes, my Rockports, the ones that people complimented me on every so often, that made me feel like a *professional* patient. Mom never brought a change of clothes.

They're here early because Dad has to work; he wanted to see me before he left. Mom is staying home today to see that I'm all right. Then, tomorrow, Friday, I'm back at school, but with the official notice that I can pop into the nurse's office at any time if I feel depressed. I don't really have to go to class for the next week; that's school policy. I'm *encouraged* to go but they don't want to overwhelm me. It's a good deal.

It's 7:45 A.M. I've taken my last vitals—120/80—and I'm standing at the crux of the hall by the nurses' office, looking at the double doors I came in five days ago. It *seems* like five days; it doesn't seem too long or too short; it *seems* like I spent the time here that I really spent. People are always talking about *real-time*—real-time stock quotes, real-time information, real-time news—but in here I think I had real-time real time.

Armelio shakes my hand a final time.

"Good luck, buddy."

Humble says I should stay in a little longer.

"You're gonna lose it on the outside, man."

Bobby mumbles at me. It's too early for him.

The Professor tells me to keep doing my art.

Smitty says he heard from Neil that I was thinking of volunteering and he hopes to see me sometime.

Jimmy ignores me completely.

Ebony says to be careful of liars and cheats and to always respect children.

Noelle pops out of her room at 7:50, just as breakfast is rolling in and my parents are stepping out of the nurses' office where they were signing papers.

"I'm out in the afternoon," she says. She's wearing sweatpants and a T-shirt. "Call me tonight?"

"Sure." I touch her number in my pocket, next to her two notes that I saved.

"How are you feeling?"

"I'm feeling like I can handle it."

"Me too."

"You're a really cool girl," I say.

"You're kind of a dork, but with potential," she says.

"That's all I'm trying for."

"Craig?" Mom asks.

"Oh, hey guys, ah, this is Noelle. We got to be friends in here."

"I saw you last night," Dad says, shaking her hand.

"A pleasure to meet you," says Mom. Neither of them takes a second look at the cuts on her face. My parents have some class.

"Good to meet you too," she says.

"Are you still in high school?" Dad asks.

"Delfin," she says.

"A lot of pressure, huh," says Mom.

"Yeah."

"I think they might have to change the whole system. Look, two people like you, smart young people, sent in here because of pressure."

"Mom."

"I'm serious. I'm going to write my congressperson about it."

"Mom."

"I'll go," Noelle says. "See you Craig." And she dips her leg up behind her as she turns away and flicks a wave at me—*that counts as a kiss, I* think. *If my parents weren't here that would be a kiss.*

"Are you ready?" Mom asks.

"Yeah. Bye, everybody!"

"Wait!" From down the hall, Muqtada moves forward as fast as he allows himself to, which isn't very fast, sort of like a speed walk, and hands me the record.

"Thank you, Craig. This boy, your son," he turns to my parents, "he has helped me."

"Thank you," Mom and Dad say.

I hug Muqtada and take in his smell one last time. "Good luck, man."

"As you go through life, you think of me and hope that I am better."

"I will."

We separate and Muqtada migrates toward the dining room and the smell of food.

I look at my parents. "Let's go."

It's incredibly simple. The nurses open the doors for us and there I am outside, looking at the *"Shhhhhhhh!* Healing in Progress" poster I saw when I came in. The bank of elevators stand sentry in front of us.

"Guys," I tell them. "Can you go home yourselves, and I'll walk after you in like one minute?"

"Why? Are you okay?"

"I just want to walk by myself a little."

"Think things over?"

"Yeah."

"You're not feeling . . . bad?"

"No. I just want to walk home myself."

"We'll take your stuff." They grab the bag of old clothes and art I had with me, plus the record; wave, and take the next elevator down.

I wait for thirty seconds before hitting the button myself.

I'm not better, you know. The weight hasn't left my head. I feel how easily I could fall back into it, lie down and not eat, waste my time and curse wasting my time, look at my homework and freak out and go and chill at Aaron's, look at Nia and be jealous again, take the subway home and hope that it has an accident, go and get my bike and head to the Brooklyn Bridge. All of that is still there. The only thing is, it's not an option now. It's just . . . a possibility, like it's a possibility that I could turn to dust in the next instant and be disseminated throughout the universe as an omniscient consciousness. It's not a very likely possibility.

I get in the elevator. It's big and shiny. There's a lot to look at in the real world.

I don't know what I'm going to do today, still. I'm probably going to go home, sort through my art, and then call everybody I know and tell them that I'm going to be switching schools and from now on they should reach me by phone instead of e-mail. But I also might go to the park—how come I never go to the park?—and throw a ball around with whatever kids are out there. Or a Frisbee. It's a real day outside. There's actual weather out there.

I walk through the lobby. The smells! Coffee and muffins and flowers and scented candles from the gift shop. Why does Argenon Hospital have a gift shop? I guess everybody has to have a gift shop.

I step out onto the sidewalk.

I'm a free man. Well, I'm a minor, but one quarter of your life is spent as a minor; you might as well make the best of it. I'm a free minor.

I breathe. It's a spring day. The air is like a sheet billowing down on me in slow motion.

I haven't cured anything, but something seismic is happening in me. I feel my body wrapped up and slapped on top of my spine. I feel the heart that beat early in the morning on Saturday and told me I didn't want to die. I feel the lungs that have been doing their work quietly inside the hospital. I feel the hands that can make art and touch girls—*think of all the tools you have*. I feel the feet that can let me run anywhere I want, into to the park and out of it and down to my bike to go all over Brooklyn and Manhattan too, once I convince my mom. I feel my stomach and liver and all that mushy stuff that's in there handling food, happy to be back in use. But most of all I feel my brain, up there taking in blood and looking out on the world and noticing humor and light and smells and dogs and every other thing in the world—everything in my life is all in my brain, really, so it would be natural that when my brain was screwed up, everything in my life would be.

I feel my brain on top of my spine and I feel it shift a little bit to the left.

That's it. It happens in my brain once the rest of my body has moved. I don't know where my brain went. It got knocked off-kilter somewhere. It got caught up in some crap it couldn't deal with. But now it's back—connected to my spine and ready to take charge.

Jeez, why was I trying to kill myself?

It's a huge thing, this Shift, just as big as I imagined. My brain doesn't want to *think* anymore; all of a sudden it wants to do.

Run. Eat. Drink. Eat more. Don't throw up. Instead, take a piss. Then take a crap. Wipe your butt. Make a phone call. Open a door. Ride your bike. Ride in a car. Ride in a subway. Talk. Talk to people. Read. Read maps. Make maps. Make art. Talk about your art. Sell your art. Take a test. Get into a school. Celebrate. Have a party. Write a thank-you note to someone. Hug your mom. Kiss your dad. Kiss your little sister. Make out with Noelle. Make out with her more. Touch her. Hold her hand. Take her out somewhere. Meet her friends. Run down a street with her. Take her on a picnic. Eat with her. See a movie with her. See a movie with Aaron. Heck, see a movie with Nia, once you're cool with her. Get cool with more people. Drink coffee in little coffee-drinking places. Tell people your story. Volunteer. Go back to Six North. Walk in as a volunteer and say hi to everyone who waited on you as a patient. Help people. Help people like Bobby. Get people books and music that they want when they're in there. Help people like Muqtada. Show them how to draw. Draw more. Try drawing a landscape. Try drawing a person. Try drawing a naked person. Try drawing Noelle naked. Travel. Fly. Swim. Meet. Love. Dance. Win. Smile. Laugh. Hold. Walk. Skip. Okay, it's gay, whatever, skip.

Ski. Sled. Play basketball. Jog. Run. Run. Run. Run home. Run home and enjoy. Enjoy. Take these verbs and enjoy them. They're yours, Craig. You deserve them because you chose them. You could have left them all behind but you chose to stay here.

So now live for real, Craig. Live. Live. Live. Live. Live.

Ned Vizzini spent five days in adult psychiatric in Methodist Hospital, Park Slope, Brooklyn, 11/29/04–12/3/04.

Ned wrote this 12/10/04–1/6/05.